APHRODITE'S CLOSET

A FRAMBLEBERRY NOVEL

SUZY TURNER

Aphrodite's Closet
by Suzy Turner

Copyright Suzy Turner 2017
The characters and events portrayed in this book are fictitious. Any similarity to real persons, living or dead, is coincidental and not intended by the author.
All rights reserved. No part of this publication may be reproduced, distributed, or transmitted in any form or by any means, or stored in a database or retrieval system, without the prior written permission of the author.

❀ Created with Vellum

AUTHOR WEBSITE

For more information about the author
and her upcoming books, please visit

www.suzyturner.com

GET A FUN FREE READ...

 # FREE DOWNLOAD

Willow Tree Farm

Nestled among a thicket of weeping willows deep in the heart of Dartmoor, lies a house like no other. A house defying the laws of logic–and gravity for that matter. Some might even say it had a mind of its own. They wouldn't be wrong.

Affectionately known as Willow, this house has been an integral part of the Winterbourne family for over 400 years, and it is very, very protective of the Winterbournes, so woe betide anyone who dares to wrong this family of witches...

Compatible with all reading devices.
Exclusively available, and never before published.

Get your FREE COPY of Willow Tree Farm when you sign up to the author's VIP mailing list. **Get started here:**

www.suzyturner.com/free-book

CHAPTER 1

"Don't be such a prude."

"I...I'm not a prude," Aggie stuttered as she pushed her long, mousy brown hair behind her ear and glanced around at the other shoppers on the high street.

"Oh, come on," Coco laughed. She grabbed her best friend by the arm and gave her little choice but to enter the famous sex shop.

Feeling her face blush a deep shade of aubergine, Aggie stumbled beside her, hiding as best as she could.

Coco, on the other hand, was in her element, picking up bras, panties, feather boas, sequinned bodices and...

Aggie gasped aloud when she saw her best friend pick up a vibrator before it dawned on her that Coco was merely teasing her.

"Can we go now?" she whispered as her best pal hooted with laughter.

"Go?" Coco giggled, "but we only just came in."

"I'm just not...not...comfortable."

"Jeeze, Aggie, it's about time you got over your nerves in places like this. It's just a sex shop, they sell lingerie and fun stuff for the bedroom. You're not an eighty-five-year-old Vicar's wife—you're twenty-eight for God's sake! Live a little. Come on, look at this," she said as she pulled a blood-red basque covered in feathers from the rails and held it up to her best friend's slim physique.

1

Mortified, Aggie gulped, and her nostrils flared.

Realising the extent of poor Aggie's embarrassment, Coco relented and immediately put it back with a shake of the head.

"Okay, okay. Just give me a minute to pay for these things."

"I'll see you outside," Aggie muttered as she tried not to trip over her own feet to get out of there as fast as she could.

The cold immediately hit her as she walked outside, so Aggie rubbed her hands up and down her arms and crossed the high street. She waited around the corner near a popular newsagent, avoiding eye contact with everybody, her embarrassment still evident on her flushed face.

Five minutes later, Coco emerged with a huge grin on her face and another large pink carrier bag in her hand. Aggie watched as her friend's smile faded, her head turning one way and the other as she scoured the crowds for her best pal.

Aggie waved from across the street as she stepped out of the shadows.

"I thought you'd buggered off and left me," Coco shrieked and tottered toward her in three-inch heels perfectly suited for a shopping expedition. "Come on, let's grab a coffee."

Arm in arm, the two women walked toward Starbucks, just a few metres further down the shop-lined street.

"I'm dying for a cappuccino," Coco added.

Aggie pushed open the door. Warmth and an inviting aroma of coffee enveloped her as she waited for Coco, who struggled with all the carrier bags. An attractive man in his forties rushed forward to help.

"Let me give you a hand," he said in such a smooth tone that Aggie's knees almost buckled. *Men never rush to my aid like that*, she thought while Coco relished the attention.

"Thank you," she breathed. "You're very kind."

"It's nothing. Can I buy you a cup of coffee?"

Coco stopped momentarily before she smiled, that beautiful bright smile that would cheer up many a toothpaste advert, and shook her head.

"No, thank you, I'm here to have coffee with my friend. Perhaps another time?"

The man, who had a head full of thick silver hair, nodded with a cheeky smile, then reached into his inside pocket, removing a silver cardholder. He withdrew his business card and placed it into Coco's front jacket pocket.

"In that case, I shall wait for your call."

And then he was gone. Aggie stood, still holding the door, with her mouth wide open.

"Shut the door will you, love? You're letting the cold air in," said an old lady to her side.

"Oh, sorry," Aggie muttered. She quickly shut the door and followed Coco to the only available table in the corner of the cafe.

"Sit down, hon. I'll get these. What do you fancy? Your usual?"

"Erm...yes please," Aggie replied as she struggled to remove her bulky coat, almost hitting a nearby person in the face. Once it was off, she sat down with a sigh.

Several minutes later, Coco returned with a cappuccino and a soy caramel latte.

"Thanks," Aggie smiled.

Sighing contentedly, Coco sat down and pulled out her flashy smartphone.

"So. Will you ring him?" Aggie asked.

"Ring who?"

"That guy?"

"What guy?" Coco asked.

Aggie rolled her eyes, "That gorgeous older guy who just gave you his card."

"Oh him. I don't know. Maybe."

"Maybe? But he was...was...so handsome, so dreamy. If not a little old."

"Yeah, I suppose," Coco murmured as she proceeded to flick through her text messages. "Oh look, I've won another competition."

"What this time?"

"Oh, just some makeup. Shit," she shrieked all of a sudden, "I mean, seriously OMG".

Aggie jumped. "What? What on earth is it?"

"Aggie, honey. Did you check your messages this morning?"

"No, why?" Aggie replied.

"You need to check your email. Now."

"Why, what's going on?" she asked.

"Just do it," Coco said, clapping the elaborate case of her mobile phone shut before she gave her friend a slightly sad smile.

"Please just tell me, Coco," Aggie replied as she delved into her handbag and tried to retrieve her own phone.

"Oh, alright then. I got an email from Amelia Hornblower. The library is closing down."

"Wh...wh...what?" stuttered Aggie.

"I'm sorry honey."

"Wh...wh...when?"

"At the end of the month," Coco added.

"But why wouldn't they tell me? And why does Amelia know about this before me? She doesn't even work there."

"Honey, Amelia is the town gossip. You know that. She knows you're going to fart before you do. What will you do?"

"I don't know. I didn't have any idea this was going to happen. I thought the library was going well," Aggie cried.

"Oh honey, even I knew it was having financial difficulties. I mean who really cares for a library that specialises in nothing but mythology?"

"I do," Aggie whispered.

"Oh babe, I'm so sorry, I didn't mean it."

"What am I going to do?"

"Don't worry," Coco placed her hand over Aggie's, "We'll figure something out."

CHAPTER 2

"I didn't even know I had a Great Aunt Petunia."

"She was your Grandma's younger sister, Aggie. I must have mentioned her once in a while when you were little. Don't you remember?" said her mother.

"No," Aggie replied.

"Well, she certainly seems to remember you, for some reason, because she's left you the old corner shop in her will."

"What? What corner shop?" Aggie asked as she shifted the phone to her other ear while she balanced several books under her right arm and walked across the room.

"The one underneath her flat where she used to work."

"Why on earth would she leave it to me? It's just weird."

"Weird? But darling, you should be happy. You won't have a job to go to in a week. At least you can do something with the shop."

"A shop? What on earth am I going to do with a shop?" she reiterated, trying and failing to stop the books from tumbling to the floor.

"That's enough, Agatha. You should be grateful to your late Great Aunt Petunia for this opportunity."

"Mum, I am grateful. Really I am. Sorry, it's just with the library closing down and me losing my job, I'm just not myself. I'm sorry," Aggie said as she crouched down and tried to pick up the books.

"I understand, sweetheart, I really do, but this could be the perfect opportunity to get you back on your feet. I know it's not your dream job, but it's a job all the same."

"I know, Mum. I just can't imagine being a shopkeeper, that's all."

"Well, whatever you do, that shop belongs to you now, whether you like it or not," her mother stated.

"Thanks, Mum."

"I'll talk to you soon. Love you, sweetheart. Toodle pip. "

"Love you too, Mum. Bye."

Aggie put the phone down and tried to remember her mother talking about her Great Aunt Petunia as a child but she just couldn't. She must've been too young. Way too young.

Before she could continue packing away the beloved books she'd spent several years caring for, her mobile rang again.

"You'll never guess what. No, you won't guess. I've won a holiday for two, and I'm taking you with me," Coco shrieked down the phone so loudly that Aggie had to hold it at arm's length.

"Huh? What are you talking about? You've won a holiday?"

"We're going to Las Vegas!" Coco yelled.

"What?" Aggie asked in shock.

"We leave in two weeks," Coco replied.

"Coco, what on earth are you talking about?"

"Honey, I entered some random Twitter competition to win a five-day trip to Vegas, and I won. I want you to come with me."

"You want me to come with you to Las Vegas?" Aggie asked.

"Yes," Coco shrieked again.

"In two weeks?"

"Yes!" Coco replied.

"I can't come to Las Vegas in two weeks," Aggie decided. "I've just lost my job, I've inherited a corner shop, and my life is insane right now. I really can't Coco."

"Of course you can and of course you will."

oOo

The breakfast buffet was more significant than anything Aggie had ever seen. In fact, it appeared to be more of a banquet than a meal to be eaten in the morning hours. It was famous, after all. Almost anyone and everyone who had ever visited Las Vegas knew about the amazing champagne breakfast buffet at the ridiculously grand hotel.

"I can't possibly drink any more," sighed Aggie before she swallowed the last drops of her third rather large glass of champagne.

"Nonsense, of course you can," Coco said as she nodded at one of the many waiters who seemed to appear out of nowhere to pour the fourth glass.

"Cheers, my dear. Now come on, let's hit the buffet one more time," said Coco.

Holding her full, slightly rounded stomach, Aggie only semi-reluctantly stood up and headed back toward the food for the third time.

"I'm going for Chinese this time. What about you?" Coco asked.

"Hm?" Aggie murmured, not really taking much notice of the question.

Coco ignored her and wandered off, leaving Aggie to decide over the massive selection of hot and cold meats, seafood, pasta dishes, salads, vegetables and much more. But she'd had her fill with savoury stuff, so she turned her attention to the sweets. A creamy chocolate mousse, topped with a generous serving of softly whipped cream caught her attention.

Back at her table, Aggie spotted Coco being chatted up, yet again, by a particularly good looking guy in his early twenties. She couldn't help but notice the manliness of his square jawline, not to mention the twinkle in his eye as he looked down at Coco. She always received attention with her caramel-coloured skin, mass of honey brown curls, huge blue eyes, and naturally dark pink bee-stung lips. The only thing that prevented her from being a supermodel was her height or apparent lack of it, Aggie thought. Coco was only five foot one. Not that she let it hinder her from doing anything. She often chose to wear at least five-inch heels—even when she was just nipping out to the corner shop.

In other words, Coco was the exact opposite of Aggie.

She sighed and turned her full attention back to the chocolate mousse at the exact time that a very attractive guy in his early thirties appeared beside her.

"Erm, excuse me, Miss," he said.

"Huh?" Aggie muttered as she looked at him.

"You dropped your jacket," he smiled, pointing to the floor behind her.

Her heart began to flutter as she watched him lean over before he stood up and put it back on the chair.

"Oh, thank you very much," she said, her cheeks changing colour.

"You've, erm, got a little cream..." he pointed to her top lip.

She blushed an even deeper shade of red and wiped her mouth with the back of her hand. The young man grinned and walked away. Aggie looked down and noticed the huge amount of whipped cream she'd wiped away.

She lost her appetite all of a sudden and pushed the offending dessert away.

"Not gonna eat that? It looks delicious," said Coco as she put down yet another plate of sushi on the table.

Aggie shook her head, "I thought you were having Chinese?" she asked.

"That guy recommended the sushi," Coco smiled as she pointed across the room to the young man with whom she'd been chatting.

"Oh, okay. I don't know where you put it all," Aggie sighed.

Coco grinned, "I'm lucky I've got a high metabolism." She pouted before placing a large piece of tuna sashimi into her mouth with the chopsticks.

Aggie blushed and shook her head.

"Want some?" Coco offered.

Aggie shook her head, dabbing her mouth with the cloth napkin for the third time.

"I think I've had enough. So who was the cute guy?"

"Just some guy who wanted to go out with me tonight," she answered as if it happened every day. Probably because it did.

"Oh."

"I turned him down," said Coco, before she put another piece of sushi in her mouth.

"He was handsome."

Coco swallowed the fish before she replied, "A bit young for me."

"He was probably the same age as you!"

"Exactly...too young. Enough about me anyway, I thought I saw someone chatting you up," Coco teased.

"Not really, he just picked up my jacket from the floor...and then told me I had a cream moustache."

"Oh, oh well. Better luck next time, hon."

"Yeah, I don't think there'll be a next time. I just don't have the kind of appeal that you have, Coco."

"Nonsense. You're beautiful. You just don't seem to see it."

Aggie looked across the table at her friend as if she was looking at a little green man.

"I'm serious! I'd kill for your poker-straight hair, perfect skin, and height."

"But not my thin lips, flat chest, and sticky-out cheekbones," Aggie almost whispered.

"Oh Aggie, there's absolutely nothing wrong with your lips, chest, or cheekbones! Honestly, woman. I do believe you've got body dysmorphia or something. Your problem is that you hide from the world. Even when you're out and about, you just want to blend in with the crowd or sink into the floor."

Aggie glanced around and pulled herself more upright in her chair.

"What you need is a makeover and some confidence-building lessons. In fact, let's go out on the town tonight, and I'll do your hair and makeup. Ooh, we could go shopping first and get you a new outfit."

"No, I don't think so," Aggie whispered.

"You're doing it again," Coco shook her head.

"What?" Aggie asked.

"Trying to sink into the floor."

"No, I'm not."

"Then let's go shopping!" Coco exclaimed.

CHAPTER 3

"I'm very sorry ma'am, but without a full description of the man who stole from you, there's little we can do."

Tears rolled down Aggie's cheeks.

"Don't worry, hon. At least he only took your money. It could have been worse, he could have taken your credit card and passport too."

"I know. I just feel so stupid."

"Hey, how were you to know he was stealing from you?"

"Stealing and making fun of my cream moustache," she wailed as they walked out of the police station a short while later.

"It was only a thousand dollars."

"It was all I had for the holiday."

"No, that's not strictly true. I won two thousand, five hundred dollars cash with this holiday and I want you to have half. I've got plenty of money anyway."

Aggie's eyes widened as she stared down at her best friend.

"No, I can't do that. I can't take your money," she said with a shake of her head.

"Yes, you can. I insist. I won't take no for an answer, okay? I've got plenty. You're taking it."

Aggie looked at Coco for a few seconds longer before she nodded and blew her nose at the same time.

"Thank you," she whispered.

"No problem," Coco added, squeezing her shoulder.

"Let's just forget this ever happened. But from now on, don't leave your cash in your pocket, okay?"

Aggie nodded.

"Perhaps it's time you thought about buying yourself a decent handbag?" Coco suggested.

Aggie raised her eyebrows, "I have a decent handbag— the one I left at the hotel."

"Aggie, honey. That's a cheap, dowdy librarian's tote, not a decent handbag. You need something with a bit of, you know —style."

Letting out a deep sigh, Aggie shielded her eyes from the bright sunlight, "Style? Like I have any of that."

oOo

"Hey, y'all. Let me know if I can be of any assistance, ya hear?" said the pretty little shop assistant in a strong southern accent as they wandered into the popular boutique. Coco smiled and nodded before she headed straight for the handbag section.

"Thank you," Aggie mouthed as she traipsed after her friend.

The assistant smiled and continued to straighten the clothes on the hangers.

"What about this one?" Coco suggested, holding up a large gold and pink leopard-print bag.

Aggie's face made her put it back down almost immediately.

"A bit much, eh?" she grinned.

"Just a bit," Aggie responded as she walked toward the brown and beige section.

Before she could get there, Coco grabbed her friend's arm and pulled her in the opposite direction.

"There's no way I'm letting you buy a dowdy brown tote again! You need a bit of colour. A bit of fun in your life."

"Coco, a pink handbag does not equal fun in one's life," Aggie stated as Coco held up a cute little pink tassel bag, followed by a fuchsia tote.

"They're just not me. I'd look ridiculous carrying around something like that."

"Oh, Aggie," Coco sighed again. "That's your problem. I keep telling you. You need to, erm…elevate your style."

Aggie looked down at herself, seeing nothing wrong with the mum jeans she'd bought especially for the holiday. She'd read about mum jeans being the latest thing in a magazine she'd found at Coco's house.

"Oh, honey. Mum jeans? With hiking shoes? Not exactly the epitome of style right now."

"Huh? But I read about them in one of your magazines."

"Honey, that magazine was, like, five years old or something. You could probably get away with them if you were wearing red patent heels or something, but those old trainers aren't doing the same trick."

"What's wrong with my trainers?" Aggie asked.

"What's right with them?" Coco replied as she spotted the perfect bag. "I've found it!" she screeched.

Rolling her eyes, Aggie followed behind her best friend, stopping at a shelf holding what looked like quite a nice compromise for them both.

Coco placed the bag in Aggie's hand with a grin, "Well?"

Holding up the soft, red leather bag, Aggie smiled back and nodded. "It's actually quite perfect."

"I knew we'd find something to suit you in here. And it is the perfect compromise for a former librarian turned sex kitten." She winked.

Aggie blushed and shook her head while swinging the satchel to hit Coco on her bottom.

"Now shoes," Coco said as she marched toward the escalator, stopping to read the map beside it. "Women's shoes," she muttered, "Oh there, third floor," she said, turning to make sure Aggie was right behind her.

"Shouldn't I pay for this first down here?"

"No need, we can pay for everything together. Have you never been to a department store before, Aggie? Honestly woman, I sometimes feel like I'm shopping with a child, not with my best mate!"

"Oh, okay," she said with a faint smile. "Sorry."

Coco linked arms with her, and together they stepped on the huge escalator taking them up to the next floor, where they stepped off before stepping on to the next escalator, continuing until they reached the women's shoe department on the third floor.

Looking around, Coco giggled like a child herself. "Just look at all these shoes," she breathed, struggling to focus.

Aggie laughed, "Well, we could always just skip shopping for me and get some new shoes for you, Coco."

"Why don't we do both?" Coco suggested with a glint in her eye as she was inextricably pulled toward the Christian Louboutins in the far corner of the massive room.

Aggie sat down and watched as her friend picked up and drooled over every single pair of the red-soled footwear until, after a while, she grew tired of perusing and turned her attention to Aggie.

"Not buying any?" Aggie asked, a little surprised.

"Actually no, not yet. I think I'll see what else they have first. But I'm not the priority today. You are. We need to find you a few new pairs."

"But not Christian Louboutins, please. As much as I think they're beautiful. I'd rather not spend all my money on two pairs of shoes when I could buy a whole new wardrobe and then some if we shopped over there for instance," Aggie pointed to the cheaper section of shoes.

"Right you are, my lovely. For now, anyway."

CHAPTER 4

*A*ggie stood in front of the mirror, turning this way and that with a slight frown on her face.

"What on earth is wrong?" asked Coco, looking a little worried.

"It just doesn't look like me," Aggie breathed as she took in the reflection of the pretty young woman staring back at her. Her long, straight locks had been blow-dried and moussed, adding a lot more volume; her flat chest was flat no longer, the Wonderbra working absolute wonders; her long legs looking even longer than usual, even though she'd insisted on buying low kitten heels as opposed to Coco's five-inch pair beside her. But it was her face that had shocked her the most. She'd watched Coco with a critical eye, making sure she hadn't gone overboard with excessive makeup. She was surprised that she hadn't. Just a little well-applied smokey eye shadow, liner and mascara, a touch of blusher, and some pink lipstick and Aggie could barely recognise herself.

Coco smiled. "You really do look beautiful, Aggie. You see, it can be done with just a little help."

Aggie nodded in agreement.

"Are you sorry you doubted me now?"

Again, she nodded.

"Will you have a go at doing it yourself next time?" Coco asked. Another nod.

"I still can't believe it's taken you a decade to let me go near your face with my makeup. You didn't trust me at all before, did you?" she asked as she proceeded to put on her own black and white striped heels that she'd bought that afternoon.

"Not really," Aggie smiled, still looking at herself in the mirror, as she pulled at the blouse. "It was the way you did your own makeup when we were thirteen that frightened me. I mean, that green eyeliner and purple mascara scared the life out of me."

Coco cringed before laughing out loud. "Oh my God, I know… but that was such a long time ago, babe. Hadn't you noticed that my makeup skills have improved just a little bit since then?"

"Yeah, I guess," Aggie chuckled.

"Those jeans look amazing on you. Your bum looks to die for. I'd kill for those long legs of yours."

"They look okay, I guess," Aggie added. "Coco, you might be little, but you're perfectly formed. Just like Kylie."

Coco grinned, "And I got the gold hot pants to prove it," she shrieked. "I still can't believe you bought me that pair for Christmas."

"I couldn't resist. See, I'm not always a prude."

Coco raised her eyebrows, "Buying a pair of gold hot pants does not make you any less of a prude, Aggie. Besides, you ordered them online. It's not like you went in to the shop to get 'em," she laughed. "Anyway, you ready?"

Aggie took one more look at herself before grabbing her new red leather satchel and headed for the door.

"Let's paint this town red, baby!" Coco squealed as the hotel room door slammed behind them. "Where shall we go first?"

"Why don't we just start here?" Aggie suggested. After all, they were staying in one of the most fabulous hotels on the strip.

"Champagne cocktails?" Coco suggested as they linked arms and headed for the elevator.

oOo

A beautiful older lady sang soft jazz songs as a younger man played the piano beside her while hundreds of people mingled around the hotel lobby. A number of them were gambling on the multitude of slot machines scattered throughout the massive area.

Coco and Aggie sat people-watching, enjoying their second champagne cocktails beside the bar, enjoying the ambience of the scene before them.

"It's like nothing I've ever seen before," Coco whispered, leaning forward so Aggie could hear her.

"I know. It's beautiful, isn't it?" Aggie replied.

Coco gave her a strange look before Aggie realised her friend had been talking about a couple sitting at the bar.

"Oh, I thought you meant the hotel."

"No, silly," Coco added. "I was talking about the weird couple over there. Just bizarre. Do you think he's supposed to look like Elvis?"

"Yeah maybe," Aggie said. "Although I'm not sure which Elvis he's going for."

"Young Elvis or old Elvis?" asked Coco.

Aggie nodded. "But what about her?"

"I've no idea. There are no words. God, I love people-watching."

A commotion further down the hotel lobby caught their attention.

"What the heck is going on over there?" asked Coco.

"It sounded like women screaming. Do you think everything's okay? God, I hope it's not a terrorist attack or something."

"In Vegas?" Coco asked. "I'm sure everything's fine. It's probably nothing."

But when more screams began to echo throughout the lobby, Aggie's heart began to beat a little faster.

"I'll go and have a look. Stop worrying. These places are flooded with security. If there were anything to worry about, we'd have been evacuated by now. Stay here. I'll be right back."

Aggie sat back in her chair and gripped her champagne cocktail with both hands. She hoped Coco was right. She didn't want to die. Not in Vegas. She shivered.

"Are you all right, sweetheart?" asked the lady singer who was taking a quick break.

"Yes, thank you. I was just a bit worried about the commotion over there."

The woman turned her head and smiled. "Nothing to worry about, my dear. It's just the arrival of a celebrity. Happens at least twice a week. Considering the screams, I'm assuming it's a famous bloke or something."

"You're English?" Aggie asked.

The woman raised her eyebrows and smiled. "Yorkshire born and bred. But the Moors couldn't keep me from the bright lights of the big city," she winked as she headed back to the piano where the pianist had already begun playing her next song.

Aggie smiled at the sound of "I Say A Little Prayer for You."

Feeling quite a bit more relaxed, Aggie leaned back into her chair again and scanned the crowd for some sign of Coco. Some twenty minutes later, she sauntered out of the throng of people with a smile on her face. She lifted her hand in a wave toward her best friend.

"Everything's fine," she said, slightly out of breath as she sat down.

"I know, I heard it was just the arrival of a celebrity or something?" Aggie replied.

"Not just any celebrity though," Coco added.

"You know him?"

"You could say that," Coco teased.

"Who was it?"

Coco was quiet for a moment before she leaned forward and opened her purse, folding a small paper napkin and shoving it in. "Someone who wrote his private number down for me."

Aggie laughed and leaned back again. "You're a man-magnet, you are! But who was it?"

"You'll never guess."

"I know, which is why you should just tell me already," Aggie smiled as the Yorkshire singer began singing "You're Too Good To Be True."

"She's really good, isn't she?" Coco said.

"She's actually from Yorkshire. I spoke to her while you were mingling with celebs. Who. Was. It?"

Giggling, Coco leaned forward and whispered into Aggie's ear.

"Sorry, I couldn't quite hear. It sounded like you said, Johnnie Blackburn?"

Coco blushed and sat back while taking a long sip of the cocktail.

Aggie's eyes rounded, and she coughed. "For real?"

Coco nodded, "For real."

"Oh my God," Aggie said, grinning from ear to ear. "And he gave you his number?"

Coco took a moment to nod again. "Yep. He invited me out for a drink."

"So what are you doing here with me?" Aggie almost shrieked.

"I couldn't leave you alone. What do you think I am?"

"Coco, we're talking about Johnnie Blackburn here. You've fancied the pants off him for the past three years. Now's your chance. You should go. I don't mind. Really I don't."

"Well I do, and I wouldn't dream of leaving my best mate, not even for Johnnie Blackburn. Not for anyone."

"Coco, you are the best pal a woman could ever dream of. Thank you."

"Well, you owe me," Coco laughed. "Big time."

"I don't doubt it."

"Come on, let's go clubbing. I need to find some eye candy to take my mind of Johnnie bloody Blackburn."

"At least you have his number. Maybe you could call him after the holiday?"

"I don't think so. Perhaps it's better to keep the memory as it is...that way I'll never be disappointed."

"Wow, Coco, you sound so wise. What on earth has happened to you?"

"My sensible best friend, that's what," she joked. "Now come on, let's have some fun. We've only got a few days left. We need to generate our own memories."

CHAPTER 5

It was still pitch black outside as Aggie stood in front of the kettle waiting for it to boil. She shivered and wrapped her dressing gown tightly around her body as she moved toward the window and tried to gauge what the weather was going to do that day. Probably rain, she thought as she returned her attention to her first cup of tea that morning. Stirring a spoonful of honey into it, the sound of post dropping through her mailbox startled her out of her thoughts of Vegas.

She and Coco had been back a week already, and her memories were slowly starting to fade, replaced instead with thoughts of what she was going to do with her life now she no longer had a job at the library of mythology. A job she'd rather enjoyed for the past five years.

Taking a sip of her sweet tea, she smiled, remembering what Coco had done for her. She was one in a million that woman, and Aggie had no idea how she could ever repay her. Not only had she shared her holiday with her, she"d also given her more than two thousand dollars' spending money. But it was giving up her chance to go on a date with Johnnie Blackburn that was the icing on the cake. Nothing she could ever do could live up to that.

Aggie sighed, wishing that one day she could repay her.

Heading toward the front door, she bent down to pick up her mail. The usual bills and her latest copy of Mythology Untold

Magazine along with a letter alerting her to the fact that her subscription was coming to an end. Hardly any point continuing with it, she thought as her thoughts drifted back to the closing of the library. She'd cried as she'd walked out of the old building. Apparently, the owner had sold it to some property developer who was going to knock it down and build a block of flats instead. She sighed as she continued to rifle through the letters, stopping at the sight of a postcard from Vegas.

Grinning, she perched on her old-fashioned telephone seat in the hallway and looked at the picture of the famous strip, lit up in all its night-time glory. Turning it over, she laughed out loud at the sight of Coco's handwriting.

Just wanted to remind you of the fun we had, not to mention the very brief encounter with Johnnie Blackburn! You owe me, you know lol! Only kidding, my lovely.

Stay happy. Love you.

Your bestest pal in the whole wide world,

Coco

Grinning, Aggie shook her head. She was such a nutcase. Picking up the rest of the mail from the side where she'd tossed it all, she went back into the kitchen and sat down to finish her cup of tea, all the while trying to get her head around her future.

Would she keep the old corner shop she'd inherited? Or would she sell it? What would she do with it if she decided to keep it? The town certainly didn't need another "corner shop" as such. There were enough grocery stores, not to mention numerous large-scale supermarkets in the vicinity. No, it would have to be something new. Something different.

But what the hell do I know about running a shop? She thought, sighing as she ripped off the plastic envelope holding her Mythology magazine. Perhaps I could create my own mythology library, she thought to herself. Excited at the possibility, she soon brought herself back down to earth as she realised nobody cared about mythology books any more. Everything was on the internet. No, that certainly wouldn't work.

Sipping the last of her tea, she looked up at the window as the sun was rising in the sky. The gentle sound of birds chirping made her smile. Even when the weather was a bit miserable, one could always count on the birds to sing in a good morning.

She stood up just as her own cuckoo clock—a gift from her mother a couple of years ago—began to sound eight o'clock. Stretching her arms above her head, Aggie yawned and went into the living room. She flicked on the TV to catch the latest headlines. As it seemed to be all doom and gloom, she changed the channel to find breakfast TV. It was more for background noise than anything as she sat down and curled her feet up under her bottom, gazing out the window at the sight of her elderly neighbours in the front garden, and the kids from next door climbing into their parents' car to head to school and their folks to work. She'd have been doing the same not so long ago. It was weird getting up and having nowhere to go. And she didn't like it.

The sound of the presenters talking on TV began to lull her into a sleepy state, so she straightened her legs out from under her and snuggled down into her old sofa, adjusting one of the scatter cushions to cradle her head.

Sighing, she let herself drift, listening in and out to the words being spoken on the telly. The TV duo was laughing as they talked about some new sex aid that was causing a bit of a scene throughout the country, making its inventors a rather tidy sum of money.

Aggie closed her ears and turned away from the TV, trying to block them out as she remembered Coco dragging her into that embarrassing sex shop in Sheffield almost two months ago. It had been quite busy too. Coco loved that sort of thing. There'd been some similar shops in Las Vegas that she'd insisted they peruse, which had caused her to blush on an almost constant basis. Whereas everyone else had seemed to act like it was quite reasonable to buy vibrators and crotchless knickers in full view of the general public. Not me, she thought.

Just as she was about to nod off again, the phone rang. Aggie sat up, catching sight of the odd-shaped gadget on the TV before she rushed into the hallway where she picked up her old-fashioned telephone and greeted the caller.

"Hello, dear, it's only me."

"Hi, Mum."

"Hello, sweetheart. How are you? Well-rested I hope? And ready to start planning your future?" she asked.

"I guess so."

"Well, that's actually why I'm calling," said Aggie's mum.

"It is?" Aggie asked. "Okay then, what's up?"

"Well, your father and I went to see the solicitor dealing with Aunt Petunia's will last night."

"Yes? Is everything all right?"

"I'm getting to that, dear. Well, it seems there's more to it than we originally realised."

"There is?"

"Yes, dear. Well, it seems that Aunt Petunia doesn't want you to sell the corner shop."

"But she left it to me. Isn't it up to me?"

"Well, that's the catch, dear. She put a, er, what do you call it? Er…" Aggie listened as her mother yelled at the other end of the phone. "Edward! What was that thing called again? No, the thing with the will and the corner shop? A what? Oh right. Are you there, dear?"

"Yes, Mum, I'm still here."

"A condition, dear. She put a condition in the will. She's only leaving it to you if you agree to get it back up and running again. It says you can choose whatever kind of shop you like, but it must remain a shop, for at least two years. After that, if it fails, you're allowed to sell. But not before. If you don't want to do that, then she's leaving it to the local vicarage."

"The local vicarage? You mean Reverend Geoff? There's no way in hell I'm letting that man anywhere near my shop," Aggie growled.

"Agatha Trout!" her mum shouted back at her. "You mustn't talk like that about a man of the cloth."

Aggie could imagine her mother cross herself on the other end of the line.

"I couldn't care less whether he's Jesus himself, Mum. That man is pure evil."

"Now why ever would you say a thing like that?"

"Don't you remember, Mum?"

"Remember what, sweetheart?"

"Colin from school? Apparently, Reverend Geoff threw Colin on his head when he was six years old, and there's that rumour about him, er, touching Catarina Eccles inappropriately on her sixteenth birthday. Not to mention the time he grabbed Georgina Wells..."

"Enough!" yelled her mother. "All rumours. None of them proven..."

"Or disproven," Aggie muttered under her breath.

"So I'm taking it you're ready to take on the shop then, Agatha?" her mother asked before anything else could be said about the rumours surrounding the Reverend in the local vicarage.

"Absolutely," Aggie said, standing up to her full height as if preparing for a fight.

"Well then, that's marvellous, darling. Have you had any thoughts on what kind of shop it will be?"

"Not really, Mum. To be honest, I was kind of hoping to sell it, but I guess Great Aunt Petunia has other ideas for me."

"I guess so, dear. Perhaps there's some way you can incorporate your love of the astrology?"

Aggie shook her head and smiled, "It's mythology, Mum."

"Oh, it's all the same to me, dear."

"It's not really. Mythology and Astrology are actually quite different."

"Tomatoes, tomatoes," her mum tutted down the other end of the phone, pronouncing the second word with a terrible American accent.

Aggie laughed again and changed the subject. "Have you spoken to Christie lately?"

"Yes, as a matter of fact, I spoke to your sister this morning."

"That must've been early."

"I rang her at half-past seven. I knew she'd be up with the twins."

"Poor thing. Josephine and Matilda run rings around her."

"They are darlings though," her mum added with a cheeky chuckle.

"So how is she doing? And why were you ringing her so early, Mum?" asked Aggie.

"Well, your Great Aunt Petunia left some money to Christie, and we were chatting about that."

"She left Christie money?" Aggie breathed down the phone.

"Yes, fifty thousand pounds to be exact."

Aggie had to sit down. Her sister, married to a very wealthy banker and living in the most beautiful townhouse, who needed money like a hole in the head, had been given fifty thousand pounds? And to me, with no job, a tiny bungalow and hardly any money to my name, she gives a corner shop, she thought.

"Are you still there, dear?"

"Y…yes Mum. I'm still here."

"I thought it was rather a decent thing of your Great Aunt Petunia to do, considering we haven't really had anything to do with each other over the years. Don't you?"

"Sure, Mum. Great."

"Well, I ought to go. I've got the Ladies Luncheon Club at the golf club today, and I still haven't decided whether to wear my yellow tweed skirt suit or my blush one. And Ebenezer is coming over to do my hair at ten o'clock, so I must dash."

"Ebenezer?" asked Aggie.

"Yes, you must remember him. He did your sister's hair for her wedding. He did such a wonderful job, didn't he? Well, he's been doing mine ever since. I'm sure I've mentioned him to you."

"Oh, yes, of course, I remember him. How could I forget? What a character. But you never told me you'd poached him."

"I did no such thing, dear. He's now a full-time mobile hairstylist, and he comes over twice a month. He does ever such a good job, you know, dear. You ought to see him. I'm sure he'll be able to do something with your long lanky hair, dear. I could make an appointment if you like?"

"I think I'll pass, Mum. Besides, it's not like I can afford it at the moment. I've got my future to sort out."

"That's very sensible, dear. Do let me know if you need any advice. You know I'm always here for you, darling."

"I know, Mum and I appreciate that. But I'll be fine."

"Yes, I'm sure you will. But keep me up to date about what kind of shop you're going to open. The ladies and I are eager to know. Right, toodle pip, dear. Talk soon. Love you."

Aggie placed the phone back on the receiver and pretty much stumbled into the kitchen where she put the kettle on to boil again. Long, lanky hair? That woman had a way with words.

And she still couldn't quite believe it. Fifty thousand pounds. Christie certainly had all the luck. Even when they were born two years apart. It had been a period in their mother's life when she had been clearly obsessed with Agatha Christie novels. Aggie would much rather have been called Christie Trout instead of Agatha Trout (Aggie for short), but she'd been born first, so it was what it was.

As for Christie, Agatha was convinced she'd searched for a husband based on his surname (as well as his bank balance, perhaps). She'd married Jonathan Valentine within a year of dating him. She'd been twenty-two at the time, and the twins had arrived soon after that. They were now approaching three years old. Jonathan, on the other hand, had already celebrated his thirty-seventh birthday. Had he not been a rich man, their mother wouldn't have been too pleased. Aggie was sure of that.

Taking her first cup of coffee (she decided she needed a little more caffeine) into the living room, she sat down. Noticing that the programme now on television was about inheritance and heir hunters, she grimaced and reached for her mobile phone.

"Coco?" Aggie asked as the phone stopped ringing, and she could hear the faint sound of breathing.

"You there? I can hear you breathing?"

"I'm still asleep," said her best friend on the other end of the line.

Aggie smiled as she imagined Coco lying in bed in her favourite satin pyjamas, her eyes covered by one of her many sleep masks, mumbling into the phone.

"It's almost nine o'clock, Coco."

"So," groaned the twenty-seven-year-old woman.

"I need to talk," Aggie whispered before she heard the bed sheets ruffle.

"Okay, I'm up. I'm awake. What's the matter? Are you okay?" asked a somewhat more alert Coco.

"Christie inherited fifty thousand pounds."

"Oh."

"And, get this. I'm not allowed to sell the shop. If I don't want it for myself, it's going to be gifted to the vicarage."

"What?" Coco yelled down the phone, making Aggie hold it away from her ear. "Bleeding Reverend Geoff?"

Aggie nodded, making a yes sound at the same time.

"Well, that's decided then. You're opening a bloody shop. We're not letting that dirty pervert get his filthy hands on it."

"My thoughts exactly," Aggie replied as she sank back into the sofa again.

"Did your Great Aunt Petunia specify what kind of shop?"

"No, that can be up to me apparently."

"Well then, how about a knocking shop?" Coco whooped at her own joke. "That would get your mum's Ladies Luncheon Club talking, wouldn't it? And the so-called Reverend? Creep if ever there was one."

Aggie laughed at Coco"s sudden alertness.

"Do you remember Kirk from Glasgow? I heard that Geoff tried it on him as well. Makes me sick to the stomach. Why ever would your Great Aunt Petunia even think to leave anything to that disgusting human being?"

"I think when she was younger, she must have been a regular at the church, but that would have been way before the arrival of the so-called Reverend Geoff. Before he was stationed there anyway. Stationed? Is that the right word? Probably not. But you know what I mean."

"Yeah, I do. But to be honest, hon. I'm kind of pleased this has all happened."

"You are?" asked Aggie, a little taken aback.

"Ever since you heard the library was closing down, you've not been yourself. You needed a project to get your teeth sunk into. And this, my lovely, is the perfect project to get you back on your feet again. Come to think of it, I have a feeling this just might be the making of you."

"I doubt it, Coco. I've always been okay with my life."

"You shouldn't just be okay with your life, hon. You should be embracing it, loving every second, taking every opportunity that comes your way and pouncing on it."

"You mean the way you do with every sexy man who looks in your direction?" Aggie laughed.

"Something like that. But it's your time now, Aggie. It's time you were noticed. I've managed to work my magic with your makeup, and a few new clothes, but now it's step two. The whole shebang. It's time to take it a step further and not only get your career on the up but maybe get you a man and…"

"Coco?"

"Yes, hon?"

"I get the gist," I smiled.

CHAPTER 6

The town of Frambleberry was located in the east midlands and had all the usual things an English town had to offer. A pretty large church (with a group of dedicated volunteers, not to mention the infamous Rev Geoff), plenty of independent shops (and chain stores) along the high street and beyond, numerous residential estates, most of which were rather nice. There were a few places that weren't so pretty, but all in all, the town had a good name for itself. Crime was relatively low too, which was an added bonus.

The Frambleberry Golf Club was known internationally for having been created by one of the world's top golfers who hailed from the town, but that was a long time ago. The poor man was long dead now.

The town even had its own Starbucks—a place Coco and Aggie frequented for their favourite coffees. A cappuccino and a caramel soy latte, respectively.

Sitting down to enjoy these coffees, the two women were deep in thought.

"What about a baby shop?" Coco cooed as a woman walked past with the cutest little bundle in her arms.

"You're not going broody on me, are you?" Aggie asked, somewhat surprised.

"Who me? Not a chance. They're very cute when they belong to someone else. And that's only until they open their mouths and start wailing. I can't be doing with that."

"Me neither, which is why I'd struggle to work in a shop where babies were brought into all day long," Aggie replied.

"That's a very good point, hon."

"What about wool?" Aggie suggested.

"What about wool?"

"A wool shop?"

"A wool shop?"

"Are you just going to repeat after me all morning?"

Coco shook her head and put her hand on top of Aggie's. "Aggie, honey. You're twenty-eight years old, not seventy-eight. Why, oh why would you want to sell wool to all the old biddies of Frambleberry all day long?"

Aggie shrugged, "It wouldn't be so bad. Some of those old biddies are quite lovely."

"Oh yeah, I forgot they're some of your neighbours. You really need to find yourself another house. Living in a bungalow is for retired people," she mouthed as an old lady walked past and scowled at her.

Coco raised her eyebrows and returned her attention to Aggie.

"Come on, there must be an alternative business opportunity needed in this town. Oh, my God. I mean, seriously O-M-G,"

"What? What Coco?"

Coco began to grin at her best friend as she sat up straight. "I've got it. It's bloody brilliant. I can't believe I didn't think of it earlier. It's perfect, and it's a proper money earner, Aggie. There's potential to earn squillions here. Oh my God…I'm so excited. I could so help with the decor. I've got ideas swimming about in my head already. We must get on to suppliers right away. I know a few people who might be able to help, come to think of it. Dickie from Saffron Walden, for example, he owes me a favour. And there's Selena from Frome. Oh and I must ring Alison, although I think she's in Edinburgh at the moment. I'll wait 'til the weekend. Oh, this is going to be so much fun. Drink up, Agg. We need to get going. We've got masses to do. Come on, let's…"

Coco stopped short and stared at her friend. "What?"

Aggie closed her eyes for a moment and shook her head.

"What's up, honey?"

"Have you listened to yourself? You're getting so carried away. But there's just one little something you haven't mentioned yet."

"Oh really, what's that?" Coco replied innocently.

"What kind of shop are you talking about?"

Coco slapped her own forehead and started to chuckle, "Oh right. Sorry...Aggie. You're going to open the town's first...sex shop!"

CHAPTER 7

"No I'm bloody not," Aggie snorted into her coffee, her face turning puce at the mere thought of it. "And keep your voice down. People are starting to stare, Coco. And I just ca…"

Coco interrupted her, "Agatha Trout, as your best friend in the whole world, beauty consultant, fashion extraordinaire, and soon-to-be business partner, you need to listen to me."

Aggie stopped, "Did you say, business partner?"

Coco's smile lit up her face, and she began to nod, "But only if you agree to open a sex shop. I will not become your business partner in any other venture. And you know that I know my stuff. I'd be the perfect partner in this situation, and you can't deny it. Plus, Vegas? Remember that you owe me? Big time?"

"But…"

"There are no buts, Aggie. It makes perfect sense. The town doesn't have a sex shop right now, and as far as I know, has never had one. The poor people of Frambleberry are crying out for some kinkiness in their lives."

"Perhaps it's never had one because the people of Frambleberry would never accept it."

"This is the twenty-first century, Aggie, not the seventeen hundreds. People are much more open to this kind of thing. Besides, people from all the nearby towns and villages will come if we do it right. This thing could make us a fortune. Think about it. You're almost broke. How are you going to continue paying your mortgage? A wool shop certainly isn't going to cut it, hon. You need to do something big, something huge, something to get the town talking. And a sex shop will do precisely that."

"Yes, for all the wrong reasons," Aggie muttered under her breath. "I just can't do it. You know what I'm like, Coco. I'm so easily embarrassed, I turn beetroot red every time we even walk past Anne Summers in Sheffield."

"Which is exactly why you need to do this. You're twenty-eight years old, Aggie. It's time we got you over your prudish ways."

"I'm not a prude, not really."

Coco's face said otherwise.

"I'm not," Aggie reiterated. "I'm just…just…shy about stuff like that."

"Well, help me help you get over that shyness. Babe…look, why don't you take tonight to think about it and we'll meet up tomorrow over lunch and discuss it further. I'll make a few enquiries of my own…"

Aggie frowned.

"Just enquiries, that's all. I won't mention your name. I promise. Think about it, okay?"

Aggie sighed and sat back in her seat, nodding just ever so slightly.

Coco beamed and finished off her coffee before glancing at her watch. "Oh shit, I'd better go. I agreed to have lunch with Kyle today."

"How is your brother doing?" Aggie asked. "I haven't seen him for ages."

"He's doing great, thanks, babe. He's just got a big contract in town. To build some new big development," Coco replied as she stood up and put on her fake fur coat.

"Oooh, that sounds brilliant. I'm so pleased he's managed to sort himself out. I was so worried about him after your mum and dad died."

"Yeah, he did go off the rails a bit. It's a good thing Dad put a stipulation in the will about Kyle not getting the inheritance money until his twenty-fifth birthday."

"It would have been horrendous had he got it before, he'd have blown much of it on drugs, I think." Aggie thought about what might have happened.

"I know," Coco nodded in agreement. "But he's worked his arse off the past three years. I still can't quite believe his property business has grown so much. I'm so proud of him. Hey, why don't you join us for lunch? I'm sure he'd love to see you."

But Aggie looked down at herself, frowned and shook her head before she followed Coco out of the cafe.

"Thanks, but I'd better head home. I've got a lot of thinking to do. Give him…my best, won't you?"

Coco smiled at her friend and gave her a long hug before releasing her.

"I'll come over to yours about eleven tomorrow. I'll bring some sushi," and with a wink, she turned and walked off, leaving Aggie alone with all kinds of thoughts rushing through her head.

CHAPTER 8

The moment Aggie arrived home, she changed out of her new black polo, skinny jeans and Ugg boots and put on the warm, baby blue onesie her nieces had given her for Christmas —something they'd chosen themselves on account of it being covered in rainbows and unicorns. But it didn't matter, whenever she put it on, it made her smile.

After re-heating a bowl of tomato soup that she'd made the night before, she put it on a tray with two slices of spelt bread and headed to the living room where she flicked on the TV and settled down with the remote control.

"...And apparently, we hit a nerve last week on our breakfast show with our little talk on the new bedroom gadget to hit stores this..." said the presenter on the screen.

Rather than change the channel, Aggie turned her full attention to the show as she started to eat her soup.

"...Sold out in stores..."

Her ears pricking, she put down her spoon and listened to what was being said.

"The small company that developed this fabulous new toy..."

At that moment, the woman's on-screen partner began to chuckle.

"Well, it is fabulous," said the presenter, "and I'm quite happy to admit it. I'm no prude." She smiled straight at the camera. "But worry not people, a spokesperson for the company has assured us that more toys are in production and will be available in stores, and online, very soon. Watch this space. And that's all we've got time for today…"

Aggie sat back as the adverts started and looked out the window. She thought back to what Coco had said about a sex shop being the perfect way to make money.

Maybe it was the right business to start. She sighed. But how? How could she get over her acute embarrassment?

She turned her attention back to her soup, dipping the bread into it before taking a large bite, followed by a small mouthful of the delicious tomato broth.

But she couldn't shake Coco's words out of her head.

"You're twenty-eight years old, Aggie. It's time we got you over your prudish ways. Think about it. You're almost broke. How are you going to continue paying your mortgage? You need to do something big, something huge, something to get the town talking. And a sex shop will do that".

Coco was right, of course. A sex shop would be the talk of the town, whether for the right or the wrong reasons.

"What am I going to do?" she said out loud.

You're going to open a sex shop, said Coco's voice in her head.

"No, I can't. I can't do it," she said aloud.

Of course you can. I'm going to help you, aren't I? repeated the imaginary voice.

All of a sudden, Aggie felt like a light bulb had been switched on in her head.

"Coco's going to help me, that means…maybe she could work in the shop, and I'll do everything else. Now that's a better idea. I wonder if she'll go for it?"

oOo

"It is a thought, babe, but I can't work full-time," Coco stated.

"Really?" sighed Aggie, a little deflated. "But why not?"

Coco popped some salmon sashimi into her mouth before replying, "I've got my weekly appointments to go to. I can't possibly miss having my hair done and my mani-pedis. Are you insane? It takes effort to look this good, you know," she grinned.

Aggie shook her head in disbelief, "Can't you just have all that done after hours or something?"

"Aggie, honey. I'm more than happy to work in the shop part of the week, but you need to be there too. How are we gonna get you over your fears if you don't jump in the deep end? But I am chuffed to bits that you're seriously considering this. So have you finally made a decision?"

Aggie shook her head as her chopsticks twisted within her fingers and she dropped a salmon roll into the bowl of soy sauce.

"Bugger, no, not yet. I've been thinking about it all night, though."

"Yeah? Me too. I asked Kyle's opinion too," she grinned.

Aggie's eyes grew large all of a sudden, and she blushed.

"Sweetie, stop worrying. He thinks it's a fabulous idea anyway. And…"

"And what?"

"You know I mentioned he's got some big new development happening in town?"

Aggie nodded.

"Well, it's actually not far from the shop, so he reckons that could be a plus for us."

"For us? You didn't tell him it's my shop, did you?"

Coco took a gulp of water and nodded.

"But you said you wouldn't tell anyone."

"My brother's hardly just anyone, Agg. He's a businessman, and he knows what he's talking about. He said we should go for it."

"Oh, Coco. I'm so embarrassed."

"Jesus, Aggie! Stop it. It's getting ridiculous. Stop being so embarrassed all the time. We've got to shake it out of you."

"Sorry," Aggie muttered. "You're right. I just can't help it most of the time."

Coco rubbed her friend's arm and nodded, "I know. But we're going to sort it out. You and I are going to change Frambleberry for the better, and it's going to make you super confident. I promise," she grinned.

"Really?"

Coco nodded, "Really."

Aggie picked up another salmon roll with her chopsticks, but this time managed to dip it in the soy sauce and pop it into her mouth as if she'd been using them her whole life.

"Way to go, girl," Coco laughed. "See…you're quickly becoming a confident young woman, and we haven't even opened the shop yet."

"Hardly," Aggie laughed. "It's only chopsticks."

"Today, chopsticks…tomorrow the world."

Both women fell about laughing.

CHAPTER 9

"... And she's believed to be the sixteenth richest woman in Britain. Can you believe it?" Coco screeched down the phone. "That could be us, you know?"

"Don't you think you're getting a bit ahead of yourself, Coco? She's running a business that has shops all over Britain. And they've been in business for decades."

"I know that, but if she can do it, we sure can," Coco slurred.

"Where are you anyway?" Aggie asked as she pulled the warm throw down from the top of the sofa, so it covered her legs. "It sounds deafening."

"The club."

"Who are you with tonight?"

"Anthony. He's just gone to get us another bottle of bubbly from the bar."

"Anthony? Is that the older guy you met at Starbucks?"

"Yeah. He's good fun, divorced, works in the city. Got a couple of kids though. Not my thing. But still, he's a good laugh to while away an evening or two," Coco said with a hiccup.

"Well, just be careful and don't drink too much. Remember you're coming with me to see the shop tomorrow. You don't want a hangover while we're talking business, do you?"

"I'll be fine. We'll call it a night after this bottle."

"Are you staying at his?"

"I haven't decided yet. Maybe."

That means yes then, Aggie thought.

"Well just be careful."

"Yes, Mum," Coco laughed. "Don't worry, I'll be well-protected."

Aggie chuckled and realised she wasn't blushing. Result!

"Anyway, I just wanted to let you know what I'd been reading about that woman. Food for thought. I'd better go, Anthony is here with the bubbles. Enjoy your evening, babe. Mwah."

And with that, Coco hung up.

Aggie smiled and shook her head as she put her mobile phone on the coffee table. Coco and her men were always very entertaining.

Sitting back in the sofa, Aggie used both hands to hold her mug of hot chocolate as she brought it to her mouth to take a sip. She hadn't told Coco that she'd been reading the very same article about the sixteenth richest woman in Britain. Smiling, she glanced down at her laptop that lay open on the Wikipedia page. She was coming round to the idea. Tomorrow, after the two of them had visited the corner shop, she would make the final decision. She was excited, although nervous, about what her future had in store for her.

Closing the laptop and pushing it aside, she flicked on the telly and scrolled through the TV guide. She stopped when she saw Meg Ryan's face and smiled. One of her all-time favourites, she settled in to watch Meg go head to head with Tom Hanks in You've Got Mail.

One of the reasons she'd always loved the film was because of the relationship between the friends who worked in the old book shop. If only I could've opened a bookshop, she thought and sighed, knowing full well that Frambleberry already had several bookstores, two of which were struggling on account of online sales taking over.

But there was no reason she couldn't create a store that made people feel at home, right? One where adults could come in and not be embarrassed. One where the staff were friendly and welcoming.

But there was just one thing in her way: her own unending embarrassment.

"I have to kick it," Aggie said aloud, as she opened up her laptop again and typed in, "How to stop being embarrassed."

Numerous results appeared, some focussing on confidence or self-hypnosis while others dealt with past situations. After a while though, Aggie grew bored and decided that if she wanted to sort it out, she had to take the problem into her own hands and simply stop. She had to accept that the things that embarrassed her were just standard everyday stuff and nothing to be ashamed of.

Sex toys, she thought to herself. Many people use them. In fact, sex toys had probably even helped countless get pregnant and have babies. They had probably helped increase the population. Not that the world needed help.

Aggie sat still and focussed on sex toys. Naturally, she felt herself blush, but only a little. She smiled and moved on to the next thing that usually turned her face crimson. Kinky underwear. Crotchless panties. Although she felt herself heat up a little, her face remained the same colour.

Could it really be this easy, she thought?

Opening a sex shop in Frambleberry. She concentrated hard on not feeling any embarrassment, and it seemed to work quite well, so she quickly moved on to the next thought. Telling Mother.

Aggie's face turned a deep shade of red.

Oh, knickers!

CHAPTER 10

"Have you got the key?" yelled Coco, from across the parking lot.

Aggie lifted up the set of keys and dangled them above her head with a grin as she increased her pace toward Coco.

"Awesome!" Coco replied as they hugged before turning away from the car park and headed towards town.

"How are you feeling? Did you have a good time with Anthony?"

"I'm absolutely fine. No hangover whatsoever. And we had fun, but I didn't stay over."

"No? That's not like you. What happened?"

"His ex-wife appeared with the kids after midnight. Can you believe it? She's a nutcase, that one."

"Blimey, that's not good. How old are the kids?"

"Fourteen and ten. Little shits too. Needless to say, I left straight away. I think his ex is trying to get him back. Well, she can have him. I was only there for the sex. Shame I didn't bloody get any," Coco moaned.

"I bet Anthony was furious."

"Yeah, he was. At her, then at the kids, and then at me for leaving him. They're not my bloody kids," Coco grumbled.

Aggie chuckled under her breath.

"It's not funny," Coco breathed, pulling her black fur-lined parka closer to her body.

"It is...just a little bit funny. Admit it," she goaded.

Looking at each other's faces, Coco started to laugh, "All right, all right, it would have made a good scene in a comedy. Happy now?"

Aggie nodded as they approached the beautiful old building on the corner of Pelican Street.

"Wow, it looks like a fabulous place," Coco said, as they came to a halt across the road so they could admire it. "I had no idea it was this old or this impressive," she added.

"To be honest, neither had I," Aggie replied, a little dubious.

"What? You haven't been here yet?"

"I didn't see the point," Aggie said, raising her eyebrows.

"You silly sod."

"Yeah, I know," smiled Aggie. "But we're here now. Come on. Let's go and check it out."

With shaky fingers, Aggie struggled to get the key in the hole. She grinned and turned to Coco as the key slotted inside. She then pushed the door open.

"Wow," she exclaimed. "It's incredible. And it's much bigger than I'd imagined."

"Hadn't you even looked at the plans?" Coco asked.

Shaking her head, Aggie stood with her mouth open, looking around at the impressive structure. Although dust had settled everywhere, and it was clear it hadn't been in use for many years, it took her breath away. "I can't quite believe all this is mine," she whispered.

"Not only that but look over here, Agg..." Coco squealed as she rushed over to the far corner of the room. It goes on even farther back here. And look..." she pointed around the corner, "stairs!"

"What? But I thought it was just on one floor," Aggie asked as she looked around.

"It doesn't look like it, honey. Come on, let's go up and have a look."

Following right behind her, Aggie's heart was beating faster and faster with complete and utter excitement.

Sure enough, the stairs opened to yet another floor the same size as the one below.

"OMG, Aggie! It's enormous. What's around here?" she asked as she wandered off, leaving Aggie open-mouthed at the scale of it all.

"How am I going to be able to afford to stock this place?" she said more to herself than to anyone else.

"Err, Aggie. I think you'd better come here," said the muffled sound of Coco's voice.

"What is it?" she said as she followed the sound of her voice.

"It's not just a shop, Aggie!" she squealed. "Look!" Coco was standing atop another set of stairs, beckoning her to follow. "Quick, come up, come up now."

The excitement was beginning to get to Aggie, and she started to come out in a little sweat as she bolted up the second set of stairs.

"What's up there? What is it?" she yelled, trying to locate her best friend.

But Coco was quiet.

Walking the last two steps, Aggie gasped as she pushed open a door a little distance away from the stairs.

"It's a flat, Aggie! You've got your own flat!"

"No, it can't be. We must have the wrong building, Coco. This can't possibly be mine. There must be a mistake. I need to speak to the solicitor. He must've given me the wrong key and the wrong address."

Coco leaned against the wall and said nothing as Aggie pulled out her mobile phone and speed-dialled the solicitor who had handled Great Aunt Petunia's will.

After a few moments, the secretary put her straight through to the man in question.

"Miss Trout, is everything all right? My secretary said you sounded a little panicked?" he asked.

Aggie turned away from Coco and began pacing back and forth as she spoke to the solicitor.

Coco tried to listen in to the conversation, but she'd moved a little too far away, and so she just stood still, waiting to hear the news. Was it really Aggie's place?

After a few more minutes, Aggie turned around and dropped her arms down by her side. Her face was pale.

"Awww, honey. It was a mistake, wasn't it? Oh, what a bummer. It would have been a bloody brilliant place to open the shop. Oh well. So where is it?"

"We're standing in it, Coco. It's mine. All of it. All four floors of it."

Coco squealed and did a little dance before she rushed toward Aggie and hugged her in a tight bear hug.

"Wait a minute," she stopped. "You said four floors?"

Aggie nodded, "There's another floor. The shop runs over two floors, and so does the flat. I…I can't quite believe it. This whole place is mine, Coco. It's all mine."

Her knees buckled beneath her and Aggie crumpled to the floor.

Coco fell to her knees along with her, and after a minute of silence, the two began to laugh. The sound of the two hysterical women became louder and louder.

CHAPTER 11

"Why didn't you tell me?" asked Aggie down the phone at her mum.

"I thought you knew, dear."

"I had no idea."

"Well, you did go there once when you were young. It was just after your Great Uncle Jim died, Your Great Aunt Petunia invited us to a memorial do there. I couldn't make it, but your father took you. Don't you remember?"

"How young was I?"

"Well, I am going back a bit. Gosh, that must've been, er, let me think for a minute, dear. Oh well, I guess you wouldn't really remember. You were barely three, I think."

"Well, I doubt I'd remember that far back, Mum," Aggie sighed.

"I suppose not. My memory must be going, I am seventy, you know," she chuckled under her breath.

"But do you remember the shop though, Mum? It's huge. And the flat? You didn't tell me about the flat."

"I don't really remember it too well, dear. I don't think Aunt Petunia lived there in her later years, so I guess I probably wasn't really aware of it. I do have a very vague memory of the shop being quite pretty, though. Aunt Petunia certainly had it jam-packed full of things when she was younger, or so I'm told."

"What did she sell? Was it a proper corner shop?"

"Well, I guess you could call it that. I believe it had everything from newspapers and sweets to milk and other groceries. Pretty much everything you'd need to live on, I suppose. But I wasn't allowed to visit so I can't remember it all that well any more. Aunt Petunia did have it from quite a young age though, you know Aggie?"

"Really? The only things I know is that the building was constructed in the late eighteen-hundreds. Do you know when she first took ownership?"

"No dear. I'm afraid I don't really know very much about that woman. But you have all the paperwork, don't you? I'm sure you'll find all your answers there. Now I should go, dear. Gretchen and Peter are coming over for supper tonight, and I must get this black forest gateau finished, not to mention the mushroom vol-au-vents. You know how your father loves his mushroom vol-au-vents."

"Okay, Mum. Have a good evening. Give Gretchen and Pete, my love. See you soon."

"Toodle pip, dear."

Aggie put her phone back in her handbag and continued sitting cross-legged on the floor of the shop. In awe of what she'd inherited, she still couldn't quite believe the size of the place. And it was hers. All hers. Giggling to herself, she climbed to her feet and leaned back against the main entrance, surveying her new kingdom.

The ground floor covered an area of about two hundred and fifty square meters, the second floor a little bit less, the third floor quite a bit smaller and the top floor, quite a bit smaller—but still very spacious for Aggie to live in.

That morning she'd been to the local estate agent and put her little bungalow on the market. It was pointless keeping it when she could go mortgage-free, and any profit she made on the sale could be put straight into the new business venture. But she and Aggie had yet to finalise their plans. That would happen in a couple of days, giving her enough time to make some notes about the actual building and how it could be put to good use.

Looking around, Aggie smiled at the beautiful architecture of the building. She just loved the reddish coloured stone that had been used on the outside, the pretty arched windows that were placed either side of the main entrance door, not to mention the old-fashioned countertop that spanned the entire length of the right-hand side of the shop floor. The stairs to the second floor, which initially had been hidden by a large pile of old chairs covered in several sheets when she and Coco had first visited, were somewhat grand. And a multitude of shelves covered the entirety of the walls, not only behind the countertop but to the lefthand side of the building too.

Aggie walked up to some of them and gently stroked the solid wood. A thick layer of dust covered her fingers, and she coughed as she released some of it into the air.

This is going to be one of a hell of a job, she thought.

oOo

"So that's it then? We've decided?" Coco asked a few days later as they pored over all their notes while sharing a bottle of white wine.

"I...I think so," Aggie stuttered.

Coco's eyes widened as she looked at her best friend, "I'm so proud of you, Aggie," she said. "Let's make a toast," she added, lifting her glass into the air. "Here's to the new business. Let's hope sex sells, eh?" she laughed.

"To the business," Aggie replied, clinking the two glasses together. "Let it be hugely successful."

"Hear hear," Coco giggled as she took rather a long swig of wine.

"So what are we going to call it?"

"I'm not sure, to be honest. I haven't even thought about that. I've been so busy thinking about the actual shop that I've barely had a chance to even think about anything else."

"What's been on your mind?" Coco asked, putting her glass down on the kitchen table and reaching for an olive.

"I've been reading over old paperwork and stuff. Trying to

find out a bit more about Great Aunt Petunia. I feel like I should learn more about her, you know? I wish I could thank her for all this."

"Yeah, that's understandable. Did you find out anything juicy?" Coco grinned.

"Well, it's funny you should say that because I did discover that she was married not once, not twice, but four times!"

"Oh the saucy devil," Coco exclaimed. "Who to?"

"Her first husband died mysteriously just before the start of the second world war, her second was murdered in Africa in 1955, the third died of a heart attack in nineteen...er what was it, oh yeah, 1970 and the fourth died on her seventy-fifth birthday. He had a heart attack too. Poor Aunt Petunia. What a terrible life she must've had."

"Or maybe she was something of a black widow?" Coco suggested.

A shiver went down Aggie"s spine before she shook her head. "My Great Aunt Petunia was not a killer, Coco."

"Well, you don't know that."

"Of course she wasn't. She was just unlucky in love, that's all. Poor girl."

"You've not really told me that much about her. Where was she up until recently? And why didn't you know she existed? It's all a bit weird, isn't it?" Coco asked.

"Yeah it is a bit, come to think of it. I got the feeling that she and Mum weren't close—at all. Mum barely even knew about the shop. Oh, she did mention that I'd been here before though. I was about three apparently, and Dad and I came over after her last husband died, but I can't remember that far back. I understand that she was in some kind of an old peoples' home for the last ten years or so and died just after her ninety-ninth birthday. It's kinda sad, really. I'd have loved to have known her—at least to have visited her at least once anyway."

"It's strange that your mum didn't tell you about her sooner. I'd have thought your mum was more sentimental than that."

"Yeah well, Mum's not really the sentimental kind. I reckon something must've happened in the family at some point. When

Mum gets something into her head, she doesn't really let it go, does she?"

"I suppose not. But why don't you ask her?"

"I don't want to pry," Aggie said. "Besides, she probably wants bygones to be bygones."

"Maybe, but don't you think she owes it to you to tell you the truth about Petunia? After all, the woman did just leave you a shop worth an absolute fortune."

Aggie screwed up her face and shook her head. "I get where you're coming from, but I don't think so. It's not worth upsetting the balance with Mum," she raised her eyebrows, "And anyway, Aunt Petunia can't have held a grudge otherwise she wouldn't have left Mum's kids anything, would she?"

"I guess not," Coco frowned, just a little disappointed not to have learned the good old gossip. "So, back to the sex shop."

"Can we not call it that, though, Coco?"

"What?"

"A sex shop. It makes is sound so…so…seedy."

Coco laughed. "What do you suggest?"

"A lingerie shop."

"But that's not strictly the truth though is it?"

"It is…kind of," Aggie added, taking another swig of wine.

"What about a 'spicy lingerie shop?'" Coco suggested.

"That's a little better."

"But still not quite right," Coco agreed. "Perhaps we should just describe it as an adult shop?"

"Yes that's better, I suppose. I've been thinking about the placement of the products," Aggie added as Coco looked up, intrigued. "Seeing as we have a second floor to the shop, I thought we ought to place all the lingerie on the ground floor and then the er…"

"Toys? Gadgets? Fun stuff?" Coco interrupted her with a laugh.

"Toys," Aggie nodded with a smile.

"Hey," Coco piped up.

"What is it?"

"You didn't blush!" Coco exclaimed.

"I…I didn't?" Aggie asked with a knowing grin before she nodded, "I've been working on my embarrassment factor."

"Embarrassment factor? Well, you should keep doing what you're doing because it seems to be working."

"Until I start working in the shop, that is," Aggie said, backtracking a bit.

"You can stop that already," Coco shook her head. "You're doing great. Don't sell yourself short. But anyway, what were we talking about?"

"Product placement," Aggie replied, picking up the bottle of wine and filling both glasses.

"I think the lingerie should be on the ground floor and the more 'adult' items should be on the upper level."

"I couldn't agree more. We'll have to splash out on CCTV though; otherwise, we'll get people nicking everything," Coco suggested.

"We ought to have a counter and till upstairs too," Aggie said. "Otherwise any shy customers might be too embarrassed to carry any…toys…downstairs in full view of the rest of the clientele."

Coco nodded, "Good idea."

"It all sounds costly, though, doesn't it?" Aggie said, resting her chin on her hand. "I just hope we can afford to do it. The CCTV might have to wait a little longer, though."

"Don't worry about it, Agg. Money's never a problem, you know that."

"Yes but I don't think you should be the one to be buying all the stock and equipment."

"Honey, you own the entire building. The least I can do is put my money where my mouth is. Besides, I reckon you'll make a little bit on the sale of the bungalow. Not that you need to, but have you thought about asking your sister if she wants to invest the money she inherited?"

"Christie? You're joking, right? She'd be mortified," Aggie said, shaking her head.

Coco's eyes squinted, and she tapped the side of her head with a finger, "You think so? I don't. I think you'd be surprised. I reckon Christie would love to get involved in something like this. It'll tickle her, I'm sure it would."

Aggie rested her chin in her hand and was quiet for a moment, regretting the jealousy she'd initially felt when Christie had inherited the cash from their great aunt. "It would be kind of nice to involve her, I guess. We're much better friends now than when we were kids," she laughed.

"I think Christie could be an asset. She knows a lot of mums and lots of mums are craving this kind of stuff," Coco grinned, pointing to a couple of the product catalogues they'd been sent. "Not to mention their husbands," she added, winking.

"You do have a point there," Aggie grinned. "I'll speak to her about it."

"Why don't you see if she fancies coming out for dinner soon? I'm sure she's craving a break from the kids."

"Now that I know she'd love. I'll ask her."

CHAPTER 12

*A*ggie had always loved the red and white checked tablecloths at Flavia's, the best Italian restaurant in the county. She always thought it was so authentic. Not that she'd ever been to Italy, but she imagined that it would be just like that.

Coco, who had once dated Luigi, the chef, could always manage to get them a table, even during their busiest season. Not that it was busy yet though—there was still a month or two until the season really got underway.

Coco and Aggie sat, after having ordered their favourite bottle of Prosecco, and compared notes about their upcoming venture while they waited for Christie to arrive.

Not five minutes later, she waltzed in, dressed in a classic knee-length black trench coat, which she took off to reveal a pretty blue floral tea dress to match her eyes.

"Sis," Aggie squealed. "You look amazing," she said as she stood up and gave her sister a squeeze.

"Aww thanks, Aggie. You look pretty good yourself. Actually, you look gorgeous," she said, pulling back and looking her up and down, "What's going on? Have you had a makeover? Oh my God, you really have. Look at you. I can't believe it. You look so different."

Aggie blushed just a little bit and nodded.

"You can blame Coco for that."

Coco grinned and hugged Christie while Aggie sat back down.

"Yep, blame me," she chuckled. "I've been trying to get my hands on your sister's hair and makeup for years. Not to mention her wardrobe. She finally succumbed while we were in Vegas, though. Since then, I convinced her to bin much of what she used to wear. Et voila—a whole new woman. Amazing, right?" Coco said, clearly quite proud of herself.

"Totally, Coco. She looks beautiful. Mind you, I always knew she was beautiful underneath those dowdy clothes and centre parting," she grinned, looking at Aggie's hair. "You've finally revealed my true sister. I'm delighted."

"Aw, you guys," Aggie cried. "You're making me blush."

"You don't seem to be blushing that much either, Aggie! You really are a different woman."

"I'm working on that too."

"Crikey, I'm so impressed. Now tell me. How was Vegas? I'm so sorry I haven't been able to meet you since you got back but what with the kids being so sick and everything, I honestly didn't want to risk giving it to you. It was horrendous. I don't think I've ever seen so much vomit and diarrhoea in my entire life. And then the spots came soon afterwards. Poor things. They've not been well at all. But enough of all that. Prosecco and pizzzzaaaaaaaaa," she almost wailed as Aggie poured her sister a glass.

"Wow, you were ready to get out, weren't you?" Coco laughed as Christie nodded.

"You. Have. No. Idea."

"Thankfully," Coco added.

"Are the kids okay now, Sis?"

"Much better thanks. Thank God. Jonathan would have struggled to take care of them tonight if they were still sick. I so needed to get out, so I appreciate you inviting me. What's the occasion?"

"Well, we're kind of celebrating a new business venture together."

"Oh, my God…I completely forgot about the shop. You must think I'm such a cow. I never even called to congratulate you on inheriting it. Blimey, Aggie. Sorry. Tell me more. What are you going to do with it? Sell it?"

Aggie smiled and shook her head, "Great Aunt Petunia put a condition in the will saying that I had to keep it otherwise, it would be donated to the local vicarage."

Christie screwed up her face, "Not to that toss-pot, Reverend whatever his name is?"

Aggie and Coco both nodded, looking disgusted at the same time.

"So you have to keep it and open it as a shop then?"

Aggie nodded and grinned at Coco.

"A corner shop? Groceries and stuff?"

"Fortunately there's no condition stating what the shop must be," Aggie grinned.

"Which is why..." Coco interrupted, "Aggie is going to open a..." she stopped and looked at her best friend.

"An adult shop," Aggie finished the sentence.

Christie almost spat out the wine she was drinking, and her eyes grew wide.

"An adult shop?" she whispered as a grin started to appear across her face.

Aggie and Coco both nodded. They were eager to discover Christie's opinion.

"You're going to use Aunt Petunia's inheritance to open a sex shop?" she said a little louder this time.

Both girls looked at each other and nodded again.

"But...but... Aggie, you're such a prude! How on earth are you going to do that?"

"I...I...I'm working on it. I don't want to be known as being a prude anymore, Sis. And I want to start a business that will bring in enough money to live on comfortably. I want to build a successful business with Coco...and, if you're interested, we wondered if you'd like to be involved."

"Oh, wow!" Christie exclaimed, "I need more wine." She laughed and lifted up her hand, gesturing to the waiter to bring another bottle of Prosecco.

"What do you think, Christie? Do you think we're nuts? Or do you think it's a viable option?" Aggie asked.

"Well, I'm chuffed to bits that you'd like me to be involved, for a start. And to be honest, I have been going a bit stir crazy at home lately. Fortunately, though, the girls are about to start preschool, which will give me some extra time. But a sex shop?" she whispered a little more quietly this time and leaned forward.

"Well, we've done some homework," Coco said. "And Frambleberry has never had one. No one has ever been brave enough to open one...until now. We reckon there's a huge market for lingerie, toys, and other sex aids. Plus, there's a bonus that the shop has two floors so the ground floor would be very tame, with pretty lingerie and stuff while upstairs will have the more, let's say, daring items. There's a new large development being built not too far away at the moment too, which will bring even more people into the town. It's one of Kyle's projects," she added.

Christie nodded and smiled as the waiter brought some more wine and left with the empty bottle.

"How is Kyle? I haven't seen him for a while."

"He's doing great, thanks. His company is growing like nobody's business. I'm a proud sister."

"I know what that feels like," Christie said, turning and smiling at Aggie.

"Shall we order before we continue? I'm starving," Aggie suggested as she called the waiter back over again and they each ordered a different kind of pizza.

Once he'd left their table, Christie continued, "Back to the business. I must say I'm very impressed with what you're telling me and I'd love to be involved. I'm sure you know I also inherited a sum of money from Great Aunt Petunia, and I think it would be brilliant to invest that in your new business."

"Our new business, Sis," Aggie said as she raised her glass.

"Our new business," Coco and Christie both repeated, clinking glasses before they all took a sip.

"So what's it called?"

"Ah, well, we haven't got a name just yet," Coco replied. "We've been so focussed on everything else."

"That's fair enough. So you don't have any ideas?"

"None whatsoever," Aggie replied. "But you should see the shop, Christie. It's freaking amazing."

"Really? I just thought it was your average corner shop."

"There's nothing average about it," Coco added. "It's also got its own two-floor flat upstairs."

"Yep," Aggie added, "and I'm moving in. I've already put the bungalow on the market."

"Oh, wow, that's fantastic. I'm so excited for you. When can I see it?"

"Well, I brought the keys with me. We could go after dinner if you like."

Christie grinned, "I'd love that," she squealed. "My sister, the beautiful businesswoman. Who'd have thought, eh?" she laughed.

Aggie stuck out her tongue just before they all took another sip of wine.

oOo

WALKING into the building and turning on the lights (which Aggie had just got put back on by Frambleberry Electricity), all three girls just stood, their mouths open, staring at the beautiful old chandelier hanging in the centre of the room.

"I hadn't even noticed it before," Coco breathed.

"It's stunning. I bet it's an antique. This place is incredible," Christie said as she walked around.

"It's still very dusty so avoid leaning on anything," Aggie warned.

"This is going to have to be a classy adult shop," Christie said. "You've got to keep all the stuff in here and use it to your advantage. People will want to come in here just to get a good look at the old building. Like those shelves, I bet they're original. Victorian, I think."

"I thought it was later than that," Aggie asked.

But Christie shook her head, "No, this place was built in the mid-eighteen-hundreds, I think. Look over there at that coving. I"m pretty sure that's original. Not to mention the floor. The black and off-white tiles are most definitely from that era. And you see those two windows up there?"

Coco and Aggie both looked upward and nodded.

"They've both got stained-glass panels, which was quite common in the Victorian era. That's what I reckon anyway."

"I'd completely forgotten you used to study architecture and design."

"Gave it all up to get married and have kids," Christie smiled. "But I wouldn't change it for the world. As long as I can have a break every now and again," she laughed.

"I wonder why Mum thought it was built in the late eighteen-hundreds then?" Aggie wondered out loud.

"Beats me," Christie replied. "Can I go upstairs?"

"You don't have to ask, Sis," Aggie grinned. "Go and explore. I don't know where Coco's got to. I'll go and have a look."

Both girls wandered about the shop, heading toward the back stairs when a yell from above caused them both to stop in their stride.

"Coco?" yelled Aggie. "You all right?"

Nothing.

Christie looked at her sister, and both ran up the grand staircase.

"Coco!" they both yelled. "You all right?"

Still nothing.

"Where are you? Aggie shouted.

A muffled sound could be heard behind a large wooden panel, at which the sisters both looked.

"Did you hear that?" Christie asked.

Aggie nodded, "Coco?"

"I'm here," Coco said back, although the sound was still somewhat muffled.

"Where?" Christie asked, putting both hands against the panel and pushing, but it wouldn't budge.

"Right here," Coco said again.

"That's weird," Aggie said as she began to feel along the wall beside the panel.

"What's that, there?" Christie suggested, pointing to a couple of books on a shelf.

"Just books," Aggie said as she went to pick them up, but the books were fixed to the shelf, and the moment her hand pushed down on them, the panel moved sideways.

"Oh wow, it's a secret door," Christie squealed with excitement.

"Coco?" Aggie asked as they stepped inside.

"I'm here," she said, as she revealed herself behind a large curtain that hung between them both. "Look what I found," she said as she pulled the curtain to one side. "I think maybe it's stuff that belonged to your Great Aunt Petunia. There are photos, letters, clothes, teddy bears, all sorts."

"Holy shit," Aggie said as she bent down to have a proper look. "You really think this was hers? It looks so old. It must belong to whoever owned the shop before."

"Maybe it was in the family before Petunia," Christie suggested as she picked up a photo and held it to the light. "Hang on, I've seen her before. Well, I've seen a picture of her before anyway."

"Really?" Coco asked, standing up and dusting herself down.

Aggie, who started coughing, stepped out of the secret room, "Surely not? This stuff must have been hidden in here for decades."

"Well, it all belongs to you now. It's up to you to decide what to do with it," Coco grinned, handing her one of the boxes she'd picked up from the floor. "By the way, there's a little wardrobe in there with even more old clothes in it. It's bloody unbelievable this place. It just keeps on giving," she smiled, leaving Aggie and Christie behind as she headed toward the stairs that led upward.

"Wait, I wanna see the flat too," Christie yelled after her. "You coming?" she asked her sister.

Aggie nodded and pulled the secret door closed again. She'd have to investigate it later.

CHAPTER 13

"I've ordered some of those new G-spot thingies," Coco said, before continuing, "you know, the ones they've been raving about on the telly?"

"What, on breakfast TV last month?" asked Aggie.

Coco nodded as she scrolled through another adults-only website. "Apparently, they're flying off the shelves, so it makes sense we should have some. How's the lingerie looking?"

"To be honest, I'm not doing so well," Aggie admitted. "I'm so used to wearing simple cotton T-shirt bras and knickers that I'm just not sure what women really want."

Coco laughed, "Well, I know you're not really going to like this, but we're going to have to go to that fair I mentioned last week."

"The lingerie fair, you mean?"

"Well, yes, there's the lingerie fair in a couple of weeks, but I was actually referring to the erotic trade fair."

Aggie gulped quite loud. "The erotic trade fair?"

Coco nodded with a huge grin on her face.

"Do…do I really need to go?" Aggie asked, quite mortified.

Coco linked arms with her best friend and nodded. "Aggie, honey. We're about to open what is for all intents and purposes a lingerie and sex shop where we'll be selling all kinds of weird and wonderful gadgets and so on. Of course you must come with me. It's where we'll get to see all the latest stuff that we ought to be selling in the shop. If we're going to be taken seriously, we need to be on top of our game, right?"

Aggie reluctantly smiled and nodded. "Yeah, you are right, I suppose. Maybe I can wear a disguise or something," she joked. "So when is it, anyway?"

"Next week. I took the liberty of buying tickets for us both," she grinned.

Aggie rolled her eyes.

"I know, I know," Coco laughed. "I knew you'd come. But before any of that, don't you think we ought to sort out the name. It'll take the sign makers a little bit of time to get the sign sorted out so we shouldn't leave it to the last minute. Plus, we'll need to do a website and the like. Not to mention the press releases. That reminds me, have you told your mother yet?" Coco asked as she walked over to the little kitchen in Aggie's new flat and put on the kettle.

Blushing almost immediately, Aggie shook her head, making Coco laugh even louder than before.

"Oh, honey. It's got to be done at some point, you know. You never know, she might be delighted."

"You do know my mother, don't you? The seventy-year-old woman who is the face of the Frambleberry Ladies Luncheon Club, as well as chairwoman to the Frambleberry WI? She's going to be shocked to high heaven."

Coco, struggling to keep a straight face, nodded while she raised her eyebrows, "Still, it's better she hears it from you rather than someone else, right?"

"I know, I know. I just can't face that right now. We've got too much else to think about. Like the shop name, for instance," she said, looking Coco in the eye. "Any ideas?"

"Everything I come up with sounds a bit cheap and cheesy, to be honest. Your sister was right when she said this place needs to remain classy, in other words, we need to come up with a classy name. Easier said than done, I'm afraid."

Aggie stepped away from the kitchen countertop, holding the cup of tea Coco had made her and leaned against the wall. "It ought to inspire love, rather than sex if you know what I mean?"

APHRODITE'S CLOSET

Coco nodded, while also scrunching up her nose, "I kind of know what you mean, but it can't be lovey-dovey either."

"What about something French? Le Petit Mort?" Aggie suggested.

Coco spluttered into her tea, "That's a polite French way of saying orgasm, isn't it?"

Aggie nodded, with a cheeky grin.

"Well, well, Aggie, it seems my cheekiness might be rubbing off on you at last."

"Never!" Aggie said, putting the mug down. "It's not right, though, is it? It's a bit too French, so most people probably won't even get it. They'll just see that it's something to do with mort: death."

Sniggering, Coco agreed, before asking, "By the way, have you been through all the contents of the secret room yet?"

"I've moved it all out of there and put it in my future bedroom upstairs. I glanced through it, but I'm waiting until I've moved in to have a proper look. That reminds me, I'd like to move that armoire from the secret room into my bedroom, but it's a bit of a struggle by myself. Maybe we could have a go?"

"Sure," Coco said, "Shall we have a go while I'm feeling fit?"

Aggie nodded, and the two of them headed downstairs. Aggie pressed on the old-fashioned book handle and waited for the solid wooden panel to open. Once it had, she flicked on the light where a single light bulb dangling from the centre of the ceiling lit up. They'd already binned the old curtain, which had seen better days, and so walked straight in.

"It's a beautiful old piece of furniture, isn't it?" Aggie said as they walked up to it.

Coco nodded and moved to the other side of it. Together they tried to lift it, barely shifting it an inch.

"Oh," Coco laughed, "I guess we're going to need more help to get it upstairs. I could call Kyle? He's only around the corner today. I saw him on the site first thing this morning. I know he's dying to get a look inside this place."

"Well, in that case, give him a ring," Aggie suggested, smiling, while she opened the armoire to take a look inside. "Hey look, there's something carved on the bottom here," she said as she grabbed her phone out of her pocket and turned on the torch app to get a good look at the words.

"Cornelia's Closet," she read out loud. "Cornelia? I wonder who that was?" she asked, turning off the torch and putting her phone back in her pocket.

"Hm, did you say something?" asked Coco who walked back into the room after ringing Kyle. "He's going to pop round in about an hour. What were you saying?"

"I found something carved into the wood at the bottom of the armoire, Cornelia's Closet."

"Cornelia, huh? I wonder who that was?"

"Me too. But it's got a ring to it, doesn't it?"

"What, Cornelia's Closet?" asked Coco.

"Yes, something about it that sounds kinda…nice."

"You mean for the shop?"

Aggie nodded, "But the name Cornelia isn't quite right, though."

"So, you're saying it should be something Closet?"

Aggie smiled and nodded, "It's got a ring to it, right?"

Coco squealed, "You're onto something, babe! What about Agatha's Closet?"

Seeing Aggie scrunching up her nose made Coco shake her head too. "Coco's Closet?"

"As cute as that sounds, I think it needs to be more…sophisticated."

"You're saying my name isn't sophisticated?" Coco asked with her bottom lip jutting forward. But before Aggie could reply she burst out laughing, "Just kidding. It needs to be something that has a stronger connection with you."

Aggie frowned and walked out of the secret room, deep in thought. Coco followed closely behind and walked right into the back of her when she came to a sudden halt.

"What about something to do with mythology?" Aggie asked.

"Ooh, yes," Coco replied. "Have any ideas?"

"Cliodhna's Closet?"

"Clio…who? I'd struggle to pronounce it, let alone spell it. Who was she anyway?"

"Irish goddess of love and beauty."

"Nice but so wrong for the shop."

"Hm. How about…" Aggie started speaking before she wandered back upstairs to her flat. "Min's Closet? Nah…that's not right either."

"And who was Min?" asked Coco, somewhat intrigued by Aggie's expertise on all things related to mythology.

"Min was a Chinese god of sexuality, love, reproduction, and sexual pleasure," Aggie stated.

"But he was a bloke? That's not good. It needs to be a goddess, naturally. Considering the shop is being run by three very unique and charming English goddesses who hail from the kingdom of Frambleberry," Coco joked as they came to the bottom of the stairs and noticed a couple of people trying to look in through the windows.

"Oh look, people are already starting to talk. Just wait until it gets out what kind of shop this is going to be," Coco said, laughing.

"I've got it!" yelled Aggie, ignoring what Coco had just said. "It's perfect," she grinned from ear to ear.

"Tell me, tell me," Coco repeated, jumping up and down like an over-excited lap dog.

"Aphrodite's Closet."

"Oh my God, Aggie. You're a freaking genius. It couldn't possibly be more perfect. It's so you! I love it, I love it, I love it. OMG," she squealed again and again, before stopping and walking toward the door, pretending to open it and bow. "Ladies and gentlemen, welcome to Aphrodite's Closet…"

CHAPTER 14

Wearing her hair down, a floppy hat that almost hid her eyes, and rather a large snood that covered most of her face, Aggie took a deep breath and followed Coco into the popular exhibition centre.

"You know you look absolutely ridiculous, Aggie," Coco had said when they'd met up bright and early that morning.

"I'm feeling a bit...cold," Aggie muttered as she snuggled into her snood while Coco started the engine.

"Nobody's going to be looking at you, honey."

"I know that. Like I said, I'm cold today."

"Hm-hm," Coco said, twisting her head to check the traffic as she backed out of the driveway.

"You've been doing so well with your embarrassment factor. Don't let it stop you now."

"I know but...but..."

"But what?"

"It's an erotic fair, Coco. I'm going to be mortified, I just know it."

Coco cracked up laughing, almost hitting a poor man on his bicycle. She swerved to miss him and waved an apology while he branded his fist at her.

"I said sorry," she muttered under her breath as she put her foot down and headed for the motorway.

"You're right. It is an erotic fair, but everybody's eyes are going to be on the products, not to mention the models. So you really have nothing to worry about. So just chill out and enjoy it. You need to get used to it."

Aggie had pretty much ignored Coco and sank back into her seat, pretty much remaining quiet until they'd arrived.

"Wow," Coco exclaimed as she turned around and pulled Aggie toward her. "Keep up, Aggie. We've got loads of people to talk to, and we need to get as many contacts as we can. Don't forget we need a whole shop floor of products to order today."

"I know, I know," muttered Aggie, as she blushed uncontrollably at the sight of two very tall and very fit men wearing very little apart from tiny thongs and what appeared to be chains.

"Are they tied together with chains?" she whispered. "And what's in his mouth?"

Coco laughed at her and nodded. "Yes they are tied together with chains and that, my dear, is a ball gag. Do you really not know any of this stuff?" Coco asked, turning to look at Aggie, who was still hiding beneath her hat and snood.

"Not really."

"Aggie, where have you been all these years?"

"Not in erotic trade fairs," she replied, rolling her eyes.

"Oh come on, Aggie. Did you and Timothy never play during sex?"

Aggie pulled her snood further up, "We played a little bit."

"You never watched any filthy movies? Or bought anything dirty online?"

"Not really," Aggie muttered.

"Well then honey, you've got a lot to learn. And you're going to need to do some homework to be ready for when our customers start asking questions."

"Oh God, I can't believe you've dragged me into all this," Aggie moaned.

Coco raised her eyebrows and pulled Aggie's hat up a little and her snood down a little. "Starting right now, you've got to be brave and just enjoy the moment. After all, this here," she pointed to all the stands around them, "is all about pleasure, honey. And there's nothing wrong with pleasure, is there?"

Aggie stood, looking around.

"Is there?" Coco asked again.

"Of course not," Aggie eventually replied. "I get all that, and I know what you're saying. I am in this business now," she said, trying to talk herself round. "I can do this. I'm an adult. I'm not a virgin. I know about all this stuff. Well...some of it. Oh, Christ, Coco. What am I doing?" she almost wailed.

"Hey darling, are you all right?" said a rather camp voice to the left of the girls.

Both of them turned at the same time, finding a man in his thirties, staring at them with the most wonderful, calming smile. "Darlings, are you lost?" he asked.

"No, we're not lost," Coco smiled, walking closer to him. "I'm just trying to convince my friend not to be so embarrassed."

Aggie rolled her eyes and shook her head at Coco's comment.

"Oh darling," he said, motioning her over. "There's absolutely no need to be embarrassed in this place. Nobody takes any notice of that sort of thing in here. I mean, look," he said, pointing in the opposite direction to the entrance. "Most of the men, the straight ones anyway, have got their eyes on those models over there."

Aggie lifted her hat so she could get a better view. About seven girls stood at the entrance to one particular exhibit. None appeared to be wearing anything.

"Are they naked?" Aggie asked.

The man nodded, "Well, they might as well be. They've probably got little G-strings on or something, but they're here today to help promote the latest buzz word," he laughed at his own joke.

"Buzz word?" Coco asked, before realising, he meant vibrator. "Oh, right. We've already ordered some of those online."

"Oh yeah," he said. "Are you in the business?"

"Yes," Coco replied, but I'll let Aggie tell you more," she said, shoving her friend forward.

"Oh, erm, yes. We're opening a shop," she said, trying to smile.

"What kind of shop exactly?" asked the man.

"Well, it's a bit unique actually," she said, warming to him. "It's part lingerie and sleepwear and stuff like that, and then the second floor is all a bit more, er, kinky," she smiled, proud of herself.

"Oooh sounds wonderful. Where is it?"

"In Frambleberry."

"Oh yes, I know the town. Lovely place. I have a cousin that lives near there, come to think of it. You must send me information so I can pass it on," he said, rubbing his chin in thought. "I'm Eric, by the way," he said, extending his hand.

"Aggie. Aggie Trout," she grinned, feeling at ease at last.

"Give him our card, Aggie," Coco suggested, who had been having a look at Eric's stand.

"I see you sell a multitude of products yourself, Eric. Sorry, I'm Coco, nice to meet you," she said as they shook hands.

"Yes I certainly do," he said, batting his fake eyelashes. "My partner and I import products from the US. All high quality, of course," he reiterated. "We can't be doing with scratchy fabrics during sex, goodness no. And the vibrators are made from natural wood, ultra-smooth and oh-so-very-nice indeed," he winked. "Nothing tacky here," he added, glancing to some of the stands across from him.

Aggie smiled. "Well then, sold. We'll be ordering from you, for sure."

Eric grinned and pawed at Aggie with his hand. "Oh, wonderful, we can offer you a very special discount, of course. Here, let me give you our catalogue," he said, handing a black and gold booklet to her.

"How soon can you deliver?" asked Coco as she flipped through the pages.

"We have plenty of stock in-house at the moment, so if you placed an order today or tomorrow, we could have it to you within the week. Anything you order from the last two pages of the catalogue is a special order from the States and could take up to eight weeks. But that is the more expensive range so we tend not to have too many in stock, as you can imagine. The swings, for instance, are also quite large and bulky."

Coco and Aggie nodded, as he pointed to a page showing a giant black leather-and-chain swing.

"Ooh Pete had one of those," Coco said to herself in somewhat of a daydream.

Aggie lightly elbowed her in the ribs and nodded to Eric.

"I think we'll be making all our orders tomorrow morning," she said. "What's your best seller?" she asked as she started to act like a businesswoman and not a prude.

Eric beamed and turned back toward his stand for a moment. When he returned, he was carrying a very sizeable wooden vibrator with a golden end. "It's the Golden Cock," he said. "Beautifully and exquisitely made in Texas, this is by far our biggest seller. The ladies love it," he said, chuckling, "and," he turned back and forth, leaning forward, "the gentlemen?" He covered his mouth for a second, "They think it's utterly divine," he mouthed. "It's the wood that does it. There's nothing better than natural materials. Feels like heaven," he chuckled mischievously. "My Edison," Eric pointed to the other man in the stand, "is wowed by it every. Single. Time."

"Well," Aggie said, swallowing and blushing a little. "Er, perhaps we should order some of those?" she turned toward Coco, who was holding the example in her hands and caressing it between her fingers.

"Coco?" Aggie said, nudging her.

"Yes, absolutely. We will definitely order some of these," she grinned.

"As you can feel, the sensation when pulsing, is really rather special," Eric smiled, taking it from her and flicking a button before handing it back.

"Oooh," Coco said. "I see what you mean," she laughed. "Here, Aggie. Feel."

Aggie, composing herself and breathing in, took the item out of Coco's hands and let it sit in her own fingers. The pulsing sensation was so intense that it made her giggle out loud.

Eric and Coco both looked at each other and chuckled.

"Well, Coco and Aggie. It's been wonderful meeting you both, but I imagine you've got plenty of other exhibits to see today, so I shall not take up any more of your time."

"Thank you so much, Eric. You've certainly helped calm her down," Coco whispered with a shake of his hand.

"My pleasure, lovely. It's why I like to have the stand closest to the door. I often meet people who haven't yet become accustomed to the business," he smiled. "But I can already tell that Aggie here is going to be a natural."

Aggie put the Golden Cock back on the shelf and shook Eric's hand, even though her fingers still felt like they were buzzing. "Thank you for helping put me at ease, Eric. I appreciate it."

"My pleasure, darling. Pop back before you leave today, I'd like to see you both again and find out how you got on."

"Absolutely," Aggie said, smiling. "We'll look forward to it. And thanks again."

Eric nodded and watched the women walk away.

"Feel better now?" Coco asked as they walked past the same two men wearing nothing but little thongs and chains.

"Much," Aggie grinned, as she bit her lip and tried to ignore them.

"I was impressed with Eric's products," Coco said. "I do think we should focus on quality, don't you agree?"

"Definitely. Quality is what Aphrodite's Closet is all about, right?"

Coco nodded. "So let's give those stands a miss then," Coco said, as they noticed some dodgy-looking plastic gadgets on show.

"What about over there?" Aggie suggested, pulling Coco toward an exhibit that was full of colourful bottles of something.

"Oh yes, we should definitely stock up on lube. I've heard good things about this company," she said.

Aggie looked at Coco and grinned, "Really?"

"I was doing a bit of research online last night, and this is supposed to be the best."

"Well then, let's find out more…"

Several hours later, Aggie was sitting at a small plastic table, swamped down with several bags full of catalogues, business cards, and leaflets while she waited for Coco to bring over some much-needed coffee and something to eat from the one and only bar in the exhibition centre.

She'd given up on her hat and snood some time ago. The embarrassment had all but disappeared from her body, having soon realised that sex was just a business there. And she was now in the trade and to get where she wanted to be, she knew, she had to be a professional.

As she waited, she enjoyed people watching. And there were undoubtedly some sights to behold in an erotic trade fair.

Every other person that walked past was demonstrating (not literally) something he was selling—either vibrators for men and women, BDSM gadgets like restraints and blindfolds, lubricants, and of course, the most entertaining, the kinky bedroom-wear.

Aggie had seen several women of all shapes and sizes wearing full-body, crotchless, fishnet suits (all wearing flesh-coloured thongs beneath to at least preserve a little modesty) in all kinds of way-out colours—even a rainbow one, which looked rather fun.

Sighing, Aggie thought of her ex, Timothy, whom she'd dated from the age of seventeen until she was twenty-five. She'd always assumed they'd get married, settle down and do the usual family thing. But it hadn't been meant to be. He'd fallen out of love with her and in love with a woman he'd met online. She lived in Australia and Timothy had moved out there shortly after that.

"Sorry it took me so long, the queue was huge," Coco said as she put the tray on the table and plonked herself down opposite.

"You okay, Aggie? You looked miles away then."

"Yeah, I'm fine," she sighed.

"Really? What's up?"

"Nothing...I was just reminded of Timothy, that's all."

"Oh...you never talk about him. What on earth made you think of him?"

Coco looked around to see if there was someone nearby who could have reminded her of him, but when all she saw was women in kinky underwear and people holding vibrators, she laughed out loud.

"What?" Aggie asked.

"I just couldn't fathom what would make you think of Timothy."

Aggie raised her eyebrows and pulled a face, while Coco

handed her a large coffee in a plastic cup and a hotdog.

"Sorry, I know you don't normally do hotdogs, but it's pretty much all they had," she said, curling her top lip.

"That's okay, I'd eat pretty much anything right about now. Awful coffee, though," she almost spat.

"Have some sugar," Coco said, handing her a couple of sachets. "It'll help a bit."

Opening the sachets and pouring the small amount of sugar into the coffee, Aggie sighed.

"You're doing it again?" Coco said.

"What?"

"Sighing like something's wrong."

"No, I was just seeing all these people selling sex stuff, and it just made me a little sad to be single, that's all."

"Wow, I haven't heard you talk like that for ages. I thought you were happily single?"

"I have been on my own for three years. Maybe it's time for a change?" Aggie replied, taking a bite out of the hotdog.

"Gosh, Aggie. You've surprised me."

"I think I've surprised myself," she sighed, sitting back into the chair.

"But why think of Timothy?" Coco asked as she unzipped her boots and rubbed her sore feet.

"Just because he was the last guy I slept with, I guess," Aggie murmured.

"It's about time you got laid," Coco chuckled. "Or, we could just get you a Golden Cock?"

Both girls laughed before they sat in silence while they finished eating.

"I think today's going really well, don't you?" Coco said a little while later, while she did up her boots again.

"Yeah, we've got some excellent contacts here for sure," Aggie replied as she finished the last of her coffee. "We'll have to go through it all tonight, and then order everything first thing in the morning."

"Definitely," Coco added. "There are just a couple more stands to do, and then we can head back."

"And then next Friday, we're off to the lingerie fair, right?"

Coco nodded, "We're going to be exhausted," she said, yawning and stretching.

"Hm-hm," Aggie agreed. "But then the hard work is done."

Coco smiled, "It's going to be amazing, you know?"

Grinning, Aggie nodded, "I know. I actually can't wait."

"Me too. Come on, let's carry on."

They both stood up, Aggie collecting the rubbish and depositing in a nearby bin, while Coco waited with all the bags.

"Hello, ladies," said a voice approaching them just as they started walking back into the crowd. "Can I interest you in our latest catalogue?"

Both Aggie and Coco looked up and smiled at the immaculate, middle-aged woman dressed in a black and white pinstriped suit. "Sure," said Coco. "What are you selling?"

"We specialise in high-end bedroom wear for both men and women," she said, handing them the thick catalogue, which had the most beautiful couple on the front. The woman was wearing an exquisite red satin negligee, which was trimmed with black lace; she also had on a pair of black stockings and rather high red shoes. She straddled the man while staring into the camera. The man, however, was staring at her. He was wearing nothing but a pair of red and black striped silk boxers but was holding a silk scarf and eye mask in his hands. It looked like such an intimate picture and was beautifully photographed.

"The photo is stunning," Aggie said before she flicked through the catalogue. Liking what she saw, she nodded to Coco. "I'm impressed."

"Do you have any samples we can look at?" Coco asked.

"Certainly," said the woman.

"I'm Alexandra. Nice to meet you," she said as she motioned for them to join her closer to the small stand some way from the cafe.

"Nice to meet you, Alexandra. I'm Aggie, and this is Coco, my business partner. We're going to be opening a shop in Frambleberry soon, and want to specialise in quality goods."

"That sounds marvellous, and exactly like the kind of place we'd like to sell to," she smiled. "Here," she handed them a couple of pieces of lingerie. One was a crotchless bodysuit in silk and the other a similar item but in fishnet. "Just to give you an idea of quality. All our goods are made in Germany and France, so they are a little more pricey, but you get what you pay for."

Impressed with the feeling of the fabrics, Coco and Aggie smiled at each other.

"This is exactly what we need for the shop," Coco said. "Do you have a business card as well?"

"Absolutely," Alexandra said, handing them a well-designed card with the name Alexandra Prince written on it.

"The Kinky Prince?" Coco grinned. "I love the name."

"It's a family business started by my parents back in the seventies," Alexandra said. "The name started as a bit of a joke, but it stuck, and it's been quite successful ever since."

"I think it's wonderful," Aggie smiled, "And exactly what we're looking for, for Aphrodite's Closet."

"Aphrodite's Closet? That's the name of your shop?"

Aggie nodded.

"Fantastic," Alexandra said, "It's certainly got a ring to it. My brother will be impressed. He's always been a fan of Greek mythology."

"Oh, really?" Coco's ears pricked up. "Your brother?"

"Yeah, he works with me in the business too. But he couldn't make it today. He's in Germany, finalising some new lines. But I'll send you information about that if you like? Again, it's top quality."

"That would be brilliant, Alexandra. Thank you so much," Aggie said, handing her a business card.

"Looking forward to doing business with you," smiled Alexandra as another client approached her. She waved and nodded as they walked away.

"She was lovely," Coco said. "And she has a brother into Greek mythology, eh?"

"Who is probably even older than her and married with a couple of kids," Aggie said, shaking her head. "Just because I mentioned Timothy earlier doesn't mean you need to find me a man, Coco."

Coco laughed and said nothing.

CHAPTER 15

"I can't talk right now, Christie, the painters have literally just arrived, and I need to finalise the details with them. Are you still coming over later? Okay, I'll see you then. I need to give you a key as well. Okay, catch you later, Sis."

"Sorry about that, Ceecee. Right, where were we?" said Aggie as she led the woman and her small team of painters toward the back of the store.

"Like we agreed before, we'd like the soft sage green for the walls of the entire ground floor," she turned her attention to the younger painters, "but the wood stays wood," Aggie chuckled, "I don't want any of that painted. My carpenter has already worked his magic on that."

"No problem, Miss Trout."

"Please call me Aggie, Ceecee."

"Aggie it is," she smiled. "I think you've made a marvellous choice to stay in keeping with the Victoria colour scheme for this room. But you mentioned you wanted something with a little more pizazz upstairs?" asked Ceecee.

"That's right. Would you like to follow me?"

Ceecee instructed her workers to get started on the ground floor before she followed Aggie upstairs.

"This is where we'd like something more, er, fun I guess."

Ceecee nodded, "Can I ask what you're going to be doing with the shop, Aggie?"

Aggie grinned, "It's a bit of a secret at the moment, I'm afraid. My business partners and I are sworn to secrecy until the grand unveiling next month."

Ceecee smiled and nodded in approval, "I got it. I'm extremely curious, though."

"Don't worry, you'll be getting an invite to the grand opening."

"I'll look forward to it."

Aggie managed to prevent herself from blushing and turned her attention back to the room. "So, colours. Coco and I were thinking about stripes."

"Oh, okay. Yes, that'll certainly be different. Colour combinations?"

"We were thinking about black and pink, but perhaps that's a little too over the top. Unless we go two-tone and go dark on the bottom half of the wall, and a lighter pink on top?"

"That would work," Ceecee said, "But black?"

Aggie pulled a face, "I'm unsure. Is it too harsh? What do you think?"

"Have you given any thought to following the pattern of the tiles up the walls?"

Aggie's eyes widened, and she smiled, "You mean a black and white diamond pattern painted on the bottom half?"

"Why not? If you want something a little different, maybe? It's more work for the painters, of course, so it will cost a bit extra, but it would look fabulous if I don't say so myself."

"Actually, I think I agree with you. And pink on top? Let me double-check with Coco first, and I'll let you know."

"And the top two floors of your flat. What would you like me to do with that?"

"Sage green in the entire living area and a soft blue upstairs. The ones you showed me before are pretty much spot on, I think."

"Okay then. Let me know about this room ASAP, and I'll get my best lads on it."

"Will do, Ceecee, thanks. And thanks for the suggestion. I think it's brilliant."

Ceecee smiled and nodded before heading back downstairs to the main shop floor.

oOo

"Christie!" yelled Aggie, waving, from across the room. "Over here."

Christie had walked into what looked like complete madness, with decorators painting the walls all over the place, carpenters measuring and fixing, and electricians doing their final checks.

"Sis, how's it going?" Christie smiled as she gave her sister a quick hug.

"Brilliantly well. What do you think?"

"Difficult to say at the moment on account of the hundreds of workers you've got in here but it looks pretty good. I love the sage green. Very Victorian," she smiled.

"Thanks for the suggestion," Aggie said with a grin. "Come on, let's head upstairs to the flat."

Once on the third floor, with all the noise well beneath them, Christie sat down on Aggie's old leather sofa.

"I'm surprised you've kept this. I figured you'd have bought a new sofa by now."

"It's still got a few miles left in it," Aggie said defensively, "besides, all my money is going into this place so I can't afford one yet."

"Soon, it'll happen soon. I'm sure of it. So, down to business. I've set up the website, and it's pretty much ready to go, and the signwriters emailed this morning to say that's ready too. They just want a day and time to come and hang it for us. I've also prepared the invitation to the grand opening and, as promised, it mentions nothing about it being an adult shop. I did add a note saying the invitation is not open to children though. I hope that's okay?"

"That's great. Thanks, Christie."

"How were the trade shows?"

"An eye-opener," Aggie laughed. "I saw things there that I can never un-see," she chuckled.

"Really," Christie's eyes lit up. "I wish I could have gone to the erotic one."

"Really? It was quite mortifying to start with."

"Yeah? I could just imagine you there, blushing like nobody's business."

"Actually, I managed to get that quite under control after about an hour," she laughed. "But seriously, my eyes have been opened to, well, many intriguing possibilities."

"Aggie!" exclaimed Christie. "You're almost unrecognisable."

Aggie just laughed and nodded her head.

"You and Coco should go to the next one. I'll happily leave it to you next time."

"Well, I'll be up for that, definitely. So," Christie stopped talking for a second before whispering, "have you told Mum yet?"

Aggie bit her bottom lip and shook her head.

"Aggie! We're opening in three weeks. She's dying to know what's going on. She's practically having kittens because all the ladies at the Luncheon Club keeping asking about the corner shop. You know what she's like."

"Which is exactly why I haven't told her yet."

Christie chuckled. "It won't be that bad. It'll be better when everything's out in the open."

"Have you told Jonathan?"

"Of course not," Christie responded. "You asked me not to spill the beans just yet so I haven't. Although it's killing me keeping this blooming secret."

Aggie laughed, "I know. It's crazy, isn't it?"

Christie nodded and asked, "Where's Coco?"

"She's busy with all the orders at the moment. Everything is being delivered to her place until the decorators have gone. Apparently, there are boxes everywhere. She says she can barely get through the front door."

"I can imagine. How are you getting on in the flat? When did you move in?"

"Tonight will be my first night."

"Fantastic. We should celebrate," Christie said before realising she couldn't, "Well, you guys should celebrate. I've got to go and pick up the girls. Jonathan is out playing cricket tonight."

"Another night then? I'd suggest bringing the girls up, but I don't think the smell of paint and new carpets will do them much good."

Screwing up her nose, Christie nodded, "I know, it is a bit stinky, isn't it? But it'll fade soon enough. We'll celebrate another night though, okay?"

Aggie smiled, "That'd be great, Sis. Oh, here's the key to the store and this one is for my flat, just in case you ever need it," she said, handing the keys over to her sister.

"Thanks. I can't wait to get started," Christie grinned. "It's going to be so much fun having a part-time job here. Thank you for asking me to be a part of it, Aggie. It means a lot. Especially considering we weren't that close growing up. I know I could be a bit of a stuck-up bitch sometimes."

"Sometimes you were," Aggie laughed, "But I was a boring old fart half the time. I don't know how you and Coco put up with me. You were always so much fun, and there was me, terrified of making a fool out of myself, or of getting hurt. God, I was pathetic."

"No, you weren't. Boring at times, yes, but pathetic, no way. And the fact that you were afraid of getting hurt protected you at times. Remember when I broke my leg falling out of the tree at Coco's house? You would never have done anything like that and see, you've never broken a bone!"

"It wasn't just physically though, Christie. I was afraid of getting hurt emotionally. That's why I rarely bothered with the boys in those days."

"The boys we hung out with were all dicks anyway, Aggie. You were better off not getting involved," Christie laughed. "Remember little Tommy? Little shit cornered me in the changing rooms, had a feel of my boobs when I was eleven and then told everyone I'd snogged him and felt his willy. And then a few years later he had the cheek to try again. Do you remember, I whacked him in the nuts?"

Aggie nodded, "Did you know he's now a surgeon?"

With her eyes wide, Christie snorted. "A surgeon? What kind?"

"Plastic," Aggie laughed.

"Wow, still likes playing with women's boobs then."

Both women snorted with laughter.

"I thought about Timothy the other day," Aggie admitted.

Christie's eyes shot upward to look at her sister, "Really? How come? Have you heard from him or something?"

Aggie shook her head, "As far as I know, he married the girl in Australia soon after he got there. We never kept in touch. Didn't see the point."

"Oh, Aggie," Christie said, "Are you all right?"

"I'm fine," she looked in her sister's eyes and nodded. "Honestly, I am. I'm fine. I just thought three years is a long time…maybe I should start thinking about dating again?"

Christie's eyes lit up, and she jumped up to hug her sister. "I've wanted to hear you say that for so long. I hate seeing you on your own. Everyone needs a bit of love and attention, you know."

"I know. But this is not an invitation to start fixing me up, okay?" Aggie insisted. "I've already said the same thing to Coco. I'm simply open to meeting someone. Not to be forced into it,"

Christie held both her hands up and backed away.

"Who me? I wouldn't dare," she winked, before changing the subject, "So, want me to help with anything downstairs? I've got a couple of hours to spare before I pick the girls up."

CHAPTER 16

"Mum, I think we need to talk. Can I come over this afternoon?"

"Why, of course, dear. But not until after three because Eileen and Kimberly will be over to discuss WI matters. I'll expect you at a quarter past three then, dear. I'll have a nice cup of Earl Grey waiting for you. Toodle pip."

Aggie put the phone down, a feeling of dread rushing through her body. How did one tell one's mother, one was about to open a sex shop? And her dad? It was so…so…embarrassing. Aggie blushed at the thought but tried to think positive, pushing her feelings to one side. It had to be done. And with only a few weeks to go until the big day, now was the time.

oOo

AGGIE'S MOTHER, Trixie, was standing at the front door at precisely a quarter past three. Aggie looked at her watch to make sure she wasn't late. It was okay, she was exactly on time.

"Darling, how marvellous to see you. Come in, come in. Take your shoes off, dear, it looks like you've been traipsing in the mud.

Aggie glanced down at her trusty old walking shoes and saw

that they were a little dusty from the shop, but by no means muddy. But she bent down and took them off anyway.

"Here's a pair of slippers you can wear," Trixie said, handing Aggie a pair of pink and orange floral slippers—the kind one would expect a great-grandmother to wear.

"Thanks, Mum. How was the Women's Institute meeting?"

"Oh, don't even mention it. That Eileen brought along her cousin with her, and she was dreadful, just dreadful."

"Why dreadful, Mum? What was wrong with her?"

Trixie rolled her eyes, "A real know-it-all she was. And Eileen's gone and invited her to join. And she was wearing jeans. Jeans, Agatha! For goodness sake."

Aggie looked at her own skinny jeans and wrapped her long cardigan around herself as she followed her mother into the kitchen where a pot of tea and two china cups and saucers sat waiting for them.

"You needn't have got the china out for me, Mum. A mug would have been fine."

"Your father broke another of the mugs last week, so we now only have one left."

"I could have still used it," she said, raising her eyebrows as Trixie poured the Earl Grey.

"You know how I like symmetry, dear. I couldn't have you drinking from a mug and me a cup and saucer."

Aggie stifled a snigger.

"But all that's unimportant right now. Tell me about the corner shop. Now I know something's going on down there. I've had several calls from several ladies from the Ladies Luncheon Club keeping me abreast of certain things. They tell me the shop's being decorated? I must admit to feeling somewhat disappointed that you haven't shared any of this with me, Agatha. After all, Aunt Petunia was my aunt, and I am vaguely familiar with the old place."

Aggie sighed and put down her cup. It rattled as she placed it back onto the saucer on account of her nerves.

"Yes I have been redecorating. The place needed it, considering how long it hadn't been used."

"I'm told that you're using Ceecee Woodley for the painting?"

Aggie nodded, "Yes, she's doing a brilliant job. Her guys are very talented. It's looking quite incredible."

"And may I ask what it is going to be?" Trixie finally asked, peering over her glasses.

Aggie sighed.

"Well, it's…"

"Good morning, my darling daughter. Long-time no see, how are you, angel?" said her dad, Ted, who'd walked into the kitchen with the morning's newspaper under his arm.

"Hi, Dad," she said as she stood up to give him a hug. "I'm great thanks. How's the shoulder?"

Ted smiled and nodded, "Not too bad, love. Although I'm told, I won't be playing golf for a while."

"A damn shame," Trixie interrupted. "The WI charity tournament is just next week too. I'm certain your father would have won."

"Nonsense," Ted replied with a chuckle. "Charlie and Pete are both far better players than me."

Trixie raised her eyebrows and pouted.

Aggie tried not to giggle at the two of them until she remembered why she was there in the first place.

"So, we're hearing you've been working on the corner shop. How's it going, love? Got a date for the opening yet?" questioned Ted.

"Yes…a…actually," she stuttered. "We're opening on the second of April."

"Oh, a few weeks then? That's exciting. Well, you can rest assured that your mother and I will be there to buy some goodies," Ted smiled innocently.

Aggie spat out her tea.

"Goodness, Agatha. Whatever's the matter?" her mother said, standing up and rushing for some kitchen roll to wipe the table.

"Sorry, it was just a bit hot," she replied, feeling the heat rising into her cheeks. It was time, she had to tell them. She had to get it off her chest.

"Mum, Dad. I really ought to tell you the truth. I've been keeping it a secret for some time now. It's about the shop…"

"What about it, love? Is everything all right?" Ted asked, with concern in his eyes.

"Yes everything's great, Dad. It's just that, well, we…Coco and me. Actually, Christie too. She's invested some of her money into it as well…"

"She has? Well, that's very sweet of your sister to do. I hadn't expected that at all. She's special, that girl," her mum smiled. "But I hadn't realised Coco was working with you too."

"Yes, Mum. The three of us are in a kind of partnership, I guess you could call it."

"That's wonderful," Ted announced.

"But the shop itself, well, it's …it's…"

Ted and Trixie both leaned forward across the kitchen table.

"It's what? Do spit it out, dear," her mother said.

"It's an adult shop."

There. She'd done it. Taking a deep breath, Aggie lifted her eyes.

Trixie had gone white. Ted wasn't saying much at all.

"Mum, Dad?" Aggie asked.

"Er, angel?" Ted asked.

"Yes, Dad?"

"When you say adult shop, what exactly are you referring to?"

Oh, God, thought Aggie. This was getting even more difficult.

"It means she's going to be selling filth, that's what," Trixie spat and stood up from the table so that her chair almost fell backwards.

"No, not filth, Mum. It's not smutty or anything like that."

"Well, of course it is. Anything to do with," Trixie looked away, turning red, "to do with…" She couldn''t quite say it.

"Sex?" Aggie whispered.

"Ha! Exactly," Trixie pointed to her. "Disgusting. I'm in absolute shock, Agatha Trout. I'd never have thought you capable of something like this. How…how could you? I shall be the laughing stock of the WI and the Ladies Luncheon Club, not to mention the golf club." Trixie was turning redder and redder.

"But Mum, it's mainly just lingerie and a few toys, that's all."

Trixie's eyes grew even wider as she turned away from her

APHRODITE'S CLOSET

daughter in disgust. "Agatha Trout, I'm so disappointed in you. And I cannot believe that Christie has been dragged into such a nasty, seedy little idea as this. You've completely let down this family. How am I going to show my face again? I'll be the laughing stock of Frambleberry," Trixie yelled before storming out of the room.

Aggie just sat, staring after her mother. Her own face in shock. She knew her mother wouldn't like it, but she never would have imagined a response like this.

She turned to look at her father. He looked at her with a sad smile on his face.

"Oh, Aggie," he said, shaking his head.

"Dad?" she croaked. "I'm sorry…I just needed something to earn a living and, you know what they say, sex sells? I didn't even think about how it would affect you and Mum."

"Shush now, Aggie," said Ted as he rose from his chair and went to sit next to his eldest daughter. "You just ignore what your mother has just said. She's a drama queen. Always has been and we both know it. I'm just shocked because it's you who's doing it. Not because it's an adult shop, sweetheart. You've always been the careful one, you used to call yourself a coward," he chuckled. "And now look at you. You're doing something that's going to get the whole town talking."

Aggie lifted her head from his shoulder and groaned, "Oh, Dad, if you're trying to make me feel better, it's not working," she sighed.

Ted chuckled, "What I'm saying, sweetheart, is that I'm quite proud of you."

Aggie sat upright and looked her father in the eyes, "You are?" she asked. "But, I'm opening a sex shop, Dad."

He chuckled again, "This is the twenty-first century, my love. These kinds of things are what the youngsters are into, I suppose. And I know you'll keep it classy. You and Christie are classy ladies."

"Dad, I've never been a classy lady," she giggled.

"You were always a classy lady, you just didn't know it," he said, pushing her hair behind her ear.

Aggie leaned forward and gave him a big hug.

"Oh, Dad," she sighed. "What am I going to do?"

"About what?"

"About…well, everything? How can I open Aphrodite's Closet now? Mum will never speak to me again."

Ted belly laughed, "Oh, sweetheart. She'll get over it. She loves you more than she loves those old biddies. It might just take her some time to accept that, that's all. I love the name, by the way. That was clearly your idea? Aphrodite's Closet?"

Aggie nodded, "Kind of. There was an old armoire at the shop, and it had been inscribed inside with the words Cornelia's Closet so I kind of played with that until I came up with the Greek goddess of love, Aphrodite."

"You were always very smart, Aggie. But Cornelia's Closet? I think Cornelia might have been Petunia's mother."

Aggie's eyes grew wide, "Really? I had wondered about that. I had intended to try and find out more about Petunia, but I've been so busy getting the shop ready that I just haven't had the time. I was hoping to ask Mum about her but…as if that's going to happen now," Aggie rolled her eyes.

"Give it time," Ted reassured her.

"Thanks Dad, you're the best."

"How's the flat?" he asked. "Sorry we haven't been able to come and see you but what with the surgery and everything, it's been a little difficult."

"That's okay, Dad. It's been pretty manic up there anyway. But I moved in last week, and I love it. It's handy for work too—I could literally roll out of bed and be there to open the doors," she chuckled. "But it's perfect. I never thought I'd enjoy living in an apartment, but I feel like I'm meant to be there if you know what I mean?"

Ted nodded and patted her shoulder. "Clearly, you were."

"And it's probably bigger than the bungalow, being on two floors and everything."

"It sounds perfect, sweetheart. I'll come and visit soon."

"Will you come to the opening, Dad?"

"I wouldn't miss it for the world."

CHAPTER 17

Coco, Christie, and Aggie stood with the main entrance behind them, all surveying the scene before them. It was ready. All the work was complete, and they were all set for the grand opening that evening. All three stood in silence as they enjoyed the moment.

The large ground floor, with its black and white tiled floor, and new sage green painted walls, and gold accessories looked astounding. The antique chandelier hung sparkling in the centre of the room, casting pretty shards of light all over the shop floor, which was now full of a wide range of lingerie. More affordable bras and knickers could be found hanging alongside some exquisite pieces, which cost a fair amount more. Aphrodite's Closet was a store for all pockets—something Aggie was particularly proud of. But most importantly, it was dedicated to selling quality.

The ground floor not only stocked lingerie, but also had a good selection of beautiful scarves, sarongs, and sleepwear, mostly in silks and satins.

The doors on the changing rooms contained painted images of the goddess Aphrodite—this had been Christie's idea, and she had invited an artist friend to do the work. The result was stunning.

The sexier the lingerie, the further back in the store it was positioned—something Aggie had insisted upon. All of that then led up the stairs to the quirky second floor.

The black and white floor tiles were duplicated in paint halfway up the wall to a black dado rail. Above the rail, the walls were painted a more muted shade of fuchsia. The effect was dazzling. Black and pink display cabinets and tables were positioned throughout the room, all containing various sex toys, some more extreme lingerie for men and women, as well as a selection of erotic books and DVDs. Beautiful old-fashioned framed images of semi-naked ladies adorned the walls.

The secret room on this floor had been cleared out and was now being used as a mini-kitchen, where the girls could make tea or coffee and have a break. It contained a fridge, kettle, and an antique cupboard they'd found downstairs while clearing out the place.

"I can't believe it's finally ready," whispered Aggie.

"Me neither," Christie replied.

"I know, right? It's going to be amazing. It looks amazing. I feel very proud to be a part of this with you girls," Coco smiled. "Aphrodite's Closet," she yelled. "Yeah!"

"Any joy with Mum yet?" Christie asked.

Aggie's face dropped, and she shook her head, "She's still not talking to me. Has she spoken to you since last week?"

Christie shook her head, too, "No."

"She'll come round," Coco insisted as she walked back into the central part of the room and headed for one of the bottles of champagne on the table that had been set up for the party.

"Let's have a glass before everyone arrives," she suggested, picking up a bottle and waving it at them.

Christie and Aggie looked at each other and smiled, "Good idea, Coco," Christie said. "Plus, I'm staying over tonight, so I needn't worry about driving."

"You can't get drunk though, Sis. We've got to be responsible adults tonight," Aggie said, frowning before she started laughing.

"Oh yeah, good one," Coco laughed as the champagne cork popped out of the top of the bottle.

"But yes, semi-responsible adults," Christie added. "We've got the press coming and everything."

"And let's hope the rest of the people we invited along too," Coco said while pouring the three glasses so that they were almost overflowing.

"Easy tiger," Christie laughed.

"Let's just enjoy the moment, girls," said Coco as she lifted her glass. "It's pretty unique what we've achieved here, and I'm determined to make it work for all of us. And like I said before, I'm so proud of what we've done. I can't wait to get this baby going. So, here's to us and Aphrodite's Closet."

"Us and Aphrodite's Closet," the girls said in unison before taking a long sip of the champagne.

oOo

AT ALMOST SIX O'CLOCK, all three girls peered out of the window and were delighted to see a small queue of people developing by the front door.

"It's happening," whispered Aggie, who was starting to feel somewhat queasy. "I…I…don't think I can do this," she whispered, moving away from the window.

"Hey, of course you can," Christie said. "It's just a shop. Don't think of it as anything else, just a shop. No need to be embarrassed by anything. You got that?"

"Breathe, honey, breathe," Coco said, "Put your hands on your knees, bend your head down, and just take a moment to breathe. You're going to be fine. "It's just nerves, that's all. I'm nervous too, okay? I'm just hiding it better than you."

"Yeah, nerves. Me too, Aggie, I'm nervous too," Christie reassured her.

Aggie did as she was told and began to breathe through her nose. In and out, in and out. After a while, the queasiness started to subside, and she lifted up her head again.

"You okay?" Coco asked as Christie walked over to the door and looked at her watch.

"Girls, it's time."

Aggie breathed in and then let the breath escape from her lungs. And she nodded.

"Let's do this," she whispered as she continued to breathe at a slower rate.

As Christie began to unlock the door, Aggie's heart rate began to increase again.

"Just nerves, just nerves, just nerves," she repeated to herself under her breath.

"Welcome to Aphrodite's Closet, everyone," Christie said loudly as people began to enter the shop.

"Help yourself to a glass of champagne," Coco added as the crowd began to disperse around the store.

Cries of "wow," "oh my goodness," and "oooh," could be heard throughout as Christie, Coco, and Aggie settled at the centre of the shop, waiting for everyone to walk inside. When it appeared that no one else was waiting outdoors, Coco stepped up onto a small pedestal.

"Hello everyone and a very warm welcome to Aphrodite's Closet," she stopped for a moment while there was applause all around. Smiling, she began to talk again. "Aphrodite's Closet is a joint venture with my best friend, Agatha Trout, and her sister, Christie Valentine. As some of you already know, this beautiful shop was left to Agatha by her Great Aunt Petunia, who sadly passed away late last year at the grand old age of ninety-nine years old."

Whispers of "wow" could be heard while others nodded amongst themselves.

"Agatha knew she wanted to re-open the store but wasn't prepared to continue it as an ordinary corner shop, which is where I came in."

Those that knew Coco began to chuckle before she continued.

"I'll admit that it was my idea to open a store for adults only. After all, Frambleberry doesn't have a store anything like this, and it seemed right to give the town a bit of cheekiness and sparkle—

and a little extra sophistication never goes amiss, right?" she said as the crowd laughed.

"We've worked hard over the past month or so to create a unique place where people will feel at home whilst buying lingerie and," she stopped for second, "other items for the bedroom," she smiled, "So please, give it up for Agatha, Christie, and Aphrodite's Closet."

At that, everyone clapped and cheered.

"Please help yourself to more champagne and hors d' oeuvres. If anyone has any questions, please don't hesitate to ask me, Agatha, or Christie. We're here to help," she smiled as there was more clapping.

"Thank you for doing that, Coco," smiled Aggie as she shoved the pedestal under one of the tables out of the way.

"You're welcome, hon. I knew you'd find that a little tough."

"You're so good at public speaking, it was much better done than if I'd have been forced into it."

"I know, you'd have been a gibbering mess!"

"Tell me about it," Aggie laughed. "Well, we'd better mingle and see how everyone's getting on. I see Christie's speaking to the local press."

"Yeah, I've overheard her talking to a couple of journalists, and I think they're quite smitten—with her and the shop."

"Let's hope so," Aggie smiled as the women walked away from each other and into the crowd. Coco headed upstairs while Aggie stayed on the ground floor.

Looking around at the crowds of people, she spotted Amelia Hornblower browsing some of the more plain pyjamas with a smile on her face. When their eyes met, Amelia waved and gave her the thumbs up.

Relieved that the Frambleberry town gossip was suitably impressed, Aggie smiled and waved in return.

"Aggie," said a familiar voice from behind her.

"Dad!" she almost screeched, "You made it. I didn't think you would."

"I told you, I wouldn't miss it for the world, love. The place looks incredible. You've done a cracking job with it. If your mother could see it, I'm sure she'd be proud of you."

"If it wasn't what it is, perhaps, Dad. But thanks for saying that anyway."

"I brought a couple of golf buddies, Charlie and Pete, with me. I hope you don't mind?"

Aggie looked aghast. "Really? They…wanted to come?"

"Are you kidding, this is exciting stuff, Aggie," he winked, adding, "best of luck, love," before he walked back toward his friends, who appeared to be deep in conversation about a slinky bodysuit that one was holding up.

Aggie frowned before she chuckled and turned to look the other way.

Kyle was standing in the doorway, taking in the newly decorated shop. An older woman was standing with her arm linked into his. She looked impressed and smiled when Aggie approached them.

"Aggie," Kyle said warmly, as he extricated himself from the woman's arm and pulled Aggie into a slightly awkward hug.

"Good to see you, Kyle. Thanks for coming," she said, blushing a little.

"Good to see you too, Aggie. The place looks amazing. You girls have done a brilliant job with the place. I'm very impressed."

"Thanks," Aggie said, blushing again as Kyle's hands brushed her own before he let go.

The older woman cleared her throat.

"Oh sorry. Aggie, I'd like you to meet Helena Bruce, my business partner in the development we're working on at the moment."

"Oh, the one round the corner," Aggie asked as she shook the woman's hand. "Great to meet you, Helena."

Helena nodded and smiled, "You too, Agatha."

"Call me Aggie, please. Only my mother ever calls me Agatha."

The women laughed.

"This place is quite charming. And how wonderful that it's the first shop of its kind in Frambleberry. I'm sure you're going to be a huge success, judging by the people's reactions here tonight."

"Well yes, I hope so," Aggie said. "But it's only the opening night. Fingers crossed the general public will be just as impressed."

"I have no doubts," Helena said. "Perhaps I ought to have a browse myself," she winked.

"Yes, yes, go and have a look, Helena," Kyle laughed. "You might find something fun," he winked back as she chuckled and turned away.

"She seems nice," Aggie said as Kyle turned his attention back to her.

"She is. I'm lucky to have found her," he smiled.

"Fancy a glass of champagne?" Aggie asked.

"Sure. I'll get it. Over there, right?" he pointed, and she nodded.

"I'll leave you to it and go and mingle."

"I was going to bring you a glass," he said, looking a little disappointed.

"Oh, thanks. In that case, I'll come with you," she grinned.

Upstairs, Coco was enjoying watching people's first impressions of the second floor. Not only did they seem delighted with the decor, but many were quite tickled by the products on display. An older lady and her husband, however, had just about run back downstairs when they'd realised what was on display. Coco couldn't help but laugh.

"What are you laughing at?" asked the voice of a man creeping up behind her.

"Luigi, you made it," she grinned at him. "I wasn't sure you'd manage it."

"I created the hors d' oeuvres, I couldn't not stay for a while," he said in a strange accent that was both a mixture of Yorkshire and Italian. "It is beautiful what you have created here, Bella Coco."

"Thanks, Luigi, and thank you for creating the hors d' oeuvres. They seem to be going down a treat."

"It is my pleasure. And it seems, pleasure is what you're selling, no?"

Coco laughed and nodded, "Yes, I guess you could look at it like that. Anything that tickles your fancy?"

"Lots…" he winked. "Isabella has already pointed out the items she would like to buy."

"Isabella came too? Oh, where is she? I'd love to say hello. I haven't seen her since the christening."

"She is downstairs, but we must go soon. The babysitter has a date," he said, raising his eyebrows.

Coco laughed, "Then let me come downstairs to see her before you go."

oOo

THE DEBRIS from the night before had all been disposed of, and the girls had continued to clean for an hour after everyone had left. It was now midnight, and all three of them were splayed out on the sofa in Aggie's flat.

"It was bloody brilliant," Coco said, as she took a sip of coffee.

"I know," Christie said. "The press seemed thrilled with it all too. I hope they write great things about us."

"How can they not?" Coco replied. "Aphrodite's Closet is A.M.A.Z.I.N.G," she spelt out. "Everyone loved it."

"Even Dad," Aggie laughed. "Did you speak to him, Christie? You know he brought two golf buddies with him?"

"They bought stuff too," Christie replied, laughing. "For the wives, apparently. Dad thought it was hilarious. He's chuffed for us, you know?"

"It's a shame Mum isn't."

"Oh Mum, Schmum …it's her loss," Christie hiccupped, causing the girls to crack up laughing again.

"Exactly how much bubbly did you have, Christie?" asked Coco as she sat forward and put her empty mug on the coffee table.

"I don't know, but quite a few glasses, I think. I hope I didn't make a fool of myself," she grinned.

"I don't think so. Not that I noticed, anyway," Aggie said with a smile. "It was great that Kyle came."

"Yeah, he was desperate to see the place finished," Coco added.

"His business partner seems nice," Aggie said. "Helena something or other?"

"Yeah, I met her once or twice recently. She's quite a successful woman, I think. She was the one who approached Kyle about working together. Apparently, she'd read about him in some property magazine and was so impressed, she gave him a call."

"A booty call?" Christie giggled.

"Well, maybe," Coco laughed. "I don't know who he's sleeping with these days."

"She's a bit old for him, isn't she?" Aggie queried, trying to remember how old she was.

"Was she? I didn't meet her. She was quite beautiful though," Christie said.

"Yeah, very," Aggie sighed. "How old do you think she is?"

"Fifty?" Coco suggested.

"And Kyle's what? Twenty-nine? A year older than me, isn't he?"

Coco nodded.

"That's quite a difference."

"Not really. Who cares about age these days? If she can get it on with a thirty-year-old, then good for her," Christie slurred.

"I think you need another coffee, Sis," Aggie suggested as she stood up and went over to the kitchen to pour some more.

"We sold quite a bit of stuff tonight, you know?" Coco said, standing up to stretch her legs.

"Really? That's great. Did you give everyone the opening night discount?" asked Aggie.

"Of course, and the twenty per cent off vouchers we made to encourage them to come back for more. Let's hope they work."

Aggie grinned. "Well, tomorrow's the proper big day, so we ought to get some sleep. Are you sure you're not going to sleep over, Coco?"

"Nah, I'll be fine. I'll call a cab now," she said as she grappled in her handbag for her phone, before stepping to the window where she dialled the taxi company.

"Ready for bed, Sis?" Aggie asked Christie as she polished off the last of the coffee.

"Yep," she hiccupped. "So ready. I'm exhausted…" she said, closing her eyes while standing up and yawning at the same time.

"Well, the bed's all made for you. There are towels in the cupboard and a dressing gown hanging on the back of the door if you need one. Feel free to sleep in tomorrow morning. I expect you'll need to head home and see the girls when you get up, though. I'll be up bright and early and down in the shop if you need me."

"Okay, Sis. Thanks," Christie muttered as she shuffled along the carpet until she reached the stairs, climbing them until she got to the spare bedroom. She barely got her clothes off before falling into bed and sleeping for a good eight hours.

CHAPTER 18

*A*ll was silent when Aggie walked downstairs to the shop the following morning. She'd managed to shower, wash and dry her hair with a noisy hairdryer, get dressed and have breakfast and still, there'd been no sign of her sister.

It was the first day of the shop opening as a fully functioning business, and although she was nervous, she was full of excitement. The opening event the previous night had given her the confidence for which she'd been looking. Positive comments from pretty much all who had been invited had given her a boost, and she, therefore, felt more than ready to start selling lingerie and other things.

Striding into the central part of the ground floor, she grinned as she took in what she had created. Aphrodite's Closet was going to be a success. She could just feel it. Flicking on the lights and the heating, she began to walk through the store, checking the cabinets and shelves to make sure everything was hanging and folded the way it should be. A couple of the scarves hadn't been hung up properly, so she adjusted them, smiling at the feel of the luxurious fabrics.

Then she moved over to the lingerie, checking that the knickers were in the right slots in the cabinets.

Heading back upstairs to the second floor, the sound of the

door being unlocked startled her, and she rushed back downstairs to make sure it was Coco walking through the door.

Sure enough, a bright and sparkly Coco was standing inside, smiling at her.

"Good morning," Aggie sang as she jumped off the bottom step.

"You're chirpy this morning," Coco said with a grin.

"And you're very sparkly," she said, looking down at her outfit.

"I couldn't help it. I had to wear something that reflected my mood," Coco grinned, taking off her little fur gilet to reveal a blush pink dress, the arms of which were covered in pink sequins.

"It's lovely. Isn't that one of the dresses you bought in Vegas?"

Coco nodded and did a little turn. "Gorgeous, isn't it?"

"Very. I feel a bit underdressed now."

"Hey, you look great. I love that green blouse and those trousers on you. I'd be more inclined to wear them with heels though," Coco suggested.

Aggie scrunched up her face. "Heels? For a full day in the shop?"

"Yeah. What about those low black heels I bought you for Christmas? They'd look fab."

"Maybe," Aggie said, "But I can't face the prospect of heels while working down here."

"Fair enough. The brogues are cute too," she grinned.

"Why thank you, Aggie smiled as she continued to prepare the shop for business. "So, you ready for the big day?"

Coco nodded with enthusiasm, "Of course. You?"

Aggie nodded, "Can't wait."

At precisely nine o'clock, the girls both grinned at each other and went to unlock the door at the same time. Together, they put their hands on the open sign and turned it to face the outside world.

"We are officially open," Coco squealed as they ran back behind the counter and waited for their first customers to arrive.

Not more than five minutes passed before the door was pushed open, and a young woman carrying a very young baby in a sling walked in.

Coco recognised her immediately, "Isabella! I didn't expect you to be in so early," Coco said as she walked back toward the door. "And you brought the little one with you. He's grown so much already."

"Hey, Coco, well he's had me up much of the night, so I figured a drive in the car might help him sleep. Would you believe it, he's conked out now? He loves sleeping in the sling."

"Well, thanks for coming back so soon. Do you remember Aggie?"

"Yes, of course," Isabella said as she walked over to Aggie and smiled. "Congratulations on the opening of the shop. It's breathtaking."

"Thank you," Aggie replied beaming. "I certainly didn't expect anyone from last night to be in this quickly," she laughed.

"Well, I saw so many wonderful things last night, but we had too little time to buy anything so I figured I'd come in today and get it all before it's all sold."

Coco and Aggie both laughed.

"Well, we'll leave you to have another look. Let me know if you need any help with anything."

"Thanks. I'm going to enjoy this," Isabella smiled as she headed straight for the second floor.

Within the next hour, a multitude of people had wandered in, had a good look around and bought things.

Christie had also appeared and disappeared, promising to return the following day to help out.

But it wasn't until around midday that things started hotting up, with the arrival of several middle-aged women who claimed to have read about the shop online.

"Oooh I wonder what they're talking about," Coco said as she ran upstairs to pick up her iPad. Once back downstairs, while Aggie helped a young woman choose a nightdress for an upcoming holiday, Coco began searching Aphrodite's Closet online.

oOo

. . .

The Goddess of Love arrives in Frambleberry

The grand opening of Aphrodite's Closet, an adults-only store on the corner of Pelican Street, was not only a huge success but a bit of an eye-opener for this reporter, writes Simon Connor.

The store, split over two floors, features everything you can imagine from simple women's cotton underwear to the more risqué lingerie to the even more daring toys and gadgets for the bedroom.

But it's not just the contents that will make you want to go back for more, it's the grand architecture and brilliantly designed interior decor. Not to mention the three women responsible for the newly opened store.

Agatha Trout is the new owner of this incredible building after her Great Aunt Petunia left the property to her in her will following her death late last year. Petunia Petal died in her sleep, aged ninety-nine. Agatha, unsure what she would do with the building, was greatly influenced by her best friend, Coco Watson, who suggested an adults-only shop was the way to go after some research showed that such a shop had never been opened in the town.

Agatha and Coco are joined by Agatha's younger sister, Christie Valentine, who, after having twins three years ago, says she was ready to get back to work.

Together, the three businesswomen are looking forward to welcoming adults, young and old, to Aphrodite's Closet and hope that the business will grow into a huge success. Undoubtedly, this reporter believes that is precisely what will happen.

"Well, that's a lovely write up," Agatha said after listening to Coco read the article online. "I loved the headline," she said as another customer paid for a couple of new bras.

"Yes, and there's lots more like it. I've read at least four posts saying what a great night it was, and what a fab shop it is. If we continue like this, it's going to be ace," Coco grinned as she followed another couple upstairs who needed a little assistance choosing something "for a friend."

CHAPTER 19

"No, sir, I'm sorry, but we don't stock inflatable dolls, I'm afraid. Sorry, what? Inflatable sheep? Er, no. I didn't even know they existed. But no, not here. Er yes," Coco listened down the phone and tried to keep a straight face. "Oh those," she emphasised for added drama to Aggie and Christie who were both listening to the conversation. "No, I don't believe so, but you can probably find them online. No, I can't suggest a site, I'm afraid. Have you thought about Googling inflatable sheep? Oh right. And what was the other thing you've been looking for? An inflatable pussy? The feline variety? Oh right. Sorry, we don't stock those either. However, we do carry a vibrating vagina if that helps? No, no, it's not inflatable. Sorry. Yes, fine. All right then. Thanks for your call."

Coco put the phone down and looked up at the girls. Both were red-faced and trying very hard not to laugh out loud.

"Everything he wanted was inflatable," Coco just about managed to say before cracking up.

"Oh my Gawd," she laughed. "I guess I'd better get used to calls like that," she said after they all began to calm down.

"Perhaps we need to start looking for inflatable sheep to stock in the shop?"

"Er, I think not," Aggie replied, looking aghast at the mere thought.

"But look, they do exist," Coco blurted out, turning her iPad toward them to show the offending item online.

"Ew," Aggie and Christie both said at the same time.

"Well, don't knock it until you've tried it," winked Coco.

"Coco!" Aggie said, disgusted, walking away and chuckling under her breath.

"I can hear you laughing, missy," Coco said a little louder.

The sound of something being shoved through the letterbox, made Aggie change direction. She scooped the letter off the floor and started to open it.

"Oh my God," she whispered.

"What is it?" Christie asked, walking up behind her.

"We've been threatened."

"What do you mean?" Coco asked, joining them to have a look.

"It's a threatening letter," Aggie added. "Look."

OPENING a sex shop in the town of Frambleberry is nothing less than despicable. You ought to be ashamed of yourselves. Look out Coco Watson, Agatha Trout, and Christie Valentine. You're about to get your comeuppance. I know where you live.

COCO READ the letter out loud as the three girls leaned against the countertop, listening intently.

"Don't worry about it, it's clearly just a pathetic joke. Nothing to worry about."

"You don't think we ought to call the police or something?" Aggie asked, taking the offending letter out of Coco's hands and re-reading it.

"Nah, it's just someone messing about. It's probably just one of my sicko friends. Let's just forget about it."

"She's right, Aggie. Let's not let it worry us."

Aggie nodded and ripped it in half and deposited it in the bin.

oOo

THAT NIGHT when Aggie went to bed, every little noise she heard outside made her jump. She didn't know why, but that letter had freaked her out a little bit. Trying to get it out of her head, she decided to get up and have a look through some of the old things she'd found in the secret room when they'd first visited the shop. She'd been so busy over recent months that she'd almost forgotten about it all.

First making herself a cup of sweet hot chocolate, she grabbed one of the boxes and hiked it into the living room, where she sat cross-legged on the carpeted floor and covered her knees with a warm throw.

Delving into the box, she pulled out a handful of old photographs. Most of them were of the same family, a tall fierce-looking woman with jet-black hair, her husband who appeared to be a little older than her with a head of thick white hair and two little girls who had the same dark hair like their mother.

On the back of the first two photographs, was the date 1921. The girls must have been Aunt Petunia and her sister Elsie.

That's obviously her mother. I wonder if it's Cornelia, Aggie thought as she looked for some other photos in the box. Pulling out about half a dozen more, she stopped when she came across an older picture of what must have been Petunia with, perhaps, her first husband. He had died in 1938, and this photo was dated 1936. She would have been around eighteen years old. Glancing at the picture again, she was surprised to see that the couple was standing at the foot of some stairs. Stairs that looked very familiar.

"It's here," Aggie said out loud. "They were here. So I wonder how the shop came to be in her possession? Hm?" she wondered aloud.

Picking out some pieces of folded paper, Aggie came across a letter. Opening it and reading it, she soon realised that Petunia's parents had died within a year of each other. Petunia had only been sixteen years old at the time. Finding more evidence, Aggie soon discovered that Petunia had been taken under the wing of a man named Henry Cleaver. And on further inspection, the two had married shortly after that.

"Gosh," Aggie said before taking a sip of her hot chocolate, which had turned cold. Screwing up her face, she put it back down on the coffee table and continued searching. This stuff was intriguing.

Finally, after going through a whole load of old paperwork, she discovered how the shop had become Petunia's. It had belonged to the Cleaver family and therefore on Henry's death, was bequeathed to his young wife, who was barely twenty-one years old at the time.

Aggie sat back and uncrossed her legs, straightening them out in front of her, as she thought about Petunia and Henry all that time ago. She'd inherited the shop from her late husband and had subsequently kept it all those years. Incredible.

But that wasn't enough, Aggie was determined to find out more about the family history, but yawning all of a sudden, she looked at the clock and realised it was after two in the morning. Putting everything back in the box, she stood up, grabbed the cold cup of chocolate and tipped it down the sink before heading back upstairs to bed where she fell asleep almost immediately.

CHAPTER 20

"...And then my Great Aunt Petunia inherited the shop from her late husband back in the thirties," Aggie said as she folded a gold satin nightgown, wrapped it in pink paper and then placed it in a bag for her customer, who just happened to be Helena Bruce.

Helena, who was clearly intrigued by the tale, handed over her credit card.

"And she kept the shop for the rest of her life, leaving it to me in her will," Aggie concluded.

"That's quite a story, Aggie," Helena said, punching in the code on the Visa machine, before taking the card out and placing it back in her purse. "It is a beautiful place. I'm so pleased that Kyle recommended I come with him for the opening. I'm sorry I haven't managed to come over until now, but we've been insanely busy. I don't know if you've passed by the development over the past couple of months?" she asked.

Aggie shook her head, "I've been dying to see it, but just haven't had the time either," she said, as she handed Helena the bag over the counter before she walked around it.

"Well, you should come over whenever you have some free time. I'm sure Kyle would love to give you a tour if I'm not there."

"That's kind of you, Helena. I will take you up on that. Just as soon as I have some free time," she smiled. "Thanks so much for coming."

"Thank you for, well, the discount," Helena grinned. "It's a beautiful nightgown. I can't wait to wear it. I'll be back soon. Bye."

"Bye, Helena. Thank you," Aggie waved.

Aggie was just about to turn back to the counter when she heard Coco yell her name from upstairs.

"Coming," she replied as she took two stairs at a time up to the second floor.

"All okay, Coco?" she asked, a little breathless. "I need to start working out again."

"Yeah, everything's fine. I just thought you'd like to reply to this email. It's from Alex at The Kinky Prince."

"Alex? Oh, Alexandra?"

Coco nodded as she handed Aggie the shop's Mac.

"I'll take it downstairs if that's okay?"

"Course. It's your computer."

"Well, it's ours. It belongs to the shop," Aggie smiled, not looking up as she read the email and walked down the stairs at the same time, narrowly escaping a fall halfway.

"Oops," she exclaimed as she heard the door close.

"Oh, hello. Let me know if you need any assistance," she said, not noticing who had walked in as she continued back to the counter where she had a stool to sit on while she worked.

"Thank you," said an odd, high-pitched voice.

Aggie glanced up and saw the back of a woman in a blue beret as she looked through the racks, but then returned her attention to the email.

DEAR MISS. TROUT,

I hope you are very well and that the opening of Aphrodite's Closet continues to be a success.

I just wanted to take the opportunity to thank you for your recent order of:

10 red and black satin and lace negligees
10 green and cream satin and lace negligees

10 crotchless panties from our "Henrietta" range
10 crotchless panties from our "Georgette" range

They are currently in processing and, as promised, will be delivered by the end of next week.

I'm also sending you a special gift, a couple of items from our newest "Eliza" range, which I hope you will enjoy. As mentioned previously, all our products are made in Germany and France, the same with this new range, which The Kinky Prince has designed exclusively for our clients. I'd love to hear your thoughts on the "Eliza" range. I've also sent you a second catalogue featuring the "Eliza" products for sale.

Enjoy!
Very best wishes
Alex
The Kinky Prince

AGGIE TYPED A REPLY TO ALEXANDRA:

DEAR ALEX,

Thank you so much for your email and for dealing with my recent order. The products we ordered from you the first time have been selling well, and our customers certainly seem pleased with them.

Huge thanks for sending me a gift! That's very kind of you. I shall look forward to receiving everything and giving you my opinion.

Have a fabulous day.
Best wishes,
Aggie
Aphrodite's Closet

AS SHE HIT SEND, Aggie heard the door close again. Looking up, she couldn't see anyone else in the shop, so she assumed the lady who had come in earlier had gone without saying another word.

Shrugging her shoulders, she closed the Mac computer and started walking back upstairs to Coco, who she met on the stairs.

"Hey, I'm done with this if you want to use it?"

"Nah, it's fine. I was just coming downstairs to you…urgh, what is that smell?" she said, screwing up her nose.

"Urgh," Aggie replied. "That's weird. And very sudden."

Both girls turned and ran down the stairs, both sniffing, their noses in the air like wolfhounds.

"Oh my God," Coco squealed from the corner of the shop. "What the hell…?"

"What is it?" Aggie asked, approaching. She almost doubled over when she got there.

"Who the hell would do something like this? Who was in here?" Coco asked with her hands on her hips in utter dismay and disgust.

"Is it human?"

Coco shook her head. "We need to clean this up now. I think it's dog shit."

"Dog shit? Nobody came in with a dog," Aggie cried.

"They must've done, Aggie. Maybe it was when you came upstairs."

"But who the hell would bring a dog inside a lingerie shop and let it shit everywhere."

"I've no idea, Agg. But bloody disgusting is what it is."

Both girls rallied around each other, cleaning up the mess on the shop floor.

"Don't you remember who came in this afternoon? I mean, this is pretty damn fresh," Coco tutted, heaving as she picked it up with some kitchen roll.

"There was just one woman who came in while I was emailing. I didn't see her, except for her hat.

"So an old woman came in with a dog, let it shit on the floor, and left? Wonderful," Coco said as Aggie carefully poured bleach on the floor before she scrubbed it with the mop.

"I know. I can't quite believe it myself. Maybe we need some cameras in here?"

"It's something to consider," Aggie agreed once everything was cleaned up and the foul smell had disappeared. "We did talk about it before we opened."

"Yeah, but I was worried about the cost."

Coco nodded, "I think I'm in shock," she said, wiping her brow.

"Hello, hello!" said a very tall woman as she opened the door. "Are you open?"

"Yes, yes of course," Aggie smiled, relieved they'd managed to get rid of the smell. "Please come in. Have a look around and let us know if we can help with anything."

"I'll get right to the point, darling. I need some new lingerie for a very special occasion," she grinned, looking at Coco and Aggie expectantly.

Coco stepped forward and said, "Is there anything, in particular, you're looking for?"

"Something insanely sexy," she said in somewhat of a deep voice.

"Well, you've come to the right place," Aggie smiled. "Perhaps you ought to look toward the back of the shop?"

Coco led the woman through the shop and began to show her some of the more kinky lingerie.

"Oooh yes, that's rather nice, but still a little…staid. Do you have anything even more…memorable?"

Coco grinned and nodded. "Why don't you follow me upstairs?"

The woman stood up straight and tossed her long wavy blonde hair backwards. Aggie thought there was something a little strange about her. But she thought nothing more of it and left her and Coco to find something suitable.

"Before we look at the other items, what do you think about this?" Coco suggested as she pulled out a delicate satin negligee in dusky pink with a cream lace trim. "It's not overtly sexual, but I thought it would look fabulous on you."

The woman's face lit up, "It's beautiful," she breathed, taking it in her hands and feeling the luxurious fabric. "I'll take it. That's a good start, but I'll need something more fun for afterwards."

"I hear ya," Coco chuckled as she put the negligee back in its box and proceeded to show the woman their more extreme ranges.

After an hour, the woman walked back downstairs with several bags in her hands and a huge grin on her face.

"Thank you so much," Aggie said as she walked past the counter and headed for the door.

"Thank you," the woman replied. "I'll be back again soon, I'm sure of it."

After a couple of minutes, Coco reappeared by Aggie's side.

"How did it go? I saw she had quite a few bags in her hands."

"Yes…he did, didn't he?"

"Huh?" Aggie said, looking up. "He?"

"Hm-hm," Coco said, grinning. "That was the most beautiful man I've ever seen."

"She was a he? Nah, you're having me on?"

But Coco shook her head.

"Wow, what did he buy?"

"Lots of goodies. He's going to have a good time tonight with his partner, for sure."

"Is his partner a man or a woman then?"

Coco shrugged her shoulders, "Who knows? He bought stuff for both, so maybe he's got several partners. Lucky him," she winked.

CHAPTER 21

Aggie had done some more reading through Petunia's old papers and had discovered that her great aunt had inherited quite a lot of money over the years but, other than the shop that she'd inherited from Henry Cleaver in 1938, all she'd had left at the time of her death was a sum of fifty thousand pounds. Aggie thought it strange that she would have spent so much money over the years, but then, she'd never met the woman so couldn't make a judgment.

She just wished she'd had the chance to talk to her and find out more about her life, other than minor details about her four dead husbands.

But then several months into the opening of Aphrodite's Closet, Aggie had received a small package in the mail. She'd ignored it during work hours but had opened it as she was climbing the stairs to her apartment on Friday evening.

Inside, was a DVD and a short note from the solicitor who had handled the will.

DEAR MISS TROUT,

I was instructed by the late Petunia Petal to mail this DVD to your attention precisely ten weeks after the opening of your shop.

Best regards,

Francis Cake
Cake & Co Solicitors

INTRIGUED, Aggie sped up the stairs, pushing open her front door and letting it slam behind her. She threw off her shoes and bounded into the living room where she scrambled with the DVD player until the DVD had been inserted. She sat down on the floor and crossing her legs, she pressed play.

"IS IT WORKING?" said an impatient very old lady sitting back in a seventies-style armchair.

"Yes, Ms Petal."

Aggie's Great Aunt Petunia shooed away whoever had pressed record, and Aggie listened as a door opened and closed in the background.

Aunt Petunia leaned forward in her seat and grinned a wicked, toothy grin.

"My name is Petunia Petal, and I'm recording this…this…video, or whatever you call it these days, for my Great Niece, Agatha Trout. Yes, love, I'm talking to you," she said, pointing toward the screen. "You're probably wondering what the bloody hell I'm doing this for, but I know you have questions and, honey, I got answers for ya. Like I said, my name is Petunia Petal. I'm ninety-eight years old. I'll be ninety-nine in a few days, and I don't think I'll be here much longer than that. Anyway, dear, I wanted to meet you. Lord, I did, but it was never going to happen, was it? That old Trout of a mother of yours would need let that happen. Not her fault, though, not really. You see, love, my sister, Elsie, was Trixie's mother and they were like two peas in a pod those two. The trouble was Elsie, and I never did see eye to eye. She was a meddling so and so, she was. She never forgave me for Jasper, did she?" Petunia suddenly started to cough, which then became an almighty coughing fit that she couldn't stop.

Aggie watched in horror as her great aunt fell off the chair with a thud.

"Uh, Petunia!" she wailed as if the old woman could hear her.

The tape stopped recording, there was a certain amount of crackling, and then Petunia was on the screen again, this time with an oxygen tank beside her.

"Ah, I'm not dead yet," grinned the old lady. "Now where was I? Ah yes, Elsie and Jasper. They were married, you see. But it seems he didn't want my boring big sister, he wanted me. And what was I to do about that? That man was something else. Larger than life and boy was he good in bed!" Petunia cackled with laughter but started coughing again. She grappled with the oxygen mask, leaned back for a few moments taking deep breaths before she removed it from her face and continued talking.

"There you have it, your mother's mother blamed me for stealing her man," Petunia shrugged. "I didn't do it to hurt her. I'd never have hurt her. She was my sister, after all. But, when men come into it, what can you do? And when there's sex like never before? Boy, that man," she sighed, before continuing. "Well, Jasper was killed in Africa in 1955. He was there on business, and someone shot him, shot him to death, they did. It was a terrible business. Tragic. And Elsie never spoke to me again; well, barely. Which is why your mother never wanted much to do with me, Agatha. Although I hear they call you Aggie, right?"

Aggie nodded.

"Well, Aggie, about the shop. You'll have probably found my papers by now, and you'll know I inherited that place from my first husband," she smiled fondly remembering him. "Henry Cleaver. He was a good man. Took me in when mam and dad died, he did. Elsie was already independent and living her own life and didn't want to have to look after her sixteen-year-old sister. I never blamed her for that. And besides, I'd never have met my Henry, would I? He was a good man. We had a special bond, the two of us. I was only twenty-one when he passed, you know? It was a hard time, but I worked through it, like a trooper. I made that shop a success for a good few years, you know? I stocked everything in there—it was a proper corner shop. People knew they could get anything they needed from me," Petunia winked. "That shop made me into the woman I am now. It gave me strength, it gave me the confidence I needed to live my life to the fullest. Aggie, that's why I'm giving it to you. Because I know you will do the same. You're probably wondering how I know this about you. Well, I've been following you."

Aggie's eyes grew wide.

"Not literally, not at this age, not trapped in this place," she sighed. "But I have eyes and ears on the outside. They keep me updated on what you're up to. I couldn't quite understand why you were working in a library, though. A library? For myths?" Petunia shook her head. "And no man? Honestly, Aggie, you can do better than that, sweetie. I want you to make the corner shop into something unique, something special like it once was. Bring it back to life, Aggie. That's what I want you to do. You hear me?"

Aggie nodded.

"As for your sister, Christie. I know she's already doing well with a good husband and children, which is why I'm only leaving her fifty thousand pounds. It's not all I've got left. There is more… but you'll learn about that soon enough. Agatha, Aggie …don't be upset with your mother for not letting us meet. She means well, that woman. She's just like my sister, and when Elsie died, I was devastated that we'd never made up. Don't ever let that happen to you, kiddo. Forgive, don't necessarily forget, but always forgive if you can. Now, I know I've not got much time left on this earth, but I've had a blast. Nearly ninety-nine years, four husbands, and some wonderful memories. But my memory isn't what it used to be. I can remember ninety years ago like it was yesterday, but yesterday? Bah! I can't remember anything. But I can remember you as a baby, Christie too. Your mother doesn't know, but your father, Ted, he brought me to the hospital to see you just after you were born. You looked like a bloody alien, so ugly! Whereas Christie was a little beauty. But I've seen pictures of you now, Aggie, and you remind me a lot of me when I was your age. I saw you again when you were three years old. I invited Trixie and Ted to the memorial I had for Jim. You and your dad turned up, but not Trixie. I wasn't surprised, though. But it was good that she let your father and you come to see me. I thought it might have been the start of better things, but I guess it was just a one-off. But never mind that now. What was I saying? Oh yes, you and me, we have the same features, don't you think? Well not now, but how I was then," Petunia cackled into the camera, her breathing becoming erratic again.

"Agatha, be brave darling...always be brave. Goodbye, sweetheart."

The recording came to an abrupt end, and Aggie found she was crying. She wiped the tears away with the back of her hand and sat back, leaning against the sofa.

What had just happened?

CHAPTER 22

"Wow," Christie sighed after she'd watched the DVD.
"I know, Sis,"
Christie just nodded and frowned.
"So...weird, don't you think?" Aggie asked.
"Absolutely," Christie replied as she took a sip of her tea. "So Mum never wanted us to meet Petunia because she blamed her for stealing Gran Elsie's boyfriend when they were younger?"
"I think it was Gran Elsie's first husband. I'm pretty sure they were married."
"But it was before Mum was even born, so why is she so upset?"
"Gran Elsie must've held one hell of a grudge against Petunia for it to last so many years and to rub off on Mum."
"It's so sad, though. Great Aunt Petunia would have liked to have been a part of our lives. I feel like Mum's taken something from us, do you know what I mean?"
Christie frowned, "No, you can't look at it like that. You can't blame her. It's all regrettable, but like Petunia just said, we all need to forgive each other. Don't hold a grudge like Mum and Gran Elsie did. It's not healthy."
"I guess you're right," Aggie said as she pressed the eject button and pulled the DVD out of the player. "But I want Mum to watch this."

"That's probably a good idea, Agg. But how are you going to do that when she's still not speaking to you? Or me, for that matter."

"I'll find a way, I'm sure," she smiled, looking downward.

"Are you okay?" Christie asked.

"Just sad, that's all."

"Yeah, I know. But remember what she said—live your life to the fullest and be brave—she has a point."

"Well I am doing that, aren't I?"

"Opening a sex shop is certainly being brave," Christie joked, picking up a soft cushion and throwing it at her sister.

"Hey."

"Now come on, let's get back downstairs and sell some stuff."

oOo

Aggie's sadness was heightened when the shop received a second threatening letter. This time, the perpetrator had gone to a lot more trouble by cutting out letters from a magazine to spell out:

APHRODITE'S CLOSET
The end is nigh
Get ready to be destroyed
Beware, girls. Your time has come...

"OH MY GOD," screeched Aggie as she dropped the letter onto the counter, causing a handful of customers to look over at her in shock.

"Hey," Christie said as she rushed over. Taking one look at the letter, she gasped.

"I think it's time we told the police, don't you?" she asked.

"What's going on over here?" asked Coco as she appeared from the changing rooms after helping a woman buy some new pyjamas.

"This," Christie cried, thrusting the letter forward.

"Oh," Coco said, looking up. "I'll call the police."

"Wait," Aggie said. "Is it serious enough to warrant calling them? I just…I wouldn't want to waste their time, you know?"

"I think it's serious enough," Christie said.

"Why don't I run it past Kyle and see what he thinks?" Coco suggested.

"Yeah, that's not a bad idea," Aggie smiled.

"Plus, he's got a few friends in the police force, so he could always ask one of them."

"That'd be good, Coco, thanks," as Aggie spoke, Coco was already dialling her brother on the phone.

Within ten minutes, Kyle was walking through the door.

"Hey, you sounded so worried, what's going on?"

Before anyone could say anything to Kyle, Coco handed him the letter.

His face turned red with anger.

"It's the second threat we've received. We threw the first one away because we thought it was just one of our friends messing about."

"Has anything else happened? Anything else that could have been a threat?" he asked. "No one has approached you or tried to hurt you have they?"

He looked at Coco, then at Aggie, then at Christie.

All of them shook their heads.

"You're certain?" he asked.

They all nodded.

"Unless you count the dog?" Coco piped up.

"What do you mean?" Christie asked.

"Oh, the dog poo incident?" Aggie said, looking somewhat dumbfounded. "You think that might have been another threat?"

"It's possible," Coco said before explaining to Kyle what had happened in the shop a few weeks earlier.

"This is definitely cause for concern, girls. It's time you got some cameras set up in here. Look, leave it with me and I'll organise it. And in the meantime, be careful. Write anything down you deem suspicious, okay? I'll have a word with a couple of my pals in the force. I'll come back tomorrow with my CCTV guy, okay?"

The three of them just stood there nodding, looking like they'd all been slapped in the face.

Before he left, Kyle's face softened. "Don't worry. We'll find out who this is. You'll be fine," he smiled. "I've got to go now though because I've got an important meeting. I'll sort this," he said as he rushed out the door.

"He's the best," Aggie whispered.

"You got that right," Coco said with a smile.

"Er, I think I'll call it a day," Christie said, her face a little white. "I need a cuddle with my girls."

"Yeah absolutely, Christie. You go on home. Look, why don't you stay at home until we've got this sorted?"

"No, I can come in…"

"Sis, I'd hate for something to happen to you. We got it covered."

"Aggie," Christie sighed as she pulled her into a gentle hug. "Okay."

"We'll call you and let you know what's going on soon, all right?"

"Okay, Aggie," she said as she crouched down behind the counter to pick up her handbag.

"Give the girls a big hug from me," Aggie said as she walked toward the door.

"From me too," Coco shouted from the stairs.

"Oh and Aggie?"

"Yeah?"

"Call Mum and Dad."

Aggie smiled and nodded as Christie walked out of the shop.

CHAPTER 23

Recognising the box, Aggie smiled at the courier as she accepted delivery of the latest order from The Kinky Prince.

Carrying the box upstairs, she opened it and checked the order was exactly as it should be. Sure enough, ten red and black satin and lace negligees, ten green and cream satin and lace negligees, ten crotchless panties from the "Henrietta" range, and ten crotchless panties from the "Georgette" range were all beautiful packaged in The Kinky Prince's subdued yet pretty boxes. There was also a separate box bearing Aggie's name. She'd completely forgotten Alex had said she was sending her a special gift from the new "Eliza" range.

Opening up the box, Aggie gasped at the sight of a very revealing, yet exquisite long dress. Clearly for nowhere but the bedroom, the silky yet clingy midnight blue dress had delicate cutouts in the chest and the crotch areas. Also in the box was a beautiful blue eye mask and a small whip. Not only that, but an even smaller box was hidden amongst the tissue paper. Opening it, Aggie found a small pen—only it wasn't a pen, it was a vibrator that could easily be mistaken for a pen. She twisted the top, and it hopped into action, pulsing and vibrating rather strongly in her hand. She blushed and switched it off.

Inside was a handwritten note,

I hope you enjoy these!
Let me know,
Alex X
The Kinky Princ"

"Oh great, The Kinky Prince order has arrived," Coco said when she noticed the box in Aggie's hands. "And what's that? Ooh, a gift? That's nice of Alex."

"Yes, very sweet."

"A pen, and a dress, ooh a whip, and an eye mask? Crikey? All you need is a man now," Coco grinned.

"It's not a pen though, Coco. Look," she said, handing the item over to her.

"Oh now, this is a great idea. You can carry it in your handbag at all times," she squealed. "I must get one for myself."

"Haven't you got enough?" Aggie teased.

"A woman can never have enough intimate massagers," she chuckled as a client walked past them on the stairs and turned a deep shade of red.

Aggie turned back downstairs and came face to face with Kyle. Her own cheeks reddened as he looked down and saw what she held in her hands.

"Ooh that looks like fun," he joked, and she bit her lip.

"Er yeah, just a n…new o…order, that's all," she managed to stutter.

"Yes I'm sure," he said, making her completely unable to function as she stood, hovering at the foot of the stairs.

He laughed then and moved out of her way as she walked past him and headed behind the counter to hide the box from sight.

"Helena told me she'd been in and bought some stuff," Kyle said, making conversation.

"Yes," Aggie replied. "She's lovely. She bought a very nice nightgown. I thought you would've seen it by now."

Kyle looked somewhat confused, "Helena's nightgown? Er, no."

"Oh," Aggie said, coming back out on to the shop floor and trying to find something to fold or move to keep her busy.

"I thought you two were…er…"

Kyle started laughing, "Helena and Me? God no. I mean she's

wonderful and all. Quite beautiful and confident but no, Aggie, no," he said, still chuckling.

"What about you? Are you seeing anyone?"

Aggie coughed and shook her head so hard that she knocked a whole load of knickers onto the floor.

"Shit," she said as she flung herself onto the tiles and began picking them up.

"Here, let me help," he said, crouching down and picking up the first pair that he found. He held them up and realised they were crotchless ones.

"Oh," he said, a little embarrassed as she reacted at the same time, and they both knocked heads as they went to stand up.

"Ouch," she said, holding her hand to her head.

"Sorry, Aggie," he muttered, rubbing his own forehead. "You okay?"

Aggie, who by now was a dark shade of puce, shook her head and rushed off in the other direction.

"These shouldn't be here," she said as she went. "This stuff should be at the back of the store."

"Oh, I can help," Kyle offered, grabbing all the crotchless knickers off the shelf and rushing behind her.

When she turned around and saw what he was carrying, her eyes grew larger, and she stood still. Closing them for a moment, she took a deep breath before opening them again.

"Thank you, Kyle, for your help. You're very sweet, but I can manage it from here," she said, managing to speak without stuttering. She had known him since they were kids so why oh why was she getting so damn embarrassed again?

Kyle nodded and dropped the knickers onto a nearby table.

"I, er, I'm actually here to talk about the CCTV," he managed to say.

"Of course. Thank you."

"It's going to be fitted tomorrow afternoon. They'll be here around three o'clock. Is that okay with you? I can come too if you'd like me to be here?"

"Gosh no, that's not necessary, Kyle. We'll manage. No problem."

He nodded for a moment, stopped, bit his lip and turned away.

"Okay then, er, I'd better be going. Busy…meeting…Helena…plans…"

Before Aggie could say another word, Kyle had gone, the door opened and shut behind him. She was left wondering what the hell had just happened.

As she proceeded to fold the knickers and put them in their rightful places, the door opened again, and a couple of ladies entered, giggling to themselves, followed by another woman who clearly wanted to be left alone.

"Hello. Let me know if you need any help with anything," Aggie said, smiling.

Both women nodded and went straight upstairs as if they knew exactly where they were going and exactly what they were getting. Perhaps they did?

The door opened again, and several people came in, and soon the shop had a good number of clients wandering around, having a look.

Once the knickers were all neatly folded and placed on the shelf, Aggie couldn't quite shake the feeling that something was off somehow.

She noticed the sound of the door opening and shutting a few times. She took her time to wander around the shelves and double-check everything. That's when she noticed that some things were missing.

The Kinky Prince boxes weren't where she'd put them on display. Neither were the silk pyjamas she'd hung up the previous night. Frowning, she scoured the ground floor and found even more items not where they should have been. And some items were missing altogether.

Knowing that Coco was busy with clients upstairs, Aggie grabbed a pen and paper and began to note everything that was missing or misplaced so she could check with the others later.

Soon, though, she heard hysterical laughter coming from outside, and so she looked up and peered out of the window. That's when she spotted a group of teenagers gathering close to the store.

Heading toward the exit, she pushed open the door and stepped outside. The teenagers were pointing and laughing at something hanging from the Aphrodite's Closet sign.

Looking up and dreading what she would find, she spotted several of the missing knickers (some of which were crotchless) had been ripped apart and were dangling from the sign.

The Kinky Prince boxes had been crushed beneath muddy feet and were strewn across the entryway to the store.

Anger filled Aggie's lungs, and she screamed at no one in particular.

The teenagers looked at each other and decided now was a good time to bugger off. She just knew that they weren't responsible for the damage, so it was pointless having a go at them.

Threats. That's what it was. Another warning.

Coco, who had heard Aggie yell, rushed outside as soon as she could.

"Oh, Aggie," she cried when she saw what had happened.

"Why?" Aggie yelled. "Why are they doing this to us?"

"Let's clean it up," Coco said. "But first, remember what Kyle said. We need to document this. Take pictures."

Aggie nodded.

CHAPTER 24

Looking at the computer screen, Aggie felt a lump in her throat, knowing that she'd have to watch everyone who came into the shop very carefully. She hated that. Hated that she couldn't trust any of her customers anymore.

The screen was split into four—each section showed a different part of the inside of Aphrodite's Closet, and if she pressed a button, she had a good view of the outside too.

Sighing, she turned away from the screen below the counter and smiled at her customer who had bought three new bras and matching knickers.

"Thank you so much," Aggie said as she handed the woman her change before she exited the shop.

Another fifteen or so people were wandering around, some were happily chatting with friends, two people were talking on their phones as they picked up items, and the others were just quietly browsing, minding their own business.

Aggie kept looking at the screen, keeping an eye out for anyone who looked at all suspicious. But she didn't expect anyone to cause any trouble—it had only been four days since the last occurrence and, although Kyle had called his police friends to stop by the shop, there was little they could do.

"I won a new washing machine," Coco said as she walked over

to her. "Do you want it? I don't need it. Mine's practically brand new."

"You won a washing machine? Why did you enter if you don't need one, Coco?" Aggie asked, confused.

"You know what I'm like. I enter just for the thrill of winning," she grinned, offering Aggie a humbug from the packet.

"No, thanks," she shook her head.

"So, do you want it?"

"If you don't want it, I'd love it. Thanks."

"Great, I'll give them this address for delivery then."

Aggie smiled, still amazed at the amount of stuff Coco was always winning. Holidays, washing machines, makeup, jewellery, designer handbags, and more.

"How did you win this one?"

"The fabric softener I use was running a competition. First prize was a car, second prize, a washing machine and a dryer, and third prize was the one I got."

"Cool," Aggie said.

"I'd have preferred the car."

"You don't need a car. You've got a perfectly good Mercedes Sports."

"I know," Coco grinned. "But the more, the merrier right?"

Aggie shook her head and turned her attention back to the screen.

"Still keeping an eye out for the person responsible, eh?"

"Of course," Aggie replied.

"Whoever it is isn't going to do anything now. I bet the person has seen that we've got CCTV installed now."

"I dunno," Aggie said, turning to look at Coco, "I just want to catch the person in the act so we can lock the person up and throw away the key."

"I know and we will. I'm sure of it."

"Hi," said a voice approaching the till.

"Hello," Coco beamed at the tiny woman who was barely taller than the countertop. "Can we help with anything?"

"Yes, please. I was wondering if you do any of those nighties over there for petites?"

"Oh," Coco said, alarmed. "No, I'm sorry, but we don't stock anything for petites."

The little lady frowned and smiled, nodding. "Oh well, nevermind. I do struggle with sleepwear for my size," she sighed and turned to walk away.

"Wait," Aggie said. "Let's see if we can order some in."

The woman beamed and walked back toward them.

"That would be wonderful, thank you."

"Coco, would you mind fetching the catalogues?"

Coco grinned and disappeared up the stairs, returning with a handful of catalogues from the various companies from which they bought stock.

"To be honest, we never even gave the petite range a second thought. So stupid of us," Coco said as the two of them began searching through the books.

"Well, I'm sure you'd be popular with my family and I if you did," smiled the woman. "We're all quite little, and we all struggle to find quality pyjamas and nighties, not to mention nightgowns."

"Here we are," said Aggie, pointing to a page in one of the catalogues. "This company does a petite range. What do you think?"

"They are quite pretty, but can you give me an example of the fabric they use?"

"Of course," Coco said, rushing to where their other stock was being displayed. "This is it, I think," she said, checking the label. "Yes, here you are."

"Oh yes, that'd be perfect. Can I order three of those? All in size eight, please. And also, can I order five pairs of pyjamas in the blue? I'll take two size eights, two size twelves and three size sixteens please."

Coco and Aggie both looked at each other in surprise as the woman took out her credit card.

"You don't have to pay now. You can pay when you collect them if you like," Aggie suggested.

"Oh, I'd rather do it now, if that's all right?"

"Of course. Well, that comes to three hundred and fifteen pounds, but we'll give you a twenty per cent discount, so that comes to two hundred and fifty-two, please."

The woman's face lit up in delight. "Goodness me, I didn't expect that at all."

"Well it's the least we could do considering we hadn't stocked any petites, and of course because you're buying so many at once," Aggie smiled as the woman punched in her credit card code.

"Well, some birthdays are coming up soon, and I don't live nearby, so I thought I'd better buy them all at once."

"You don't live nearby?" Coco piped up.

"No, I'm just here visiting an old family friend, and she told me about your shop, so I thought I'd come and see for myself before I head home."

"That's so nice of you, and of your friend to tell you about us. Perhaps we can send you everything in the mail, to save you driving all the way back here again next week? Where do you live?" Aggie asked.

"I live in a small village in Somerset. Thank you, that would be marvellous."

"Oh, that's a long way away," Coco added, handing her a pen and paper so the woman could write down her address.

"It's not too bad. I enjoy the drive when the roads aren't so busy."

Aggie coughed, "But they're always busy."

"Yes," the woman laughed, "But not so bad if you avoid the motorways."

Smiling, she handed the pad of paper back. "Thank you so much. Your shop is an absolute delight."

"Aww, thank you," Coco and Aggie both said as she waved and left the shop, grinning.

"Now that's why we opened this place in the first place," Coco said as she typed in the woman's address on the computer.

"Yep, it certainly is," Aggie grinned, forgetting just for a moment about the awful threats they'd been receiving.

CHAPTER 25

"Hi, Dad!"
"Aggie, sweetheart. How are you? How's the shop? Busy?"

"It's great thanks, Dad. And yes, we are keeping busy with a steady flow of customers every day. How's the shoulder?"

Aggie could just about hear her father rubbing his shoulder while he spoke.

"It's getting much better. The physio is impressed with my progress."

"That's great. You'll be back swinging that golf club in no time. I bet you miss it, don't you?"

Her dad sighed down the phone, "I certainly do. It often drives me crazy being stuck in the house with your mother all the time," he chuckled.

"How is Mum?" Aggie asked.

"Oh well, she's the same as always."

"I take it she still hasn't forgiven me?"

Ted sighed again.

"She's not quite ready for that yet, sweetheart."

"Well, you should know that Great Aunt Petunia sent me a video of herself before she died. She told me everything, Dad. I know all about Gran Elsie and Jasper. She told me why Mum wouldn't have anything to do with her."

"Well yes, it was an unfortunate affair, and your mum blamed Petunia for her own mother's unhappiness."

"That's mad...it happened in the nineteen-fifties!" Aggie exclaimed.

"I know, I know. But you know how your mum gets."

"Tell me about it," Aggie sighed.

"What else she did tell you?" he asked.

"Well, she did mention that you took her to the hospital to see Christie and me when we were born, which surprised me, Dad."

"Oh, she told you that, did she? You mustn't tell your mum about that. She wouldn't be too happy to know that I was the one who kept in touch with Petunia over the years."

"But why did you, Dad?"

"Because she was alone, Aggie. She had no one."

"Dad, you're such a softie," Aggie smiled. "Great Aunt Petunia was lucky to have you."

"Perhaps, love. But still, she was alone when she passed, and that makes me very sad. I wish I'd have been more assertive with your mother about her. She was a cracking lady, and she didn't deserve to be shut out of the family the way she was. But..."

"But what, Dad?" asked Aggie.

"But your mother, once she gets a bee in her bonnet, there's no talking her out of it. I tried a few times, and she refused to speak to me. I once took you to meet Petunia, just after Jim died. It was at his memorial at the shop. When Trixie found out where we'd been, she didn't talk to me for two whole weeks. Can you imagine?"

"Oh, Dad, you do put up with a lot of sh..."

"Now, now, she is still my wife and your mother, Aggie."

"I know, Dad. She's just so damn stubborn all the time. Where is she anyway?"

"At some ladies' luncheon in town. I'm enjoying the golf on the telly," he chuckled, "not to mention the quiet."

Aggie laughed. "What else can you tell me about Great Aunt Petunia, Dad?"

"What do you want to know, love?"

"Anything and everything. I just feel like I should know her, you know? She left me such an enormous gift, and I didn't even know her. I couldn't even thank her. And yet she seemed to know almost everything about me. Was that because of you? Did you keep her up to date?"

"I sent her pictures and letters every once in a while. But I hadn't been to see her for a few years. That home she was living in was a bit far for me to get to without your mother knowing about it. We spoke on the phone, though, about a week before she died."

"Really, Dad? What did she say?"

"She told me she was dying and that she wanted to leave her legacy with you."

"But why me, Dad?"

"Because she knew you were special, that's why."

"But I'm not, Dad. I'm not special. Why not Christie?"

Ted chuckled, "Because you are a lot like she was when she was younger. You're independent, not reliant on a man, you do your own thing regardless of what people think."

"But that doesn't sound like me. I worked in a library of mythology for most of my adult life."

"Exactly, Aggie," he chuckled. "You did that because it was your passion. Your mother said you shouldn't do it when you left school. She wanted you to become like her. And you refused. You chose your own path, Aggie. That's why Petunia chose you. That's why the corner shop became yours. She knew you'd make a go of it."

"But why then, did she put a condition in the will? Why did she say if I didn't want the shop, she'd leave it to Reverend Geoff?"

Ted started laughing.

"What, Dad?" she asked.

"She knew that would spur you on even more. She knew the rumours about that man, and she figured if you were as much like her as she thought you were, you'd never let him get his paws on that shop. And she was right," he laughed.

Aggie stopped talking for a minute, taking it all in. Shaking her head, she laughed to herself.

"So Petunia and I were alike?" she asked again.

"Very much so, sweetheart. The only difference between the two of you is that you're not much of a man-eater like she was," and he burst out laughing. "But other than that, you could quite easily have been a direct descendant. You even look alike. Have you not looked at the pictures of her at your age? Apart from your lighter hair, your features are almost the same. You look more like her than you do Trixie."

"I suppose I do, come to think of it."

"Anyway, I'm missing all my golf, and my armchair is calling me."

"Okay, Dad, I'll let you go. I'll call again soon, okay?"

"Okay, sweetheart. And don't worry about your mother, she'll come round, eventually."

"I suppose you're right, Dad. Speak soon. Love you."

"Love you too, sweetheart."

As Aggie put the phone down, she walked over to the cupboard where she'd put all of Petunia"s belongings. She looked through some of the photos until she found one where Petunia looked to be about thirty years old. Carrying it into the bedroom, she sat down at her dressing table and looked at the photo before looking at herself in the mirror.

It was true, if Aggie had shorter dark brown hair instead of long light brown, she'd be quite strikingly similar to her great aunt.

Both had quite narrow noses, and dark eyes, high cheekbones, and very straight hair. In that picture, Petunia's dark hair was in a bob and sat above her shoulders, whereas Aggie's light brown hair hung down her back. In that instance, Aggie decided to do something most unlike her.

CHAPTER 26

Taking her time to walk down the stairs into the shop, Aggie smiled to herself when she heard Coco taking off her jacket and hanging it away.

"Good morning," Coco yelled without turning to look at her.

"Morning," Aggie said back. "How was your long weekend? Did you enjoy having a few days off? Did you get up to no good?"

Coco laughed, still rummaging around in the storeroom cum kitchen.

"I'm always up to no good according to you. Fancy a coffee?" she yelled.

"Yes please, that would be lovely. So what did you get up to?" Aggie asked.

"Well, I went out for dinner again with Tony on Thursday night, but there's not really much of a spark there, so we agreed just to be friends. I think he's considering going back to his crazy wife anyway, but he's going to...Aggie!" she squealed as she walked out of the room carrying two cups of coffee which she had to put down to prevent herself from dropping on the shop floor.

Aggie grinned with delight and did a twirl on the spot.

"You like it?" she asked.

"OMG...Oh my God, girl, you look amazing. What on earth made you do that? And why didn't you tell me?"

"I wanted to surprise you."

"Holy shit, girl, I'm surprised all right. You've never done anything like this before. I mean, in all the years we've been friends, you've never once wanted to dye your hair. Or cut it, for that matter. I can't believe it. You look like another person altogether. Actually, you look like...Oh my God... you look just like your Great Aunt Petunia!"

Aggie laughed and nodded with enthusiasm. "I do, don't I? I did it on purpose. I was talking to Dad the other day, and he commented on how alike we were at the same age, so I looked at one of her old photos and just decided to do it. Do you like it?"

"I love it," Coco squealed. "I can't believe how different you look with shorter, darker hair. It's seriously incredible, Agg. I'm just in shock right now. If it weren't Monday morning, I'd have to have a drink."

"Well, let's save that for tonight. We could go out for a drink to celebrate?"

"Who are you, and where is Agatha Trout?" Coco asked, winking before she picked up the coffees and handed one of them to her best friend.

"Thanks. So are we on?"

"You bet we are," Coco shrieked. "A girls night out on a Monday night. Whatever next?"

oOo

THE DRESS AGGIE wore had been one she'd found in the charity shop in town a few days earlier. It was the emerald green colour that had first drawn her to it, and when she took it off the rail, it was the vintage design that had blown her away. Since Petunia had come into Aggie's life, she felt like she was being gently tugged into another direction. As if Petunia's soul had connected with her own. Not only was she becoming much more confident, but her tastes were changing too.

Just a year ago, Aggie wouldn't have even considered wearing a dress unless it was to somebody's wedding. But here she was wearing a nineteen-forties' style feminine dress in emerald green with heels no less! And with her new haircut and colour, she felt like a new woman.

"I still can't quite believe my eyes," said Coco as she returned from ordering their drinks at the bar. Placing two glasses of white wine on the table, Coco sat down and grinned. "It's almost like you're not you any more. Well, I mean, it's you underneath, but I just can't quite explain it. You're blossoming. Ew, I hate that word. Like the ugly duckling becoming a swan? Oh my God, where are these expressions coming from? Cinderella...now that makes more sense."

Aggie threw her head back and laughed.

"Cinderella, huh? Well, I'll take that," she smiled. "I feel different too. I know it sounds cheesy, but I almost feel like Petunia is here, you know?" Aggie said, placing her hand over her heart. "Or maybe here," she said, pointing to her head.

Coco nodded, taking a sip of wine. "Maybe she is. I kinda like that. Here's to Great Aunt Petunia," Coco said, clinking her glass with Aggie's.

"To Great Aunt Petunia," Aggie repeated, grinning before taking a sip.

"Coco?" said a woman's voice approaching them.

"Hey, Helena isn't it?" Coco replied, standing up. "Lovely to see you. How are you?"

"Marvellous, thank you. How are you? How's the shop doing? I must pop by again soon," Helena Bruce nodded to Aggie and smiled, "Hello."

"Hello, Helena," Aggie said. "Nice to see you."

Helena's face changed, her eyes growing wider. "Oh, goodness me. Agatha? Is that you?"

Aggie and Coco both laughed while she nodded.

"It's a pretty amazing transformation, isn't it?" Coco asked as Helena sat down beside them as she stared at her.

"It certainly is. I'm flabbergasted. You look...quite beautiful."

Aggie began to blush a little. She picked up her glass of wine and took a sip to try and hide the sudden onset of shyness. "Thank you," she murmured in reply.

"Has Kyle seen you yet?"

"Kyle?" Aggie said and sat upright, looking around.

"Is my brother here with you?" Coco asked.

"Oh no, not here. I just wondered if he'd seen you, that's all."

Aggie frowned and shrugged.

"Well, I ought to be going. I'm meeting someone…oh there she is," she smiled and stood up, waving to a pretty little blonde who was standing at the bar smiling.

"That's my date tonight," Helena grinned. "Gorgeous, isn't she?"

"Er, yes she is," Coco said, smiling, before giving Aggie a quick look of shock.

"Well, it's been wonderful to see you both again. I shall be back in the shop soon to stock up on goodies," she grinned. "See you soon."

Before she left, she turned to Aggie again and walked away, staring at her.

They all waved, and Helena and her date were soon gone.

"Oh, my God. Did you know?" Coco asked.

"What? That Helena is gay?" Aggie asked.

Coco nodded, sitting down and taking a swig of her drink.

"I had no idea. I kind of assumed she was with Kyle."

Coco shrugged, "Really? Well, I had no clue, either. Not until I saw her practically fall over her own feet to stare at you."

"At me?" Aggie squawked.

"Yes. Haven't you noticed that most eyes are on you tonight?" Coco asked, looking around.

"Don't be ridiculous, Coco."

"I'm not ridiculous, Aggie. Look, people are staring."

She discreetly looked around before covering her mouth with her hand. "Have I got spinach in my teeth," she asked, flashing a toothy smile before covering it again.

Coco let out a deep belly laugh. "Oh, Aggie, you're so naive sometimes. And no, you do not have spinach in your teeth."

Aggie dropped her hand and took another sip of wine. Sure enough, several men were eyeing her up. Her heart began to race a little and blood rushed to her cheeks.

"Hey, don't start that blushing business again. You got that

APHRODITE'S CLOSET

under control before. You can do it again now," Coco reassured her. "Guys are noticing you. Enjoy it. Lap it up. Get some numbers. Go on some dates. Get laid," she mouthed, making Aggie laugh.

"That's better, loosen up, Agatha Trout. Or should I start calling you Petunia?" Coco asked as one of the men plucked up the courage to approach them.

"Hello there. Can I buy you ladies a drink?" he asked.

Coco grinned at the man but said nothing, using her eyes to encourage Aggie to be the one to do the talking for a change.

Aggie sat in silence for a moment, before she realised what Coco was doing.

The poor man shifted his weight from one foot to the other before Aggie finally spoke.

"Thank you, that's very kind of you. But…"

She felt Coco give her a little kick under the table, and so she changed what she was about to say, "That would be so nice of you."

The guy visibly relaxed and he smiled. "A couple of white wines?"

Coco and Aggie nodded while he ordered the drinks from the waitress who had appeared beside him.

"Please sit down," Aggie said as Coco stood up. "I'll be right back. Just have to powder my nose," she winked at Aggie before disappearing with her handbag toward the ladies' room.

"I'm Aggie," she said, turning her attention back to the attractive guy who she imagined was around thirty, maybe thirty-two.

"Tom. Nice to meet you, Aggie. Are you from around here?" he asked.

"Born and bred in Frambleberry. You?" she inquired.

"I was born in Cheshire, moved here two years ago."

"What do you think of our little town?" she asked as the waitress brought over the two glasses of wine and a beer for Tom.

"I am rather enjoying living here, to be honest. The people tend to be pretty friendly," he smiled.

"Generally speaking, we are. But what brought you here, Tom? Work?"

Tom nodded as he took a swig of beer. "I'm a podiatrist. There was an opening at the local clinic, and I figured I'd apply and got the job."

"You treat people's feet," she said, trying not to look grossed out.

"That's right," he smiled. "Not a common job, I admit, but one I do love. It's amazing how people mistreat their feet. They tend to forget that we walk miles and miles and miles over the years and our feet become terribly neglected. I've seen some bad bunions, callouses, ingrown toenails and terrible deformities over the past few years, I can tell you."

"Oh right, yes I can imagine," Aggie said as she tried to smile and search the bar for Coco.

"Take today, for instance, I had a woman come in with the most atrocious smelling feet. It was clear she had an infection under her big toe nail. When I put pressure on it, pus just oozed out all over the place…"

Aggie glanced at Tom's fingers and stood up without thinking.

"Sorry, Tom, urgent need for the ladies' room. I'll be right back," she smiled awkwardly and rushed past him.

"Coco," she whispered when she arrived at the loos. "Coco!" she whispered again, somewhat louder.

"What's up?" said a voice from behind one of the cubicles before the door swung open revealing Coco sitting on the closed toilet lid, which was covered in toilet roll while she texted on her phone.

"He's a podiatrist."

"So? He's still cute."

"But…but… he's just been telling me all about a woman's foot infection with pus oozing out all over the place. It's absolutely disgusting. I can't bear it. We've got to go."

"Let's finish our drinks first. We shouldn't be rude."

"We can't. I left them on the table. Anyone could have spiked them while we were in here."

"Oh yeah, you're right about that."

"Did you bring your handbag?"

Aggie nodded.

"Your jacket?"

"I wasn't wearing one."

"So we're good to go?" Coco whispered.

"Are we going to do a runner?"

"Clearly we have no choice in the matter," she replied. "Come on, follow me. Fortunately, the door isn't too far from the ladies' so we can probably get away without him seeing us. You ready?"

Feeling awful, but not able to digest any further talk about disgusting foot ailments, Aggie nodded, and the two of them edged their way out of the ladies', their backs against the bar and through the door.

The waitress, who had served them, spotted them through the window. She checked out the guy at the table and grinned, winking and nodding as Coco gave her the thumbs up.

Once they were a couple of streets away, the two came to a halt, both out of breath and both giggling like school children.

"I can't believe we just did that. I feel so evil," Aggie admitted.

"Well, we could go back," Coco suggested, her brows raised as she smirked.

"No!" wailed Aggie. "Please, no."

"Come on then, let's head to the Green Goddess for a drink."

Aggie grinned and the two began walking toward the nearest taxi rank just as trickles of rain started to drop on them.

"The Green Goddess, please," Coco said as they climbed into a cab.

The taxi driver nodded, eyeing up the two women in the back of his car before driving off.

Five minutes later, just as the heavens opened, the cab pulled over right outside the pub, which appeared to be very busy for a Monday night.

"Typical," Coco said as Aggie paid the driver. "We're going to get soaked."

"We'll be fine. We're right outside."

"Your hair doesn't react to water the way mine does," Coco scowled.

"Wait one second," Aggie said as she opened the door and rushed into the pub. Seconds later, she reappeared with an umbrella for Coco. Opening it, she motioned for Coco to get out of the vehicle.

Once they were both in the pub, Aggie put the umbrella down and thanked the man who had lent it to her.

"A pleasure, my love," he grinned, his girlfriend nodding as well but not quite smiling.

"Thanks, honey," Coco smiled as they headed toward the bar, where two bar stools had just become available.

"Perfect," Coco said as she ordered a couple of glasses of white wine. "This is more like it. Much busier than the other place. I wonder what the occasion is?"

"Two glasses of white wine for the ladies," said the barman. "Courtesy of that guy over there." He pointed to a man about twenty-three years old with a mass of curly black afro hair.

Aggie smiled, lifting her glass to thank him as Coco seemed to frown, her mood instantly changing.

The young man nodded but made no effort to join them.

"Well, that's sweet of him," Aggie said.

"I guess," Coco said, looking a little like she'd seen a ghost.

"You okay?" Aggie asked, concerned.

Coco nodded and just about downed the drink but said nothing.

Before Aggie could say anything else, the barman placed two more in front of them.

"Courtesy of that fella over there," he winked, pointing to another guy at the opposite end of the bar but they couldn't quite see him. "He wants to know if you own the bar?" he said, looking at Aggie.

Confused, she frowned and shook her head. "Why would he ask that?"

"Because, love. He said you're clearly a Green Goddess in that dress. Sorry, he asked me to say that," the barman chuckled, shrugged and walked away.

"Well, that's one I've never heard before," Coco smiled as the two of them raised their glasses once again to thank the man. This time he turned around and revealed himself to be rather a handsome guy in his early thirties. Built like a rugby player, Aggie felt her cheeks flush with appreciation as he began to approach them.

As he stood in front of them, Aggie could barely take her eyes off him. The attraction was instant.

"Thank you so much for the drinks," Coco said. "Why don't you sit here? I need to go and have a chat with someone," she offered, standing and heading over to the young guy who'd bought their previous drink.

"Thank you," said the gorgeous guy.

Aggie bit her lip and smiled, "Thanks for the wine," she said, before adding, "I'm Aggie."

Holding out her hand, she felt a spark at their touch.

"Cole," he said. "Is Aggie your real name?" he asked, eventually releasing her hand.

She screwed up her face a little and said, "Agatha, but only my mother calls me that."

He smiled. "Aggie is cuter. Are you from around here, Aggie?"

"I am. Are you?"

"Nah, just visiting."

"So where are you from, Cole?"

"Canada, actually."

"Really?" she asked, not having detected an accent.

He smiled and nodded, "I'm a Londoner originally, but I moved to Canada about ten years ago. I'm just here visiting family and friends who live nearby for a few weeks."

"Well that's a shame," she said, blushing as the words came out.

Cole grinned. "So what do you do, Aggie?"

"I own a shop," she smiled.

He raised his eyebrows, "A shop?" he asked. "What kind of shop?"

"I sell...sleepwear, silk scarves, lingerie and..."

"And?" he asked, intrigued. He licked his lips.

Gulping, Aggie took a large swig of her wine before she looked into his eyes and said, "Gadgets."

Cole began to laugh. "Gadgets? As in boys' toys gadgets?"

"That depends what you mean when you say toys," she grinned.

"Oh," Cole said, blushing. "You mean toys," he laughed.

Feeling a little more confident, Aggie smiled and nodded. "That's exactly what I mean. We opened the shop a few months ago. It's called Aphrodite's Closet."

"The goddess of love?" he asked.

"You know Aphrodite?" she replied, somewhat surprised.

"Not personally, but yes," he grinned, taking a swig of his beer. "It's a great name."

"It's a great shop. You should stop by," she flirted.

"Now that…sounds like a good idea."

"So how much longer are you in the area, Cole?"

"Two weeks," he said. "Then I must get home, back to work."

"What do you do?" she asked.

"I build houses. Wooden houses, log homes, stuff like that."

"Oh, wow, that's impressive."

Cole smiled seductively. "I try."

"So where in Canada do you build these houses?" she asked.

"All over the place, but primarily over toward the western part of the country. From Banff to Vancouver and around there. Have you ever been?"

Aggie shook her head, "I haven't had the pleasure of doing much travel, unfortunately. Perhaps one day I'll get there."

"You should. It's probably one of the most beautiful places I've ever been to," he said. "I mean it's spectacular. Especially the Rockies."

"I've seen pictures, and it does look incredible."

"Have you ever been to Scotland?"

"Only when I was a baby. Don't really remember it much."

"Well, if you can't make it to Canada, then I'd recommend you visit Scotland. It's a bit like Canada just on a much, much smaller scale," he grinned.

"I shall bear that in mind," she smirked at him.

Briefly looking over her shoulder, she noticed Coco having a bit of an argument with the young man who had bought their first glasses of wine. Frowning, she continued looking for a moment. Cole noticed and turned around.

"Is everything okay?" he asked, a bit concerned.

"I'm not sure," she said. "I think I'd better go and see."

APHRODITE'S CLOSET

"Sure," Cole said. "Do you want me to come with you?"

"No," she stopped and smiled at him. "Thank you. I'll be right back."

Noticing that Coco's words were getting louder and louder, Aggie rushed over to the other end of the bar.

"Coco? What's going on? Are you okay?" she asked.

"I'm absolutely fine," fumed Coco.

"Well, it certainly doesn't look like it from over there, and we can practically hear you both shouting."

"Aggie, there isn't a problem."

"Well then perhaps you ought to leave?" Aggie said to the young man.

"I'm not leaving," he said.

"Really?" Coco said in anger. "Well, we'd better go. Come on, Aggie. Let's get the hell out of here."

"Coco, why are we leaving? Who is this guy?" she asked as Coco grabbed her arm and marched her away from him.

"I'm not ready to go yet, Coco. I've met this really nice guy."

"Well then you should stay," Coco said with tears in her eyes.

"What's happened? Coco, talk to me. Look, I'll go and tell Cole that I have to leave. I'll come with you."

"No, Aggie, no. You clearly like the guy. You should stay."

"No, I'm coming with you. You look like you need me more than Cole does. Just wait here. Wait a second."

Coco nodded and turned away from the crowd. "I'll wait outside."

"But it's raining," Aggie said. "Your hair?"

"It doesn't matter. It really doesn't matter," Coco said as she pushed open the door and walked out into the rain.

Aggie, torn, rushed back over to the other side of the bar.

"Cole, I'm so sorry, but I have to go. My friend needs me right now. It's been wonderful meeting you, but I must go. Sorry."

Before Cole could even say a word, she turned and rushed away from him. He stood up, shaking his head.

Once Aggie reached the door, she opened it and stopped for a second. She turned to look at him standing there before she rushed outside to be with her friend.

CHAPTER 27

"What's happened, Coco? I don't think I've ever seen you like this before. Who was that guy? Why didn't you tell me you knew him?" Aggie soon realised she was babbling, so she stopped and looked at her friend who was already soaked to the skin.

Both stood, with the rain pouring down, shivering. Luckily, Aggie soon caught sight of a taxi, and so she flagged it down, and the girls climbed inside.

After Aggie had given the driver her address, she pulled Coco toward her and hugged her, saying nothing during the short drive home. Coco was very quiet other than the occasional sob that came out of her mouth.

Once they'd arrived, Aggie paid the driver, and the two rushed indoors, careful not to drip too much water on the shop floor as they rushed up the stairs to the apartment at the top. Grabbing a large fluffy towel from the airing cupboard, Aggie draped it across Coco's shoulders and rubbed away the excess water, before handing her a small towel so her friend could dry her hair a little.

"Do you want me to run you a bath?" she asked.

"No, I'll just change out of these clothes. Can I borrow something to wear?"

"Of course. I'll get you some pyjamas, and then you can sleep here tonight, okay?"

Coco nodded with the saddest smile Aggie had ever seen. Her heart just about broke watching her like that.

After both had changed, Coco lay on the sofa with her eyes closed while Aggie made them both a hot drink. She was worried, having never seen Coco react quite like that. Who was that guy?

"Here you go, Coco," Aggie sat as she sat beside her and waited for her to sit up. "I made your favourite kind of hot chocolate," she said. "With almond milk."

Coco smiled, "Aww thanks, Aggie."

"So," Aggie prompted.

Coco leaned back in the sofa and closed her eyes for a moment. "I'm sorry I freaked out," she whispered. "And I'm sorry I messed it up with that guy you were talking to. He seemed cool too."

"Hey, it's all right. He was just a guy. I'm much more worried about you right now anyway."

Coco took a sip of her almond-flavoured hot chocolate and opened her eyes. "Remember, after Mum and Dad died, and I took off for a year?"

Aggie nodded, "You went to Spain. Yeah."

Coco turned to look at her best friend and shook her head. "Aggie, I'm sorry, but I lied."

"What do you mean?"

"I didn't go to Spain for a year."

"What? But I thought you spent a year in Barcelona?"

Coco shook her head, "I did go, but I came back after a month."

"You...you never told me. Where were you?"

"I was in Scotland."

"Oh my God, Coco. Why? Why would you feel the need to lie? I've always been here for you. You know that. You didn't have to keep anything from me."

"I know, and I'm sorry, but something happened and I...I... couldn't come back here for a while."

"I don't understand, Coco."

"I was pregnant, Aggie."

Aggie almost dropped her drink in her lap. With her eyes wide open, she placed the cup on the coffee table and turned to look at her friend.

"You…were…pregnant?"

Tears started to roll down Coco's face, and she nodded.

"Why didn't you tell me?" Aggie asked, clearly hurt. "I'm your best friend. We've been buddies for years. I…I don't understand. And…what about the baby?"

By now Coco was starting to sob.

Realising how much she was hurting, Aggie took the cup out of Coco's hands and put it on the coffee table with hers. She pulled her toward her and rocked her back and forth.

"I'm sorry," Aggie whispered. "Whatever happened, it doesn't matter now. You obviously had your reasons. But it's okay, it's over now. Shhhhhh."

"But it's not okay, Aggie. I lied to you. I lied to my brother."

"It's okay, Coco. It's over."

Coco sat forward, forcing Aggie to let her go. "It's not over, Aggie."

"What do you mean? Did you…did you have the baby?" Aggie whispered.

But Coco shook her head. "I had a miscarriage. It was horrible. I was five-and-a-half months pregnant, and he died inside me, Aggie. I had to give birth to a dead baby."

"Oh my God, Coco. I'm so sorry. I'm so sorry I wasn't there for you."

"I should have told you, but I was so ashamed."

"But why would you be ashamed? You were eighteen, practically an adult."

"Because of the baby's father, Aggie."

Aggie looked into her eyes and frowned. "Who was it?" she whispered.

"Remember Mr Cook?"

"From school?" Aggie asked, and Coco nodded. "You were dating his son, weren't you?"

Coco stood up and went to look out the window. She watched as the streetlights lit up the rain, which was still lashing down from the sky. Slowly she turned around to look at Aggie and nodded.

"Yeah I was dating his son, but we never had sex, Aggie."

Confused, she said, "So who?"

"Mr Cook, Aggie. Mr Cook was the father."

Aggie gasped and stood up. "You were sleeping with your boyfriend's dad?" she said.

Coco nodded.

"But he was like, sixty or something? And, wasn't he married?"

"Forty-nine," Coco corrected her before she nodded, "And yes, he was married."

"Oh, Coco," Aggie sighed. "But it's all in the past now. It's finished," she said, remembering what had caused all this to start in the first place. "But who was that guy?"

"That was Mr Cook's younger son, he recognised me in the bar."

"Oh, honey," Aggie whispered. "What did he say?"

"That I ruined his family," Coco said.

"That's rubbish," Aggie tried to reassure her.

"He's right, Aggie. He told me everything that happened after I left."

"What?" Aggie said, "What did he say happened?"

"That Mr Cook's wife had found out that he'd slept with a student and so she left him. They got divorced a few months later."

"So, people get divorced all the time. Surely he can't blame you?" Aggie exclaimed.

"Of course he can blame me, Aggie. I'm the one to blame."

"Why didn't you tell me, Coco? I would have been here for you, you know that."

"I know, honey, and I'm sorry. It's just that…Mrs. Cook was on the board of the Women's Luncheon Club, and she was a friend of your mum's. I couldn't risk it. I'm sorry," Coco blurted out and started crying again.

"Oh, Coco, you must've felt so alone."

Coco went and sat back down, picking up her drink and taking a sip. "Seeing Danny this evening just brought it all back, you know?"

"Did Danny or his brother know? About the pregnancy, Coco?" whispered Aggie.

"No, thank God. None of them knew. I didn't even tell Ron…

Mr. Cook, I mean. I didn't tell anyone, not even Kyle. I just got on the plane to Barcelona. I spent a whole month throwing up in a hostel over there. I had terrible morning sickness, Aggie. It was hell. Then when it calmed down a bit, I decided I couldn't bear the heat, so I went to the airport and got the next available plane out. I ended up Edinburgh where I stayed until I lost the baby."

"Oh, Coco," Aggie soothed, rubbing her back.

"So you didn't even know anyone up there either?" Aggie asked, and Coco shook her head.

"I met a few people who were friends while I was there, but I left without saying a word. I didn't want reminding of any of it. I just wanted to put it all behind me."

"Which you did," Aggie smiled.

"Until tonight," Coco sighed. "A few years ago I'd heard that Mr Cook had moved to Cornwall with Danny, so I figured I'd never have to see any of them again."

"And what about Mrs. Cook? Do you know what happened to her?"

Coco looked a little blank for a second before turning to Aggie, "I think your mum mentioned something about her a couple of years ago. Said she'd remarried and moved to Croatia?"

"Oh yeah, now that you mention it, you're right. I hadn't put two and two together."

"And what about Mr Cook's eldest son? The one you were going out with at the time? What happened to him?"

"Preston? He came out about a year later. I should've known he was gay."

"He's gay?" Aggie exclaimed. "That's why you never slept together?"

"I guess," Coco sighed. "He was such a sweet guy. We did have some good times, but when I got drunk, and his dad came on to me, well..." she shrugged. "Shit happens. The funny thing was, Preston never blamed me as such. He emailed me after I buggered off to Spain and said he didn't understand why I'd slept with his old man on account of him being an old man, but he said he understood that I needed things he couldn't give me. He didn't tell me he was gay there and then though."

"What a mess," Aggie sighed, leaning back in the sofa.

"I know. I fucked up big time, Aggie."

"Maybe, but it's over now. Plus," she turned to face Coco. "You can't blame yourself. Mr Cook is as much to blame, if not more. He came on to you. He came on to his son's girlfriend. I mean, who does that?"

"Yeah, I guess you're right."

"Of course, I'm right. He's more to blame than you. And you had to deal with the consequences. That bloody Danny doesn't know what he's talking about. To treat you like that after all these years—who does he think he is?"

"He needed to blame someone for the divorce, Aggie."

"How can you be so understanding?" she replied.

Coco shrugged, "He was just a kid, Aggie. Divorce is tough on kids."

Aggie leaned back again and kind of nodded.

"He would've been nine now, you know?" Coco whispered.

"Huh?"

"If I hadn't miscarried, he'd be nine years old."

"Oh, Coco."

CHAPTER 28

A few days went by without Coco saying anything about the events of that night, or about what she'd been through years ago. She just went on with her work as if nothing had ever happened. Aggie was a little worried but said nothing, allowing her best friend to deal with it all in her own time.

Business was going well, with a steady stream of customers throughout each and every day, but one day while it was a little quieter than usual, Aggie took the opportunity to pop to the bank to make a deposit. When she returned, she could hear Coco's laughter from the back of the store.

"I'm back," she said as she closed the door behind her.

"Hey, we're back here," Coco yelled.

"We?" Aggie wondered out loud.

Taking off her jacket and plonking it down behind the countertop with her handbag, she followed the sounds of talking until she found Coco in the back near the changing rooms with a man who was bending down and looking at some of the artwork on the doors.

"Hey," Aggie said, wondering whom Coco was talking to.

"Aggie," squealed Coco. "Look who I found!"

And then the man stood up and turned around, revealing himself to be none other than Cole from the night at the Green Goddess.

"Well, if it isn't the Green Goddess herself," he said with the sexiest smile she'd ever seen.

"Cole!" she exclaimed. "What are you doing here?"

"Well," he said, approaching her with rather a sexy swagger. "I looked you up. You told me the name of your shop the other night, and I'm pretty sure there aren't many Aphrodite's Closets in the area, so it wasn't difficult," he chuckled. "I hope you don't mind, but I wanted to see you again, especially after you ran off like that."

"Well, I…"

He put a finger over her lips, and she tingled all over. "Not to worry, Coco explained what happened."

Aggie's cheeks burned red, and she cast a quick look at her friend who was giving her the biggest thumbs-up sign behind his back.

"She told me she'd had way too much to drink and had bumped into an ex who had broken her heart, so being a man who understands the intricacies of the human heart," he patted his chest, "I understand perfectly why you had to run away like that, and therefore I forgive you."

Aggie grinned.

"But," he held up a finger, "there is one thing you must do for me to make it up to me."

"Oh," she said.

"You must come out with me for lunch today," he looked at his watch. "Actually, that would be about now."

"But…" Aggie looked at Coco.

"No buts allowed. Don't worry, Coco has courteously agreed to take care of the shop for a couple of hours. So, are we on?"

"Of course she is," Coco shooed them away from the back of the store.

"Er, are you sure, Coco?" Aggie managed to say.

"I absolutely insist," Coco grinned as she started to push them both out of the shop.

"Wait, my bag," she said, rushing over to pick it up, along with her jacket.

Coco stood at the door, "I'll see you in a few hours."

"My mobile's on if you need me," Aggie yelled as Coco shut the door behind the couple.

"I won't," they heard her yell back.

Aggie grinned at Cole, and he smiled back.

"Ready?"

"Where are we going?" she asked.

"Anywhere you like," he offered, leading her away from the shop.

oOo

REALISING FAR TOO late that ordering spaghetti was not such a good idea, Aggie tried and failed to suck the final bits into her mouth without ending up with tomato sauce all over her chin.

"Here," said Cole, "allow me," as he used his napkin to wipe away the sauce.

She blushed, "Thanks. A bit stupid to order spaghetti," she muttered under her breath.

"Not at all. It's kinda sexy," he winked. "So, Aggie, now I've heard all about Aphrodite's Closet, are you going to tell me a bit more about you?"

"There's not much to tell."

"Of course, there is. There must be. I already gathered from our previous engagement," he chuckled, "that you were born and bred in Frambleberry but that's about all I know. Other than you used to work in a library of mythology—which is kind of cool."

Aggie smiled as she took a sip of her water. "Honestly, there isn't that much to say. I'm just not a very exciting person."

"I don't believe that for a second. Anybody who opens the town's first sex shop is very exciting," he grinned.

"It's more of a lingerie store. You saw for yourself."

"Ah, but I have heard all about your infamous second floor, Miss Trout."

Aggie blushed again. "And who told you about that?"

"The townspeople talk," he said, taking a slow swig of his shandy. "That and Coco mentioned it earlier."

"I'm surprised she didn't take you up there to see for yourself."

"I was hoping you would give me the grand tour," he winked.

"Seriously though," she asked, "How did you find the shop? Who did you ask? And what did they say?"

"Well, I Googled you first, and I asked a couple of people as well, for good measure. Most people have nothing but great things to say about the shop."

"Most?" she asked.

Cole laughed, wiping his mouth after finishing his mushroom tortellini. "I asked the barista in one of the coffee shops in town who raved about it, as did a couple of others in the queue behind me, but two older ladies were sitting down who overheard us talking. They made it quite clear they were disgusted with you."

"Oh dear," Aggie breathed, putting her glass down on the table and almost missing it. "Oops," she said, making sure it was firmly on the glass top. "I wonder if they're the ones responsible for all the threats we've had."

"You've been getting threats?" Cole asked, his brows furrowing together.

Aggie nodded and proceeded to tell him all about the horrible things that had been happening since the shop was opened.

"But that's terrible. They must be stopped."

"My thoughts exactly," Aggie agreed. "We have told the police. But nothing's happened since we installed the CCTV. We're hoping that's the end of it."

"I hope so, for your sake. That can't be very nice at all, having to worry about that."

"Thanks, Cole," she smiled, pushing her plate away from her so she could put her elbows on the table, almost knocking the glass of water on to the floor again. "Shit," she exclaimed, grabbing it before it went. "Sorry," she added.

Cole just grinned.

"Do you think that a couple of old ladies could be responsible for something like that, though?" he asked.

"I honestly have no idea," she sighed. "I would hope not, but then I guess I'd rather it was someone like that other than someone more menacing, don't you think?"

"You do have a point," he said as she looked at her watch.

"I ought to get back there. It's been more than a couple of hours. It's not fair, leaving Coco to handle the place."

"Okay," he said. "I'll walk you back. Perhaps you could give me the tour?"

CHAPTER 29

As Coco folded clothes and put them on their respective shelves, she smiled at the thought of Aggie and Cole. It was about time her best friend was finally lucky in love.

Still feeling guilty about keeping such a big secret from her, she felt a stab of something in her chest. Heartache. She sighed. It had been almost ten years since she'd run away and had a miscarriage. Something she'd thought she'd dealt with, but after seeing Danny the other night, it had brought everything back, including the pain.

She tried to push it aside again, but Danny's face kept filling her mind. He'd seemed so angry with her. Even after all this time, it was clear he still held a grudge against her. He blamed her for his parents' divorce. Even though they had moved on, he hadn't. The way he'd approached her in the bar, sending her and Aggie a glass of wine and pretending to be an admirer was freaky.

The thought clung to Coco, and she couldn't help it as a stray tear dropped out of the corner of her eye. Brushing it away, she tried to think of better things and thought of how luck had entered her life when she'd turned twenty, winning competitions on an almost monthly basis. She focussed on her close friendship with Aggie and of the wonder of Aphrodite's Closet; her wonderful brother, Kyle, who had also been through hell and back, after sinking so low with a serious drug addiction but breaking through to have a success story of his own.

Thinking of Kyle, Coco soon realised that her story was nothing compared to his. Both had suffered at the sudden, tragic loss of their parents, but he had hit rock bottom, nearly losing his own life in the process. It had been a tough time for them both, and both had survived.

Surely her being blamed for someone's divorce was nothing in comparison to that?

Standing tall, she nodded to herself. "I won't let him bring me down," she whispered to herself. "I won't. He can blame me all he likes, but it was his father's doing, not mine," she said a little louder.

"Sorry, love, did you say something?" said the voice of a woman who had been browsing the satin nighties.

"Oh sorry," Coco said, realising where she was. "No, I was just mumbling to myself. Is there anything I can help you with?"

The woman smiled, "I think I'll take this, please," she said, handing Coco a pale blue nightdress.

"Of course," she replied, taking it back to the till.

After the woman had gone, Coco wandered around the shop, smiling at some other customers who were browsing, while she made sure everything was tidy before Aggie came back. She walked up the stairs, checking that no one was waiting to be attended to in the shop.

A couple of boxes had been knocked aside, so she bent down and restacked them on the shelf, smiling to herself as she remembered people's reactions to the popular vibrators at the shop's opening. Most had giggled in delight, others had been too embarrassed and had returned back downstairs.

"Excuse me, I'd quite like to take one of those," said a man beside her.

"Of course. What colour would you like?" she asked without even turning to look at him.

"Er, not sure, what are the options?"

"There's black, pink, gold, silver or...let me see. I think we also have it in red. Yes," she exclaimed, pulling the red one from further back. Having to bend over to pull it out, she suddenly felt the man lean against her.

"Oh," she said. "Do you mind?"

The man's hand covered her mouth as he stopped her from standing up. His other hand felt firmly between Coco's legs.

"Get your hands off me," Coco tried to yell, but his large hand was muffling her voice.

"Listen to me," he said while rubbing his hand hard in the crotch area of her trousers. "Is this what you want?" he asked.

Terrified, Coco shook her head. He rubbed harder while still holding his hand over her mouth.

"It is, I know it is," he said, leaning over her so he could smell her hair.

"You opened this shop which suggests this is exactly what you want."

"No," she tried to say.

"We've told you before, you're not welcome here. This shop is not welcome here. We want it finished. Closed. Do you hear me? If you do not abide by our rules," he stopped for a moment and rammed his own body against her backside, "we'll be back to sort you all out, and this time we won't stop."

Before Coco could react, he pushed her so hard that she fell against the shelving unit, whacking her head before she hit the floor.

CHAPTER 30

*G*iggling as Cole opened the door for Aggie, the two of them stepped inside.

"Are you ready for the grand tour then, Cole?" breathed Aggie.

"I certainly am. I can't wait to see what's in store," he chuckled at his own joke.

"That was bad," she laughed at him. All of a sudden, feeling like something was very wrong, she turned to look at their surroundings and realised Coco wasn't alone. And it wasn't clients surrounding her. It was the police officer they'd spoken to before, as well as Kyle.

"Kyle? Coco? What's happened?" Aggie asked, rushing to Coco's side; she was sitting with a cold compress to her head. It was obvious she'd been crying.

"Aggie," cried Coco, trying to stand but stopping herself when she realised she was still a bit dizzy.

"Stay seated, Coco," Kyle said.

"What happened?" Cole asked.

Kyle, realising Aggie was with someone, narrowed his eyes and stepped forward.

"It's okay, Kyle. This is my friend, Cole. Cole, this is Coco's brother, Kyle."

Both men looked at each other for a second and nodded.

"Coco was attacked," Kyle said.

"Attacked?" shrieked Aggie. "Here? In the shop?"

Kyle nodded, "Unfortunately, yes."

"Holy shit, Coco. Are you all right? Are you hurt? Did we catch them?" Aggie asked without taking a breath.

"I'm all right I think, just a bit shaken up that's all. Sorry, but we didn't get him. He threw me across the floor, and I banged my head. I think it knocked me out for a minute. When I came to, he was gone, and a couple of customers were taking care of me."

"Shit, Coco. I'm so sorry. I'm sorry. I should have been here."

Coco winced as she shook her head, "Don't be silly. We weren't to know. Besides, you needed some time with Cole," she tried to smile.

Kyle raised his eyebrows but said nothing.

"I should have been here."

Kyle inched forward and agreed, "Yes, you really should have been."

Cole looked from Kyle to Aggie and back again and frowned.

"It's probably not a good idea for either of you to be in the shop alone at the moment. Not until we catch the people responsible."

"I think I've got all the information I need, Miss Watson," said the police officer as Kyle walked him out.

"Did you recognise him, Coco?"

Coco shook her head, "I didn't see him, Aggie. He grabbed me from behind and threatened to…do stuff to us if we don't shut the shop."

Aggie gasped, "Who the hell are these people? It's just a bloody shop. He didn't try to rape you…?" Aggie whispered as she suddenly realised what could have happened.

"No, but his words suggested he wouldn't be so…lenient next time."

"Jesus," Cole whispered. "We've got to get this guy."

"It's not something you need to worry about," Kyle said to Cole as he approached them. "I think we've got this covered."

"Really?" Coco said. "I wish I shared your confidence."

"Seriously, I'm here for another week or so. If there is anything I can do to help, you can count on me," Cole offered as he leaned against the countertop beside Aggie.

Aggie smiled and reached for his hand, which she squeezed before letting it go, "Thanks, Cole."

Kyle watched and turned away.

"Like I said, we can handle this," he repeated.

"What about the CCTV? We must have him on camera?" Aggie thought.

"Can you believe it, he was wearing a damn mask."

"But the police must be able to identify his height, weight, any unusual identifying marks, that sort of thing. Surely that will help in catching the guy?" offered Cole.

"They've got all the information they need," Kyle replied. "They're on it. So, like I said, you don't need to worry about it. Especially if you're only here for a week. You may as well just go and leave us to it."

"Kyle," scolded Coco, before Cole took the hint and stood up to his full height.

"Well, I guess I'll be going then, Aggie."

"Oh, there's no need to go, Cole," she said. "I was going to show you around."

But Cole was looking at Kyle and knew when he wasn't wanted.

"Perhaps we can reschedule," he suggested. "You've got a lot to discuss with Coco and…Kyle."

"Yes we do," Kyle reiterated. "Nice to meet you. Bye, Cole," Kyle said as he lifted Coco off the stool. "Aggie, help me get Coco upstairs to your place. I think she needs to lie down."

"Of course," Aggie said, looking from Kyle to Cole. "Just give me a few minutes," she said as she walked beside Cole and they headed for the door.

When they reached it, Cole opened it. Both stepped outside.

"I'm sorry about Kyle," Aggie said. "I don't know what's come over him. He's usually much more…friendly."

Cole shook his head and smiled at her. "Not to worry. I think I know what's up. But it's fine. You need to look after Coco right now anyway. Can I see you tomorrow? I know you won't want to leave the shop, but I can come over here if that's okay?"

Aggie's smile lit up her face. "I'd like that a lot."

"Cool," he said. "I'll come over about eleven then."

Aggie nodded. "I shall look forward to it."

"There's just one other thing, Aggie?" he said.

Frowning, she looked up at him, "What's that?"

Without another word, Cole bent down and planted a very gentle kiss on her lips, causing her heart to do somersaults in her chest.

"Until tomorrow then," he said as they pulled apart and she leaned against the door, letting her body weight push it open.

"Until tomorrow," she breathed before she slipped inside and let the door close behind her.

Leaning against the door on the other side, Aggie took a moment to stand there, her eyes closed. A small smile lit up her face as her heart continued to jump around in her chest. It'd been a long, long time since she'd been kissed like that. Actually, it had been a long, long time since she'd been kissed at all.

oOo

THE SOUND of someone clearing his throat made Aggie open her eyes, and she blushed when she saw Kyle still waiting, with Coco in his arms. He didn't look so happy.

"S...sorry," she said, rushing to his side. "Let me help."

Coco, on the other hand, was smiling.

"Ah young love," she said as Aggie tried to help carry her.

"It's fine," Kyle said. "I've got her. If you could just open your apartment, I'll put her on the bed."

"I don't need to lie down on the bed, Kyle. I'll be fine just sitting on the sofa for half an hour. And you certainly don't need to carry me. I'm not injured, you know," she said.

Kyle ignored her while Aggie rushed up the stairs and unlocked the apartment.

"Not the bed," Coco insisted. "The sofa is fine."

Reluctantly, Kyle listened to her and walked into the living room and placed her on the sofa, making sure her legs were extended out.

"I'll make us some sweet tea," Aggie suggested.

"No, Aggie. The shop's still open. I'll be fine up here on my own. You two just go down and keep an eye on everything. Seriously, I'll be okay. I just need a bit of time alone."

Kyle nodded, and he followed Aggie back down the stairs to the second floor of the shop.

"This is where he attacked her," he said, pointing to where some coloured vibrators were strewn across the floor.

Aggie gulped and shook her head. "Why are they doing this to us?" she whispered as she bent down to start collecting them to put them back on the shelf.

Kyle just stood for a second, breathing quite loud.

"Ouch!" Aggie exclaimed as her foot slipped and she fell backwards.

"Are you okay?" Kyle asked as he crouched down to help her.

"Yeah. This is hard though," she said, pulling out the offending vibrator that she'd fallen on, holding it up between them.

Kyle's eyes widened, and a moment later, they both began to laugh.

"Oh dear," Aggie whispered as Kyle took the red vibrator out of her hand and pulled her up to her knees. "Are you all right?" he asked, as the two of them knelt, looking at each other and at the vibrators around them.

"I'm fine," she said. "I will be fine. I'm worried about Coco though," she breathed.

"Me too," he said as he put his hand over hers and lifted her up so that they were both standing, staring at each other just a moment longer than necessary.

"I'd better try this again," she said, bending forward to put the gadgets back on the shelf.

"Don't forget this one," he said, handing the red one to her.

She took it and stood it on the table, "Thanks."

"So what now?" he asked.

"Back to work I guess," Aggie said.

"Really?"

"Why not?"

"Well, I just thought after what happened that perhaps you might be rethinking the shop."

"You're joking?" she said, stepping away from him.

"I'm just worried about Coco…and you."

"Coco and I can take care of ourselves, Kyle."

"I just want you to think deeply about what you're doing."

"Kyle, how can you say that? You know how much this place means to us both. We won't let some crazy folks drive us out of our own backyard. No way."

"I'm sorry, Aggie, I just don't want anything to happen to you, either of you."

"Then help us catch this bastard, Kyle."

He stood back and nodded, "You know I'll do everything possible to do that for you, Aggie."

"Yes, I know, sorry."

As they started walking back down to the ground floor, Kyle suddenly took her hand in his, making her jump, "Aggie?"

"Kyle?" she asked as they stood on the stairs.

"What do you know about this Cole guy?"

Aggie raised her eyebrows and snatched her hand away, "You are joking, right?"

Her eyes searched his, and she shook her head before she continued to walk down the stairs.

"I think you'd better go, Kyle. I've got a business to run."

"Aggie, I just don't want to see you get hurt. This guy, Cole. Who's to say he's not responsible for all this?"

Just as she was about to respond, the shop door opened, and a small group of women walked in.

"Goodbye, Kyle, thanks for your help," and she turned around, making it quite clear she didn't want to speak to him anymore.

The nerve to accuse Cole, she fumed to herself. What the hell had gotten into him?

She listened as the door opened and closed before she cleared her throat and smiled at her customers.

"Let me know if I can help," she offered as she went to sit behind the counter, a strange feeling settling in her stomach.

CHAPTER 31

"Dad?" Aggie asked as the front door opened, and her father appeared.

"Aggie, sweetheart. Whatever's the matter? Come in, come in," he motioned. "I love the new look. Smashing," he smiled.

"Thanks, Dad."

"Who is it, dear?" her mother yelled from the kitchen.

Ted's eyes shot from the direction of his wife's voice to his daughter's face. "I'm afraid she's in," he whispered to Aggie.

"That's okay, she's got to speak to me sometime," Aggie sighed.

"It's your daughter, Trixie. It's Aggie."

"Oh," said the voice before her mother appeared in the kitchen doorway. "Agatha," she said with her lips pursed, looking somewhat shocked at the sight of Aggie's new look.

"Mum," Aggie said, moving toward her. "Can we talk?"

Trixie's eyebrows twitched, and she was squeezing a tea towel tighter and tighter in her hands. But when she looked closer at Aggie's eyes, her own eyes softened, and she visibly relaxed, "Of course we can," she sighed. "Go on into the lounge, and I'll make us some coffee."

"Thanks, Mum," Aggie smiled as she and her father headed into the living room and sat down.

"Is everything all right, love?" Ted asked as they waited for Trixie to bring in the coffee.

"Not really, Dad. But I'll wait and tell you when Mum comes in."

Her dad sighed and sat back in his chair, wincing a little.

"Your shoulder again?" she asked, and he nodded.

"I thought the surgery was a success?"

"It was, I think I just went a bit overboard playing golf today."

"You played golf? But Dad, you're not supposed to even pick up a golf club for another month or so. You could've done some damage…"

"My words exactly," said her mother as she pushed open the living room door with her bottom and walked in backwards carrying a tray with three cups and saucers and a cafetiere filled to the brim. "But he was having none of it. Men," she sighed as she put the tray on the coffee table.

"I'll let it brew for a minute or two," she said, sitting down. "I must say, Agatha. I didn't expect to see you."

Aggie smiled, "I didn't think you'd want to see me. You made it quite clear the last time I was here, Mum."

Trixie looked away from her daughter and up toward Ted as he stood up. "I'll pour the coffee," he said, hoping to avoid the conversation.

"Well, I meant what I said, Agatha. I was most upset with your choice, of…business. And I still am. It's quite disgusting."

Aggie tutted and sighed. "Well, if it makes you feel any better, you're not the only one who thinks so."

"Why do you say that love?" her dad asked as he handed her a cup full of coffee.

"Don't forget the saucer, dear," Trixie muttered as Ted raised his eyebrows and handed Aggie the saucer.

"We've had some threats."

Trixie's ears pricked, and she sat upright, "Threats?" she asked. "What kind of threats?"

"Well, they started out as harmless letters, followed by some general mess in and outside the shop but today…today…" Aggie burst out crying.

"Oh dear," Trixie said, unsure what to do.

"Oh, love," her dad said as he got up and sat on the sofa next to her, pulling her into his arms. "There, there," he said, patting her on the back.

"Whatever has happened?" Trixie asked, standing up and going to get the box of tissues from the mantelpiece. "Here you are, dear," she said, handing them to Aggie, who took them with thanks. "Thanks, Mum," she sobbed before continuing. "Someone… someone came into the shop today and got physical with Coco. He threatened us, he threatened us all. All three of us. He pretty much said that if we don't shut the store down, he'd…he'd…hurt us," she sobbed again.

"Oh my goodness," Trixie said as her knees buckled beneath her and she had to steady herself with the back of the sofa. "I can't believe it," she whispered. "My girls, my girls," she said.

"There, there," Ted said to reassure her. "I take it you called the police?" he asked.

Aggie nodded.

"Is Coco all right? Ted asked.

Trixie shuffled over to the chair and flopped down into it. "Yes, yes, of course. Is she all right, darling?"

"You know Coco," Aggie looked up and smiled a bit. "She's one tough cookie. She's fine. A bit shook up but fine."

"What are you going to do? Are you going to shut the shop?" her mother asked, perking up somewhat.

"Absolutely not," Aggie growled. "We're not going to let some pathetic man do this to us. We won't be bullied into changing who we are."

"That's right, you should be strong right now, Aggie, love," Ted said but added, "But perhaps you ought to just think about it?"

"Dad," Aggie exclaimed. "How can you even say that? You know how much this shop means to me. How much it meant to Great Aunt Petunia."

Trixie, who had been rubbing her forehead, looked up. "I'm sorry? What did you say?"

Aggie gasped at her own words and looked from Trixie to her father, who sighed and turned toward his wife.

"Petunia, she said Petunia, darling."

"But how would she know what it meant to Petunia?" Trixie asked.

"Because she made me a video, Mum. She told me everything. I know why you and she never spoke. But it doesn't matter any more. It was ages ago. Your mum was hurt decades ago, and it means nothing now."

Trixie stood up and stormed out of the room.

"There she goes again," sighed Ted. "Always runs away."

But before he'd even finished his sentence, Trixie was back. "What did Petunia say?" she asked.

"That she stole your mum's first husband," Aggie sighed. "And that she understood why you didn't want anything to do with her, but she wished it had been different because she would have liked to have known Christie and me…"

"But…"

"You may as well tell her, love," Ted said to Aggie as he stood up and went over to the drinks cabinet, pulling out a bottle of brandy.

He held the bottle up to Aggie who nodded and then to Trixie, who shook her head for a moment before she sighed and nodded too.

"In the coffee?" he asked them both. Trixie and Aggie nodded.

"Yes, please."

"Tell me what exactly?" Trixie asked after they'd all taken a sip of their brandy and coffee.

"That Petunia had seen us as babies, when we were firstborn, and that she'd kept an eye on us all through the years. But she'd never made any attempt to reach out and get to know us because she didn't want to upset you."

"And how, may I ask, did she see you as babies?"

"I took her to the hospital," Ted muttered. "It was me that kept in touch with her all these years. I felt she had a right to know about her own family."

"My mother's family, not hers," Trixie growled.

"Mum!"

"Trixie, really?" Ted said, shaking his head. "The woman is dead. She hurt your mother when they were young. That's going on some eighty years ago. Christ, how long are you going to do this? It's complete and utter madness, and I think it's time you gave it a damn rest. Let the poor woman rest in peace and let Aggie enjoy her life for once," Ted said, putting his cup and saucer back on the coffee table so hard that the saucer broke in two.

Trixie immediately began to sob.

Aggie, who had never in her twenty-eight years seen her father speak to her mother like that, just sat back in complete shock.

All three sat in silence, the only sound being the gentle sobs coming from Trixie's mouth.

"It's all I've ever known," Trixie murmured.

"What's that, Mum?" Aggie asked.

"Hating Petunia, it's all I've ever known. I grew up with it," she said, looking up as Aggie passed the box of tissues to her. "Mother hated her so much, she passed it on to me. It's all I've ever known," she whispered.

Ted, who was still in shock having spoken to his wife the way he had, stood up and sat down on the arm of the chair where Trixie sat.

"Darling, we understand that, but enough's enough."

Trixie patted his hand as he tenderly rubbed her shoulder. "Enough," she whispered and nodded. "Eighty years is a long time, isn't it?" she asked.

Ted smiled.

"Do you want to see the DVD, Mum?" Aggie asked, biting her lip.

Her eyes wet with tears, Trixie dabbed at them, careful not to smudge any more of the mascara she was wearing. "I...I'm not sure I do, dear."

"I think it would be a good idea, Mum," Aggie suggested. "I brought it with me, just in case."

"You did?" Ted asked, surprised.

"I've been carrying it around with me for weeks, trying to get enough courage to come over."

"Oh, sweetheart," Trixie sobbed again, dabbing at her eyes some more. "I'm so sorry you've felt that way. That you couldn't even come home. I feel dreadful about it. Really I do. I've been wanting to call you ever since you were here, but just...just couldn't."

"That's okay, Mum. I understand."

"I feel dreadful that it took some horrible man attacking Coco in the shop to bring you here. What kind of a mother am I? How could I?" Trixie's sobs turned louder.

Ted looked toward the floor, his chin quivering somewhat.

"How about a drop more brandy?" Aggie suggested as she stood up and took the bottle off the sideboard and poured them each a separate glass. "I know I could use one."

Ted lifted his head and agreed, "Good idea," he whispered.

"Before we watch the DVD, dear," Trixie said as the sobbing finally subsided. "What exactly happened today? Do you know who it was?"

"Unfortunately not," she sighed. "Coco never got a good look at his face, and when we looked at the CCTV footage, we realised he'd been wearing a mask anyway."

"Oh, dear," Trixie said. "I feel I may have been responsible," she muttered, her forehead creasing as tears continued to fall down her cheeks. By this time, the brown mascara was now streaked across her face.

"How on earth do you feel responsible, Mum?" Aggie said aghast.

"I...I...oh dear, Aggie, please forgive me."

"For what?" Aggie said, standing up.

"I told some of the ladies at the club about the shop when you first opened, and they were just as shocked as I was. There was some talk of trying to shut you down, dear. Oh, I am sorry."

"But you never instigated this talk?" Ted asked. "Did you? Did you love?"

Trixie looked instantly guilty.

"Trixabelle Trout," he said. "How on earth could you do something like that to your own daughter?"

"I...I...didn't do anything; honestly, I didn't. I merely asked, hypothetically, what we could do to change Agatha's mind. To encourage her to open a different type of shop. I never once suggested threats or violence. I would never do anything to harm my children. They mean the world to me. I know I don't always show it in the best way. I didn't exactly have the best role model, did I? Oh dear, Agatha. But I do feel somewhat to blame for all this. What if, what if someone overheard us talking about it all? What if? What if one of the members took it upon herself to do this? Oh, goodness me, goodness me. Whatever have I done?" Trixie wailed.

"Mum?" Aggie said. "Mum?" she said louder while looking at her father.

"Trixie?" he asked.

Trixie lifted her head up, her face a total mess from the combination of makeup and tears.

"It's not your fault," Aggie said, kneeling down by her mother's feet. "I know you would never do anything like this, but someone you spoke to. Someone you trust, Mum. That person must be responsible. Is there anyone in your circle of friends who you think could be capable of this? If there is, we need to tell the police."

Trixie"s eyes opened wide. "The police?" she whispered. "Oh, the shame."

"Wouldn't you rather have justice for what's happened to Aggie and Coco than risk the shame of the Ladies Luncheon Club?" Ted asked, shaking his head.

For a moment, Trixie looked from Aggie to Ted and back. "Of course I'd rather have justice, Edward. Do you think I'm a monster?"

"Of course not, Trixie. I'm just making a point."

"Well, you've certainly made it," she said, folding her arms across her chest and sighing before she unfolded them just as quickly and sighed again. "If the person responsible for hurting my girls is in the Ladies Luncheon Club, I will find out about it, and that person will pay for what she has done. I promise," Trixie said, reaching out to touch Aggie's face. "I promise," she repeated. "Now, let me see this video that your Great Aunt Petunia made."

Aggie and her father shared a smile between them as she got up to get the DVD out of her handbag. That's when she noticed her mobile had been ringing. Five missed calls from Coco and two from an unknown number.

. . .

oOo

Aggie, Ted, and Trixie stood alongside Coco as well as several other locals in the street, watching the fire brigade put out the flames.

Aggie and Coco were hugging each other tightly as eventually, the last fireman came out of Aphrodite's Closet and nodded to the small group.

Their supervisor came over and spoke to them.

"You were lucky you have a fire alarm installed, and it went off when it did," he said. "There's minimal damage to the shop, but I'm afraid there was a vast amount of smoke, which will probably lead to your stock being worthless. It's not an easy smell to get rid of, I'm afraid."

"Do you know how it started?" Coco asked as she shivered.

"Arson, we believe it was arson," he said. "The police are on the scene. It's best you talk to them now."

"Thank you, thank you so much," Coco said. "Thank God for you guys," she smiled as she rubbed the tears from her eyes.

Aggie hadn't said a word since they left her parents house. Luckily Ted hadn't drunk his brandy before she'd picked up the message that Aphrodite's Closet was on fire. They'd immediately climbed into his Volvo and sped off toward town.

Coco was already there, standing outside watching in disbelief as smoke poured out of their shop.

"It was him, wasn't it?" Coco asked. Aggie's eyes were wide in shock as she nodded.

CHAPTER 32

Everything was black, covered in soot. Tears flowed down Aggie's cheeks as she, Coco, and her parents visited the shop the following morning. They'd been advised not to enter for a few hours so they'd all gone back to Ted and Trixie's house where they'd tried, unsuccessfully, to sleep.

"I can't believe it. I just can't believe it. You could have been here. You could have been killed," Trixie whispered, pulling Aggie close to her and shaking her head as Ted looked on.

"It's all ruined. Everything's ruined," Coco said. "We can't sell any of this. Everything stinks. What are we going to do?"

"We'll figure it out, girls. Don't worry. We'll figure it out," Ted reassured them.

The door suddenly burst open, and Christie ran inside. "Oh my God, I came as soon as the girls were at preschool. I can't believe it. What a bastard," she yelled. "Mum? Dad? You're here?"

"Yes, yes, love. We're here. And we'll always be here for you and Aggie, you know that right?" Trixie said as she hugged her youngest daughter.

Christie, looking like she was being hugged by an alien, eyed Aggie who nodded and shrugged.

"Yes, everything's okay now," Coco whispered to her as she walked past. "Bygones and all that."

Christie nodded. "Do we have any idea who the perpetrator is yet?"

"Not really," Aggie replied. "Although Mum thinks it might be someone at the Ladies Luncheon Club."

"What? You're joking, right?" Christie asked aghast.

But Aggie shook her head. "It is possible. She's going to try and find out more."

"Well, you be careful, Mum. They're clearly quite insane, dangerous," she said, looking around. "I mean, Aggie could have been in here. Can you imagine what might have happened?"

"Let's not think about that right now, Sis," Aggie added, looking at their mum and dad.

"But I don't think it's a good idea you go investigating the Ladies Luncheon Club, Trixie. Christie's right. This person is dangerous. They were willing to kill just to close the shop," said Coco.

"Yes, indeed," Ted said. "Let"s just leave it to the police."

"No, I will not. This person might be doing this because of something I said. Me," Trixie said, aghast, "I can not. No. I will not let them get away with this. I'm going to do everything in my powers to do that. And if that means going undercover at the Ladies Luncheon Club, then so be it."

"You wouldn't be going undercover, Mum, because everyone knows who you are," Christie said.

"Well, you know what I mean, dear. But enough of all this for now. We need to clean all this up. What can we do?" she asked, looking at the three girls.

"You want to help?" Aggie asked, looking a little confused.

Trixie nodded.

"You want to help us get Aphrodite's Closet back up and running?" Coco asked.

Trixie nodded again.

"You mean you want to help us get Aphrodite's Closet, the adult shop, back up and running and open again?" Aggie asked again, her brow furrowed.

"Yes!" exclaimed Trixie. "For goodness sakes. How many times do I need to say it? I want to help. I feel somewhat responsible, and

I also feel like I've been a dreadful mother, and I want to make amends. If that means helping my girls, and that includes you, Coco, to re-open the town's only sex shop, then yes, yes, yes!" Trixie yelled as she turned a little red in the cheeks.

Aggie, Coco, and Christie each looked at each other.

"I'll have what she's having," Coco said, sniggering before they all started laughing.

"Just look at us," Ted said after a minute or two. "This place has almost been burned to the ground, and here we are, standing amidst all this soot, laughing. Whatever is the matter with us?"

"Oh, Dad, if we weren't laughing, we'd been crying even more. Surely laughter is better than tears?"

Ted smiled at her, "I'm so proud of you, love".

"Right, I'm going to call Elsebeth," Trixie said, rolling her sleeves up and rifling about in her handbag to find her phone.

"Elsebeth?" Ted asked, "Whatever for, darling?"

"Elsebeth's niece runs an industrial cleaning company," she said, "I'm sure I can get them here as soon as possible."

"Thanks, Mum," Aggie said. "I'm going upstairs to see if there's much damage to my flat. I'll bring some bin liners down so we can start chucking things away."

"Okay, love," Ted said. "I'll call Bruce, Charlie, and Pete. See if they've got a few spare hours to help sort things out."

"Dad, you're a star," Christie said. "I'll see if the coffee machine is still working."

CHAPTER 33

Mid-morning, the door to the store was pushed open, and Cole stepped in.

"Sorry, dear, but as you can see, we're very much closed," Trixie said, stepping over all the soot-covered rubbish and walking toward him.

"I'm here to see Aggie," he said. "What the hell happened here?"

"Fire, some scoundrel set the place on fire," Ted said, rubbing his forehead with the back of his hand, leaving a black soot mark.

"Shit," Cole whispered. "Is Aggie all right?" he asked, his eyes scouring the place for some sign of her.

"She's fine, she's fine. Fortunately, she wasn't here. She was with us," Trixie said. "I'm Trixie, her mother," she held out her hand. "And this is Ted, her father. And you are?"

Shaking her hand, Cole stepped forward. "I'm Cole, a friend. We just met recently, and we'd arranged to meet up today."

"Oh," Trixie said. "Well, it's clearly not the best time. But she's upstairs with the police at the moment if you'd like to wait?"

"Yes, yes, of course," he replied. "Is there anything I can do to help?"

Trixie handed him a bin bag and pointed to a pile of charred clothes and blackened products on the floor in the middle of the room. "You could throw all that lot in the bin bag," she instructed. "You might get a little dirty, though."

"That's all right, Trixie. A little dirt never hurt anyone," he smiled, taking the bag out of her extended hand and started to clear the rubbish away.

After about ten minutes, the door was opened for the second time, and Kyle appeared.

"Kyle," yelled Coco from the back of the store. "Over here."

"Hey guys," he said to everyone busy clearing up as he began stepping over items on the floor. He stopped when he noticed Cole and stood still for a second. "Cole," he nodded. "Good to see you here to help out," he said through gritted teeth.

"Actually I was here to see Aggie. We arranged it yesterday. I had no idea about the fire. I can't believe it's happened, but I'm happy to help out, obviously."

"I'm sure you are," Kyle replied.

"Do you have a problem with me, mate?" asked Cole, putting down the bin bag and straightening himself up to his full height, which was about half a foot taller than Kyle.

"I'm not your mate, am I?" Kyle growled.

"Everything all right here, boys?" Coco appeared and stood between them, looking from one to the other.

After a moment or two of too much testosterone, the men both nodded, and Kyle walked away.

"Kyle, what's wrong with you?" hissed Coco once they were out of earshot. "Can't you see we're having a bloody horrible time here at the moment and Aggie really likes the guy. She certainly doesn't need you butting in and causing further problems for her."

Kyle stopped and turned to look at his sister. "That's why I'm here, Coco. To help you and Aggie. We don't need his help."

"Have you heard yourself? You sound like a child. What the hell's wrong with you at the moment? You're acting so weird."

Kyle looked at her and shook his head. "I'm fine."

"Yeah clearly," she said. "While we're here dealing with a potentially lethal threat, you're acting like a five-year-old with a bee in his bonnet. He's a nice guy. Jeeze, Kyle. Give the guy a break already."

When Aggie appeared on the stairs, Kyle rushed over to her, ignoring his sister's comments.

"Aggie, are you okay?" he said concern written all over his face. "I came the second I heard."

Aggie nodded, "I'm okay. Luckily I wasn't here, so yeah, I'm fine. Thanks for coming, Kyle. I appreciate it," she said, noticing Cole out of the corner of her eye. She smiled and carried on walking down the stairs, leaving Kyle alone.

"Cole," Aggie said. "You came."

"Well, we had a date, didn't we?"

"Not one that included a charred building though," she muttered. "Have you seen what that bastard has done?"

Cole looked around and nodded, "Yeah, it's unbelievable. I'm just glad you're okay," he said, pulling her toward him into a gentle hug. "I met your parents," he smiled when he spotted Trixie and Ted both eyeing them up. "I'm not quite sure what they make of me though. I thought your mum wasn't talking to you at the moment?"

"We sorted it out last night," Aggie sighed, pulling away from him. "We're good now."

"I'm pleased. So now the only thing you're dealing with is a nutter with a grudge?" he asked.

"I guess so," she replied. "I just wish I knew why they've got such a grudge. But I can't even think about that right now. I need to get this place back up and running."

"Well, I'm here for you. What can I do to help?"

"How much time have you got?" she smiled.

"Almost a week?"

"Is that all?" she pouted, trying to make light of the fact that he'd be going back to Canada in less than eight days.

"If I could extend it, I would," he said. "But for now, use me however you can. I'm yours for the duration."

Aggie grinned, "Thanks, Cole. I appreciate it. I just wish it wasn't a week of cleaning up this mess."

"It doesn't matter what it is, as long as I get to hang out with you for the next few days," he said, finally letting her go as her dad approached them.

"Everything all right, love?" he asked.

"Of course, Dad, everything's great. Well, under the circumstances, everything's great," she smiled.

"Can you give me a hand, Cole? I need another strong man to help me lift these cupboards to clean underneath."

"Happy to help," Cole smiled as he let go of Aggie's hand and followed her dad.

Aggie smiled from the doorway and watched them go. Turning back to walk further into the store, she couldn't help but notice Kyle watching her. She'd never seen him look like that before.

CHAPTER 34

"I'm lucky my flat wasn't affected," Aggie said later that evening when the others had gone home after a day of sorting through everything. "Just a faint smell of smoke up here, but otherwise okay."

Cole handed her a glass of wine after she'd had a quick shower and put on a pair of jeans and a sweater.

"Thanks. The shower's all yours if you want to get cleaned up."

"Absolutely," he smiled, highlighting the several black smudges across his cheeks. "It's a good thing you suggested I pick up some clean clothes earlier," he said as he picked up his bag and walked toward the bathroom.

"I've hung a clean towel on the rail for you."

"Cheers," he smiled before disappearing behind the closed door.

Aggie sighed and sat down, leaning back in the sofa before taking a long, much-needed swig of her white wine. She listened to the sound of the shower being turned on and imagined Cole's naked body beneath the water and shivered, almost dripping wine all over herself in the process.

"Christ," she muttered. Her business and home had almost been burned to the ground, and all she could think about was the naked man in her shower.

"You need to get laid, Aggie," said Coco just before she'd gone home. "After everything that's gone on over the past few weeks, you need to get that delicious man into your bed and let him do things with you using all those goodies The Kinky Prince sent you last month."

Aggie's cheeks had blushed to high heaven as she'd playfully punched Coco in the shoulder. "Coco!" she'd exclaimed. "I've only known him a few days."

"So? He's bloody hot, and he's proven himself to be a gentleman. What more do you need? And why wait? He's only here for another week. Get in as much sex as you possibly can, Aggie. Enjoy him. I know I wouldn't bloody wait! I'll leave you to it. I'll be back in the morning. Enjoy," she'd winked before heading home.

Kyle, on the other hand, hadn't stayed around very long at all. He'd helped out for about an hour, but then he'd been called back to the office, complaining about a plumbing problem or something. But he hadn't been that friendly to anyone, come to think of it. Aggie put the glass of wine down on the floor and tipped her head back, closing her eyes for a moment, as she remembered everything that had happened over the past week.

It had been one thing after another. Good and bad. The good was standing in her shower. Naked. The bad was threatening to mess with her head. Screwing up her face, she opened her eyes and took a deep breath. Who was messing with her and the shop? And why would that person go to such extreme lengths to try and shut her down?

Thoughts led her to her mum and dad, and she smiled. She was so relieved she'd gained the courage to go over there and talk to them. Her mum had seen the error of her ways and was willing to put it all behind her, even helping make Aphrodite's Closet great again. Grinning, Aggie leaned forward and picked up her wine, but knocked it in the process, making it wobble on the carpeted floor.

"Bugger," she said as she grappled with the glass, trying to keep it upright and failing.

"Shit," she said as she stood up and rushed to the kitchen to grab some paper with which to mop it up. Enroute though, she tripped on Cole's bag at the exact time he decided to exit the bathroom, and the two collided. To try not to fall to the ground, she grabbed the nearest thing. Which just happened to be the towel around his waist. She fell to her knees, taking the towel with her.

Dazed for a second, Aggie shook her head and opened her eyes, only to find herself face to face with Cole's manhood.

"Oh my God," she said, trying to look away but finding it difficult. Her gaze just kept pulling itself back to Cole's rather large piece of equipment.

Trying hard not to laugh, Cole took Aggie's hands and lifted her up so that they were almost face to face (he was somewhat taller).

"Seen enough?" he asked with a cheeky grin on his face.

"No, not at all," she replied, not realising what she was saying.

"No? Perhaps you'd like to have another look?"

"No, that's not what I mean at all. Oh God, can this get any more embarrassing?" she groaned, looking downward and realising he was just a tad excited by it all.

"Aggie? I'm up here?" he chuckled, using his fingers under her chin to lift her face upward.

"Sorry, I'm just not…it's been a long…I…it's not…"

Chuckling, Cole lifted her face toward his, and before she knew it, he was kissing her with tenderness on the lips.

Her want soon became more and more urgent, and she let the towel, which she'd been gripping between her fingers, fall to the ground. Cole's hands moved to beneath her arms, and he lifted her sweater until she was wearing just her jeans and one of her favourite new pretty satin bras.

Then he moved his fingers to the buttons of her jeans, undoing one by one until they were all open and ready for the jeans to come off.

He stopped kissing her for a moment so he could slide the jeans down her thighs. When they reached her knees, she tried to step out of them. Easier said than done, though, and she almost fell over. Grinning, Cole held her steady as she bent forward to pull them off by herself.

While Cole stood butt-naked in the hallway of the flat, Aggie stood wearing bra and knickers, waiting for his next move.

It had been such a long time since she'd had sex, and she felt a little rusty.

Suddenly, she was whisked off her feet as he carried her through to the living room, where he placed her on the sofa.

"More wine?" he asked.

She nodded and watched as he stood up and confidently strolled out of the room in all his gorgeous nakedness.

Coming in moments later with the bottle and two glasses, he poured them both a drink and handed one to her.

She downed it in seconds.

"Whoa there," he laughed. "What's up, Aggie? Nervous?"

She nodded. "It's…been a while since I've done this."

"Well don't worry, I won't bite, unless you want me to," he said, after taking a long swig of wine and putting the glass down. "Now, where were we?"

CHAPTER 35

It had taken a week of substantial cleaning and sorting out to get the shop back to the way it was before the fire. Still, there had been no clues as to who was responsible, but no one was willing to give up.

Cole had been there at the shop every single day, helping with the cleaning, re-painting, the rearranging of things as well as reordering all the new stock. He'd even driven Aggie and Coco to a couple of their suppliers to pick up some stock to save time.

But when the time had come to say goodbye, Aggie had found it heart-wrenching. She knew it would happen. She'd known she'd fall for him and then it would be over. A holiday fling. It's what it had been for him. But she hadn't been on holiday.

But he'd gone, and she had to get back to her life the way it was before. She had to forget about the man who had shown her it was okay to have some fun and enjoy her own body. And she certainly had done that. Cole had been incredible in bed, occasionally a little distant, but that was to be expected of a man whose life belonged in another country.

"Hey, you," Coco said as she walked into the shop the following morning to find Aggie hanging the new "open" sign on the door. "Ready for business again?"

Aggie grinned, "Absolutely."

"How are you feeling, honey?" Coco asked, looking a little sad.

"Okay I guess, a bit down to see him go but, hey, c'est la vie, right?"

Coco rubbed her friend's shoulders and nodded. "He was good for you, but now you can move on and have some fun with someone else."

"He's only just left, Coco," Aggie sighed as they both turned and walked back into the shop.

"Yes he has, but he was just a fling, right? You were together less than a couple of weeks. Just a short-term love affair," she smiled, putting her small handbag behind the counter.

"I suppose so," Aggie sighed. "I'm going to miss him, though."

"Of course you will. You hadn't had sex for years before he came along!" Coco laughed.

"Yoo-hoo," said the familiar voice of Aggie's mother from the door. "Open for business?" she chuckled. "Hello, dears, your father and I just wanted to pop in and make sure everything is all right for the opening today?"

"Hey, Mrs Trout," Coco said as Trixie air-kissed her cheeks.

"Tut tut, Coco Watson. What have I told you about calling me, Mrs Trout? It's Trixie from now on, dear."

Coco laughed, "Okay, Trixie."

"Morning, girls," said Ted as he trundled in carrying a large round box.

"I brought you a little something to keep you going today," said Trixie as she followed Ted to the countertop as he put down the box. She took off the lid to reveal a large cake.

"I baked you a cake. Ta da!" Trixie giggled as she showed them the miniature version of the building. "Plus, I knew that you'd be feeling a little lonely, what with Cole's return home and everything," she said, looking at Aggie, who smiled in appreciation.

"Oh my God, Trixie that's incredible. You made that? Wow," admired Coco, taking her finger and nicking a little bit of the chantilly cream that surrounded it. "Mmmmmm, vanilla flavour," she cooed.

"Well, I made most of it. I did have a little help with the decoration from some of the ladies of the Ladies Luncheon Club who popped over last night for supper. We had a very good chat. Didn't we, Edward?" Trixie said before cutting him off. "I'm afraid I'm no nearer to finding out who the dreadful criminal is who caused the fire though, dears."

"Mum, I've told you about that. It's too dangerous. You shouldn't get involved," Aggie scolded.

"And I've told you that I will do everything in my power to get justice for my girls. Everything."

Ted raised his eyebrows, "Any news from the police, Aggie?"

"Unfortunately not," she said, putting the lid back on the cake and taking it through to their little kitchen. "But Coco has had a bit of a breakthrough."

Ted and Trixie both inched closer to the girls.

"I don't know why I didn't remember before, but I had a dream last night. It was a bit of a nightmare, really. I dreamed about him attacking me again," she cringed before continuing, and he had a smell about him." Coco screwed up her nose. "He smelled like cigars."

"Cigars?" asked Trixie, "Well, that's interesting."

"Do you know anyone that smokes them, Mum? Dad?"

Both of them shook their heads.

"But it certainly gives me something to work with," Trixie smiled. "Now, we should be leaving you. I'm sure you'll be inundated with customers today, after more than a week of being closed."

"Don't you want to have a look around Mrs. ...er, Trixie?"

"But I've spent a week here every day, Coco."

"Yes, but you never had a look at our products," she grinned.

Trixie, getting a little flustered, shook her head. "Well no, I don't think so, dear. Perhaps another day. I...we must be going. I've got a busy day myself. Come on now, Ted. Let's leave the girls to it. Oh, is Christie not coming in?"

"We made her promise to stay away until we catch him, Mum."

"Oh right, of course," Trixie smiled. "And she does have the twins to look after. Perhaps we'll pop in to see her later. All right then. Toodle pip."

Coco chuckled, "Thank you for the cake, Mr. and Mr.s Tr... Trixie and Ted."

"My pleasure, dear," Trixie said as she gave both girls an air-kiss before heading for the door.

"See you soon, love," said Ted, giving Aggie a hug and Coco a quick peck on the cheek. "Stay safe, keep your eyes open at all times and don't leave each other alone. You hear me?"

Aggie and Coco nodded.

"Thanks, Dad, we'll be fine. Promise."

"You better be," he smiled as he closed the door behind him.

"Your mum is like a different person, Aggie," Coco sighed. "Has she had a lobotomy or something?"

Aggie laughed. "Yeah most likely. She is very different. I think Dad yelling at her for the first time in their fifty-year relationship shocked her into it. She's trying very hard, I know that, and I love her for it."

Coco grinned, "Like mother like daughter, eh?"

"I don't think so," Aggie guffawed. "I'm nothing like her, not really."

"Actually..."

"I'm not," Aggie continued to screech.

"Okay, okay, maybe not quite. But there is a certain stubbornness there that you must have gotten from Trixie."

Aggie raised her eyebrows, looked to the ceiling for a second and then nodded. "Okay, maybe a little. She's clearly still a bit embarrassed about what we sell though."

"Well so are you and it's your shop," Coco grinned.

"Our shop," Aggie added.

"Well, kind of," Coco winked before the new bell above the door dinged, announcing the arrival of their first client.

CHAPTER 36

There had been no further attempts of violence, no threats in the mail and no suspicious behaviour in the month since the shop reopened. Aggie and Coco were so confident that the matter was finally put to bed that they invited Christie back to work whenever she wanted to. Happy to get out of the house, Christie had begun to work every morning after she'd dropped the girls off at preschool.

A steady stream of customers filled the shop, keeping all three of them busy. Coco had even given up her mid-week manicures and hair appointments so she could spend all her time at Aphrodite's Closet. It should be noted though, that she hadn't given them up altogether. She had moved them to the weekend instead. It was Coco, after all.

When the shop phone rang one Monday morning, Aggie picked it up, "Aphrodite's Closet, how may I help?" she asked, putting on her telephone voice just like her mother.

"Good morning, may I speak to Agatha Trout, please?" said the polite voice on the other end.

"This is Agatha."

"Hello, Agatha. I'm calling from Liberty Magazine, the monthly women's magazine?"

Aggie chuckled, "Yes, of course, I know Liberty. What can I do for you?"

"Well, it has come to our attention that you are the owner of a shop called, er..." she waited a second before continuing, clearly reading her notes, "Aphrodite's Closet? Is that right?"

"It certainly is."

"Well, Agatha..."

"Please call me Aggie."

"Sure, Aggie. We'd like to write a piece about you and your store if that's something that interests you?"

Aggie, taken aback, sat down on the stool behind the countertop. "Er, yeah, yes that would be brilliant. But why me? Why Aphrodite's Closet?"

"Well, last month we asked our readers to tell us about their favourite independent shops, and your name popped up quite a few times it would seem."

"Really?" asked Aggie, shocked.

"Yes, Aggie," chuckled the woman on the other end of the phone. "It was also noted how you almost lost it all in a fire."

"Unfortunately yes, but we reopened about a month ago. Luckily the damage wasn't so extensive that we were only closed for just over a week but still, it was pretty bad."

"I can imagine. Look, can I make an appointment to come and see you with a photographer?"

"Sure, yes, that would be fantastic. When would be good for you...sorry I've forgotten your name already."

"Emily...Emily Franks."

"Great, Emily, thanks. So, name a day and time, and I'll be here with Coco and Christie."

"They're your business partners, I assume?" asked Emily.

"Yes, that's right. I own the building, but Coco and Christie are both investors who work in the shop with me. Coco's my best friend," she chuckled. "And Christie is my younger sister."

"Oh, that's wonderful. Another great angle for the story," Emily said. "So, how's Thursday suit you? About ten?"

"Thursday at ten is perfect. I look forward to it. Thank you, thank you so much, Emily."

"My pleasure. See you Thursday."

Aggie put down the phone and whooped out loud, blushing when several clients eyed her up.

"What's going on?" asked Coco from the top of the stairs.

Aggie motioned for her to come downstairs, which she duly did in a hurry.

"What is it?"

"You'll never guess…" Aggie breathed.

"No, you're right. I won't. So tell me," Coco said, raising her eyebrows.

"Liberty Magazine is sending someone to interview us on Thursday."

"Whaaaaat?" yelled Coco.

"Shhhhhhh, there are clients in the store, Coco."

"That didn't stop you from whooping out loud."

Aggie grinned, "I suppose not. Anyway, they're coming on Thursday at ten."

"What on earth am I going to wear?" Coco said, pouting as she started to give her outfit some serious thought.

"Well, you've got a few days to make a decision. But maybe we ought to wear some of our own pyjamas and nightgowns?" Aggie said, excited about her own idea.

"Ooh yeah, what a fab idea. Have you told Christie yet?"

"No, I've literally just got off the phone this second. Where is she anyway?"

"She's upstairs explaining how the Sonic Flutterer works to a couple keen on trying new things."

"Does she know how the Sonic Flutterer works?" Aggie asked.

Coco grinned, "Well, she does have one of her own, so I'd assume so."

Aggie laughed out loud. "I'll tell her about it when she comes back downstairs."

"So," Coco said, hanging around the till. "Anything interesting to report?"

"Like?"

"Like news from Cole?"

Aggie's face dropped, and she shook her head. "Nothing."

"It's weird. You were like this," Coco crossed her fingers in front of her, "for over a week, and then he goes back to Canada, and you get one email in a month."

Aggie shrugged, "Like you said before, it was just a holiday fling. He has no need to keep in touch now that he's home."

"Are you okay?" Coco asked.

Nodding, Aggie began to fold a couple of pairs of pyjamas that were left on top of the counter. "Yeah, I am now. I've had a month to get over him. It's not like we were married or anything. He's got his life. I've got mine," she shrugged again.

Coco stroked her shoulder, "True, but you would tell me if you needed to talk, right?"

"Of course I would, but I'm fine. Honest."

Coco nodded, "Well, in that case, there's this guy who has a pretty hot brother…"

Aggie looked at Coco sideways, put the folded pyjamas back down and then proceeded to push Coco toward the stairs.

"Go. Away. Now," she said grinning. "I don't want to be set up. I don't want to date. I don't want to blind-date. I don't want a man," she said. "I just want to be left alone to do my own thing. I'm happy as a single woman, Coco. Live with it."

"Okay, okay," Coco relented. "You want to be left alone. I get it, I get it."

Coco walked up the stairs, stopped and looked back at her. "He is cute, though."

"No!" Aggie said, shaking her head in dismay, but laughing all the same. "You're unbelievable."

CHAPTER 37

Trixie flicked through the magazine for the seventieth time, "I just can't believe it. My own daughters. Famous," she giggled.

"We're hardly famous, Mum. We're just in a magazine, that's all."

"In the magazine, Aggie. This is the best-selling women's magazine in the UK."

"You're just reading what it says on the cover. It's only the best-selling magazine to women in their twenties and thirties."

"Yes and that's huge," Trixie exclaimed. "And you've got a four-page spread. It's incredible. And look at these photos of you in the pyjamas. You all look so beautiful."

"It is pretty cool," Aggie agreed. "It was a fun interview to do. Emily Franks was lovely as was her photographer, Julie, I think her name was."

"I'm pleased you told them about the threats, the attack of Coco and the fire," Trixie said.

Surprised, Aggie looked up from the magazine, "Really? Why?"

"Because the more people know about your attack, the better the chance we'll finally get the person, or persons, responsible."

"Do you think so, Mum?"

Trixie nodded as she picked up the cup and saucer and took a sip of her Darjeeling tea. "Of course."

"I'm not so sure we'll ever find the person now. It's been ages since the fire, and nothing else has happened. I reckon the person has given up."

"Perhaps he has, but he should still be brought to justice for what he's done to you and Coco. It's the most despicable behaviour and should not be tolerated."

Impressed, Aggie nodded. "I agree, Mum. But I just can't share your confidence that we'll find him."

"Oh we will," Trixie said. "I'm going to find out who did this, even if it takes me to my grave."

"Mum, that's no way to talk," Aggie cried. "You've been watching too many of your police detective dramas."

"Nonsense," Trixie said. "Now, speaking of going to my grave, I was wondering about…"

"What?" Aggie cried out. "I hope you're not planning your funeral already, Mum. You're only seventy-one."

"Actually, Agatha Trout, if you'd given me a moment to speak," her mother said as if she'd smacked her hand out of the way. "I was going to say, I've been giving my life an awful lot of thought over the past couple of months, and I've come to realise something…"

"What, Mum? What have you come to realise?"

Trixie raised her eyebrows and looked across at her daughter, "That's what I'm trying to say, dear. I've come to realise that I haven't been the most…understanding or accepting person over the years, which has led me to keep someone important from you," she said.

"You have? Who?" Aggie butted in again.

"If you'll let me finish, I'll tell you. Now, where was I? Oh yes. I realised that I kept you from knowing someone so very important. Someone responsible for changing your life, actually, for changing all our lives, for the better, now I come to think of it. I'm talking about your Great Aunt Petunia, dear."

"Oh," Aggie said, looking at the teapot while her mother poured them some more.

"I realise now that I acted most despicably myself and for that, I am terribly sorry to you and to her. And so I'd like to do something…"

"You would?" Aggie looked up, confused. "What?"

"Oh, Aggie, just listen, will you? I'd like to organise an event—a memorial at the church and then a little party—for her."

"Oh, Mum, that's lovely. What a great idea."

"Do you think so, dear? Really? You don't think it's too little too late?" Trixie asked, clearly unsure of herself.

"Oh, Mum," Aggie smiled and shook her head. "I think it's bloody brilliant, sorry," she apologised, "But Great Aunt Petunia would love it, I'm sure of it."

Aggie hopped up from the kitchen table and rushed around to the other side and pulled her mum into a sincere hug. "I can't believe it," Aggie breathed. "You've changed so much over the past few months, and I appreciate it so much, Mum."

Tears began to well in Trixie's eyes, and she patted Aggie's back. "I know, dear," she whispered. "You, your dad, and Petunia all made me realise what a horrible, bitter old lady I'd become."

"Mum, you weren't a bitter old lady at all," Aggie said, not entirely convincingly.

"I was. I had turned into an exact replica of my own mother, Aggie and I never wanted that. When your dad raised his voice to me, that was it. That's when the penny dropped. That's when I knew I had to change. That's when I knew I had to do everything possible to make things right again. I hope it's not too late."

"Of course it's not too late, Mum," she said, leaning backwards and looking down at her mother's eyes. "Gosh, I'd never realised it before," she said.

"What's that, dear?" Trixie asked.

"We have the same eyes."

Trixie smiled, "We do. Petunia's eyes."

CHAPTER 38

Aggie's mum had gathered her "troops" and pulled out all the stops to make the church event one to remember. She had a lifetime of wrongdoings to put right, and so she wanted everyone to know all about her own Aunt Petunia. The lady who had died alone in an old people's home the previous December. When in truth, as a younger woman, she had been a firecracker, full of life. A real character who people loved. And Trixie wanted to celebrate her for who she really was, not for the husband-stealing hag she'd pretended her to be.

"Mum," Aggie gasped when she saw the flowers that decorated each row of seats, as well as the several large bouquets that sat at the front along with a huge blown-up photo of Petunia Petal.

As people began to enter the pretty old building, some did double-takes as they glanced at the picture and then looked at Aggie who, with her bobbed hair and fringe, did look the spitting image of her great aunt.

She smiled at the sight of so many people gathering to pay their respects to a woman they hadn't even known. All to support Trixie and her family at this time of remembrance.

Trixie was beaming, rather like the mother of a bride, even though there was no wedding. Dressed in a new outfit, Trixie looked beautiful with her hair done in a whole new style—much to the shock of her fellow churchgoers. Trixie had done her hair the same way for the past fifty years! Her dress was also bright and cheerful, quite the opposite of her usual tweed skirts and jackets. It was clear that she'd changed, not just in appearance but within too. Her smile was beaming like her heart was on show for all to see.

Ted, the proud husband, beamed alongside her. And beside him sat Aggie, Christie, and Coco. All dressed up, ready to show the world the wonderful woman who had been a part of their family—albeit many, many years ago.

When the church was almost full, Reverend Geoff stood up and faced the flock.

"Good morning and welcome to this fine and sunny day. A glorious day to celebrate the life of Petunia," he glanced down at his notes, "Peaches Paula Petal. Aunt to our beloved Trixabelle Trout and Great Aunt to Agatha and Christie, who have all organised this wonderful memorial event in memory of such a darling lady who moved over to the realm of God some months ago."

"Realm of God?" whispered Aggie to Coco before they both sniggered.

The Reverend continued, "Petunia Peaches Paula Petal was born into this earthly realm some ninety-nine years ago, back in September of 1917 when the world was rather a different one. When times were tough and, lives were…er…tougher. Petunia Paula Petal Peaches…"

Aggie rolled her eyes.

"…met her first husband, the late Henry Cleaver, at the tender age of sixteen and would later marry him a year later at the age of er…seventeen. Their short marriage would succumb to his death when she was no more than twenty-one years old. Although the marriage produced no children, Paula Petal Petunia Peaches inherited what is now a well-known building within the town of Frambleberry on the corner of Pelican Street. A building so beautiful one can only imagine what might have been."

Reverend Geoff lifted his head and glanced at the people in front of him.

Aggie and Coco shared a confused look.

"A building left to her great-niece, Agatha Trout, who has built up her own, unique…" he pursed his lips before continuing, "business. But back to Paula…"

"For God's sake, can't he get his bloody facts straight," Coco said a little louder on purpose.

Reverend Geoff cleared his throat, glanced at his notes and corrected himself, "Petunia. She would later marry Jasper James, followed by Frank Thomas, and finally Jim Petal. She outlived them all and is now in the heavenly realm with all four. Let us pray," he added at the end.

Once the congregation had said the Lord's prayer, Reverend Geoff began singing "All Things Bright and Beautiful," to which everyone joined in. Finally, he invited Trixie to say a few words.

"Hello, everybody. Thank you all so much for coming. I'm delighted to see so many friendly faces. I know none of you knew Aunt Petunia, and I'm therefore so grateful that you'd give up your time to be here with us to celebrate her life. Admittedly, I wasn't there for Petunia for much of hers. She and my mother had a terrible falling out when they were younger, and my mother, God rest her soul, could never forgive her. Mother, Petunia's sister, insisted I not forgive her either. She instilled in me a…hatred…of Petunia that I carried with me for years, and I am deeply ashamed of myself for that. But lately, I have learned the importance of forgiveness. How opening your heart and letting the love in can make you a better person," Trixie stopped for a second and glanced over at her family. "I held a grudge. A grudge that wasn't even mine. It was my mother's. My mother had no right to hold that over me. But that she did. And because of that, I neglected to welcome Petunia into our family. But she was family, and I want to rectify that right now. Petunia Petal was my auntie, and I wish, oh how I wish, I could change the last years of her life. How I wish I could have invited her into our family. How wonderful it would have been to have spent Christmases with her, birthdays, weddings," she glanced at Christie. "Petunia, if you can hear me now. Please forgive me, dear. I made some terrible mistakes, and I'm sorry."

The crowd, which had been very quiet, erupted with applause and Trixie blushed as she stepped down from the podium. As she did so, the door of the church suddenly burst open and the large framed photograph of Petunia was lifted by a gust of wind and landed in Trixie's arms.

Reverend Geoff stood up quickly, looking from the door to Trixie and back. Clearly in shock, he proceeded to address the church.

"What a wonderful speech, Trixabelle. Thank you. The importance of forgiveness, one which we should all carry with us."

Trixie, looking a little shellshocked, smiled and placed the picture back on the large easel, which had held it previously, before returning to her seat.

"Now, let us sing another song…"

"What on earth happened?" Aggie asked Trixie as she sat down beside her.

"What? The picture? I'm not sure," Trixie breathed.

"I think it was Petunia giving you a hug of forgiveness," Coco whispered, leaning over so Trixie could hear her.

Trixie smiled and patted down her hair, "I don't think so, Coco. Now shush, we should sing."

Coco and Aggie laughed before returning their attention to the order of service to read the words of the song they'd never even heard of before.

oOo

"Thank you so much for coming. It is very much appreciated," Trixie repeated again and again as she stood at the foot of the steps to the church, while people stepped out. "Please do pop over to my daughter's shop for drinks and nibbles this afternoon. We're having a little get-together to remember Petunia. We felt it only apt to hold the event in the shop she bequeathed to my daughter," she smiled. People nodded and smiled, promising to appear later.

"Reverend Geoff," she smiled as he stepped down toward her. "Thank you so much for the lovely service. I know Petunia would have been delighted."

"Yes, I'm sure," he said. "Tell me, Trixabelle. Why choose the shop for drinks and nibbles? Don't you think that a little… unusual? And perhaps a little…unsavoury?"

Trixie's eyes grew large, "Unsavoury? Why, Reverend, I wouldn't have expected you to say that. But not at all, no. The shop belonged to Petunia, and so we felt it only right to hold the memorial there. I think it's rather wonderful. I do hope you'll join us," she said, somewhat dismissively as she stepped away from him, with Ted on her arm.

"Dreadful man," she whispered to her husband. "Did you hear what he said? Unsavoury? He's talking about my daughter's shop. The nerve," she whispered.

"Well, darling, the girls did say they'd prefer not to have the event in the church on account of their dislike of the man."

"Clearly, I should have listened. I must apologise to them at once," she said, turning back to see if she could spot Aggie, Christie, or Coco. "You go on to the car, darling, I'll be there in a minute."

Ted nodded and smiled and left his wife to look for the girls as he wandered down toward the car.

"Aggie, dear," Trixie said as she spotted her daughter chatting to an old school friend around the corner from the church.

"Good to see you, Jane. Bye," she said before turning toward her mum. "Hey, Mum, you okay?"

"No, not really. I wanted to apologise."

"What for?"

"For insisting we do this here. I think you were probably right to dislike that man."

"What man?"

"Reverend Geoff," Trixie whispered.

"Oh?" Aggie was surprised.

"He just called Aphrodite's Closet unsavoury, dear," she said, quite disgusted.

"Well, that's pretty much what you called it before, Mum," Aggie smiled, linking arms and turning back toward their Volvo.

"Well, that's different. I'm your mother. He has no right. Horrid man."

"I've been telling you that for years, Mum."

"I know, and I'm sorry for not listening. I should have taken notice. I wonder now if the rumours were true?"

"Mum! I can't believe you've just said that. You were always so anti that kind of talk about a man of the cloth."

"Man of the cloth? Not my cloth, dear."

As they turned the corner of the church, they spotted Coco, who appeared to be hiding behind the church.

"Coco?" Aggie asked.

Turning, Coco's eyes were wide open in shock. She put a finger over her mouth and motioned the two women over.

They tiptoed over as quickly as they could, both wondering why such mystery.

"What is it, dear?" Trixie asked.

"It's him," she whispered, pointing.

"Who?" Trixie asked.

"The man?" Aggie questioned.

Coco nodded, causing Aggie to gasp. "Are you sure?"

Coco's expression said it all.

"The man who attacked you?" Trixie asked as it dawned on her what they were talking about.

The other two women followed Coco's gaze to a tall, heavily built man wearing a black suit. He was talking to the Reverend.

"How do you know it was him?" Aggie asked.

"Walking out of the church, I recognised the smell of the cigars, and then I noticed the scar on his hand. It's definitely him. That's the man who attacked me and threatened us all."

"We need to find out who he is," Trixie said, straightening her dress and patting down her hair.

"Mum, no!" Aggie whispered as the two women watched on as she walked off toward the Reverend.

"Reverend," Trixie shouted. "Reverend. Sorry, I forgot to…"

"Yes, Mrs Trout. Trixabelle?"

"I just wanted to find out if…"

"Yes?" he asked as the big man stood by his side.

"Oh, hello. I don't think we've been introduced," Trixie said, offering him her biggest, brightest smile. "I'm Trixabelle Trout."

The man just stood looking blank.

"I'm Trixabelle," she said, enunciated the words. "And you are?"

Reverend Geoff elbowed him in the ribs.

"Gavin, Gavin Jones," he said as he held out his hand with some reluctance.

"Oh, hello, Gavin Jones. How nice to meet a fellow churchgoer. I haven't seen you before, are you new to town?" she inquired.

"Er…, I'm…" the man stuttered.

"Mr Jones is here from Manchester…on business," Reverend Geoff finished off the man's sentence.

"Oh, is that right? Well," Trixie smiled, "nice to meet you, Mr Jones," she said. "Perhaps we'll be seeing you at the memorial this afternoon?"

The Reverend and Mr Jones both nodded tersely as Trixie turned on her heel and walked off toward the car.

Coco and Aggie were waiting with Ted and Christie.

"Well?" they all asked.

"Guilty as sin," Trixie seethed.

CHAPTER 39

"What are we going to do? We can't just go up to him and make a citizen's arrest, can we?" asked Aggie as they sat in the car.

"We should call the police," Ted suggested. "Let the police deal with it."

"I agree with Dad," said Christie.

"What if we don't have time? What if he's planning to do a runner?" Coco asked.

"That's unlikely," Trixie said. "He doesn't know we know. What I can't understand is why he's talking to the Reverend."

"Because the Reverend is a jackass," Christie muttered under her breath.

"Oh my God," muttered Aggie all of a sudden.

"What? What is it, dear?" Trixie asked as they all turned their attention to Aggie.

"Reverend Geoff. It's him. He's behind it all."

"What? The Reverend? Don't be ridiculous, dear. He's a man of the cloth, not a criminal."

"It makes perfect sense," Coco and Christie both agreed.

"Mum, remember you told us that if I didn't agree to open the shop myself, there was a condition in the will stating that it would be donated to the church? To the Reverend? Well, he must've found out. The will stated that if I failed to make a go of the shop within the first two years, he would get his hands on it. He's been behind this all along. He's been trying to get me to give up so he could have it," Aggie said, losing her breath.

"But...but...but he's the Vicar. Vicars aren't criminals. I've even had his wife over for tea. She sits on the board, for goodness sake. She..."

"What, Mum?" asked Christie.

"She was there when I told them about the will," she whispered. "That's how the Reverend knows about the condition in the will. I told her. I actually told her myself. I gave them a reason to do all of this," she cried, putting her head in her hands.

"Now wait a minute, love. We don't know that the Vicar is even involved. We're probably blowing this right of proportion. Let's at least give him the benefit of the doubt," Ted said, giving everyone a second to sit back and just think about it in silence. "Now, before we go all gung-ho and start creating scenarios that are straight out of one of your mum's crime drama series she loves so much, we've got a party to host, and if we don't get to the shop soon, people are going to be queueing up outside. So, let's stop mooching about and go," he continued, barely taking a breath.

"Your father's quite right, girls. We must get to the shop. We can't have our guests waiting. I told them to be there for two, and it's already twenty past one," Trixie said as she shuffled around in her handbag as Ted started the engine. "Just one moment, dear," she said as she pulled out her phone.

"Who are you calling?" Ted asked.

"I'm not. I'm going to take a photo of that blessed man so we can show it to the police later. Now how do I do it?" she said, pressing every button on the phone to try and get it to work.

"I'll do it," Coco said. "I'll use mine, it'll take a better picture from here."

She took her own flashy phone out of her bag and proceeded to discreetly snap away at the Reverend and the man who had called himself Gavin Jones.

"Wait!" Christie exclaimed as they began to drive off.

"What is it now?" Ted asked.

"I came in my own car," she said, getting into a tizzy as they drove past her own blue BMW parked down the lane from the church. Ted stepped on the brakes as Christie released her seatbelt and jumped out.

"I'll come with you," Aggie said.

"Me too," Coco shouted as they all hopped out of the car. "Meet you there," they all said to Ted and Trixie.

oOo

THE SHOP HAD BEEN RE-JIGGED to allow for a party of people to mingle without causing any damage to any of the products on display. All the cabinets had been pushed up against the walls, while still retaining the feel of a shop floor. The main countertop was where all the food and drinks were placed, making it easy for people to reach, and several long black ribbons had been tied together across the staircase to prevent people from heading up to the second floor. The afternoon was about Petunia, not about selling sex aids!

Several photographs of Petunia had been specially framed and hung around the shop to remind people why they were there; who they were remembering. One of Aggie's favourite photographs was the first one people could see as they opened the shop door.

Probably taken in the late nineteen-thirties, Petunia's bobbed hair was parted at the side, with waves created close to her face, which looked flawless. The long, clingy, sequinned, green dress draped almost to the floor, as she leaned against a staircase, not unlike the one in the shop. She looked like she was having fun, and that's one of the things Aggie loved about it.

"You look so much like her, you know?" said Ted as they waited for their guests to arrive. "She was a beauty in her day," he smiled. "Especially with your haircut like this," he pointed. "It suits you."

"Thanks, Dad," Aggie said. "This is one of my favourite photos of her. I'd love to know where it was taken. But I guess we'll never know."

"Never mind, sweetheart. At least she's part of the family again. In a manner of speaking anyway."

"Yes, I know," she smiled as Trixie walked over with a glass of champagne for her.

"Bubbly?" she asked, handing it to her. "Bruce's getting you a beer, dear," she said to Ted.

"I'll go and get it, thanks darling," he said as he wandered off toward his old friend.

"She was beautiful, wasn't she?" Trixie sighed, taking a swig of the champagne. "She always had such lovely taste in clothes too. I think Mother had always been a little jealous, even before, well, you know."

"She looked like a classy lady. That's how I imagined her to have been. But fun too. Was she Mum? Was she fun? Can you remember?"

"I can't honestly comment because I only ever met her on a few occasions—weddings and funerals. Mother kept her away, I'm afraid. But from what I gather, you're probably right. Also, judging by the recording she did of herself for you, I'd say she had a little bit of a wicked sense of humour. But we'll never really know, will we?" Trixie asked.

All of a sudden, the door whooshed open, causing the new bell to ding a couple of times and the picture they were looking at seemed to rock back and forth before settling back again. Nobody walked into the shop, though.

Aggie rushed up to the door and peered outside. Not a single person stood anywhere near it. Frowning, she pulled the door closed and walked back inside.

"Weird," she said, looking up at the photo of Petunia. For a split second, it looked like she winked. Stepping back, Aggie blinked a couple of times then looked at her drink.

"This is some strong champagne, Mum," she said to Trixie, who had been gazing at the picture without blinking.

"Hm, dear? What did you say?" she said, coming out of the strange daze.

"Nothing, nothing," Aggie said, turning toward Coco, who had been on the phone to the police officer who had been dealing with their case.

"What did he say?" she asked.

"Just that they would look into this Gavin guy. I emailed the pictures to him, so I guess we'll just have to wait and see for the time being."

"But what if he tries something else?" asked Christie, who had walked over when she heard them talking.

"I don't think he'd be stupid enough to try anything now," Trixie reassured them. "They're probably fully aware that we've got even more CCTV cameras on the go plus there are more locals aware of what's been going on now thanks to the article in Liberty. I'd say the girls are pretty safe today," she smiled, an odd sensation coming over her every time she looked up at the photos of Petunia.

"Are you all right, Mum?" asked Christie, looking at her oddly.

"Yes, yes, fine. I think this bubbly has gone to my head already, though," she smiled.

"But you've barely had half a glass, darling," Ted said, knowing full well that Trixie could put back several glasses of the stuff when she wanted to, without it having any effect.

"I know. It must be a little stronger than the usual brand we buy," she suggested. "Oh look, people are starting to arrive. Let's welcome them," she hiccupped.

Sure enough, the door began to open and close, the little bell dinging away every few minutes as guests started to arrive into the shop.

"Welcome to Aphrodite's Closet for Petunia's memorial," Trixie said to people as she wandered around greeting everyone with a smile. "If you wouldn't mind keeping on the ground floor, we'd appreciate it. However," she winked, "if you do want to see what's on offer upstairs, just ask one of the girls."

"Mum!" exclaimed Aggie as she overheard her talking. "I didn't think you wanted anyone to go upstairs?"

"I didn't, did I? I don't know what's coming over me."

"I do," laughed Aggie, looking at Trixie's empty glass.

"No, it's not that. Not that at all," she giggled. "I don't know what it is. I just feel a little, different," she said, wandering away.

Aggie watched her mother walk away before she glanced up at Petunia again. Everywhere she went today, Petunia seemed to be smiling down at her. Aggie started to think that perhaps Petunia was smiling down on them all—Trixie included.

CHAPTER 40

It had been some time since Aggie had seen Kyle, so she was quite surprised to bump into him after she'd headed to the bar to top up her glass of bubbly.

Turning around after she thought she'd heard someone call out her name, Aggie's hand, with which she'd been holding the glass of champagne, hit him in the chest, causing the liquid to pour out all over him.

"Kyle! Oh shit," she cried out. "Sorry." She looked on the counter for a paper towel she could use to dry him.

"It's okay, it's okay," he said, pulling his shirt away from his chest to try and avoid his skin from getting too wet. "My fault," he said. "I shouldn't have come so close."

"I thought I heard someone call out my name," she muttered. "Must've been hearing things. Sorry."

"It's all right, it's only wine. It'll come out in the wash. How are you anyway?" he asked politely.

"Okay. We had a nice ceremony at the church this morning, well, kind of nice," she smiled, filling up her glass again and offering Kyle a drink.

He shook his head, "I think I'll have a beer instead," pointing to the other end of the temporary bar.

"Let me get it for you."

"No, it's okay. I can do it," he said, walking away.

Feeling a little abandoned for some reason, Aggie shrugged and walked away in the opposite direction.

With a beer in his hand, Kyle turned, smiling, but found that Aggie had disappeared. Frowning, his eyes searched the busy shop floor for some sight of her. Following what looked like her, he stepped away from the bar and headed toward the back of the room, where their small kitchen was situated. What appeared to be Aggie, wearing a long green 1930s style dress, headed inside.

"Odd", he thought, "I could have sworn Aggie was wearing a pink dress."

But thinking nothing of it, he followed her in. Once inside, he was baffled to find no one in the room.

"Aggie?" he asked, but the little room was empty.

Walking back out, he spotted her across the other side of the room, not far from the main entrance to the shop. Doing a double-take, Kyle was at a loss. There she was again, but this time in a pink dress.

He looked down at his beer. "What the heck is in this stuff?" he thought to himself before he followed her yet again.

"Aggie?" he said, but she couldn't hear him above all the voices talking inside the shop. "Aggie," he said, a little louder.

She heard him and looked up. Catching her eye, Kyle smiled and tried to encourage her to join him where it was a little quieter. But someone had just cornered her and wanted to know something about the shop, so she shrugged in his direction and stayed where she was.

Sighing, Kyle turned away and took a long swig of his beer. He watched as Coco entertained a small group of people who seemed eager to hear more of her story, while Christie was enjoying chatting with a couple of other younger mothers from the community. Aggie's mum was pointing to some of the photos of Petunia while discussing what she did know of her aunt's life to a larger group of women a similar age to herself. Kyle chuckled to himself as he watched the husbands sneaking past the black ribbons to head to the second floor, like a group of schoolboys doing something they weren't meant to be doing.

Kyle had known Aggie and her family since he was a teenager.

They'd always been there for him and his sister and had proved invaluable after the car crash that had killed their parents. They'd been there through heartbreak and the hell of Kyle's drug addiction and not once had they judged him for his sometimes terrible decisions.

He realised they were like a family to him. A family that meant the world.

Smiling as these things dawned on him, Kyle finished the last of his beer and put the glass down on the temporary bar. Aggie was still deep in conversation with the same couple who had cornered her, so he decided to leave them all to it and head home. He'd had a long day, arriving back from some business he'd had in Dubai early that morning. Knowing that everyone was having a good time, he decided to sneak out. Opening the door, he'd forgotten the new bell would ring, but he ignored it and walked outside.

After such a lovely morning, the grey clouds had settled above and were about to start depositing their heavy load. Looking up, Kyle winced as the first of the rain began spitting on him.

Wiping his face, he started to walk back to his car, which he'd been lucky enough to park just around the corner. Climbing inside, he was about to start the engine when he saw Aggie appear outside the door to the shop. He waved, but she didn't see him. Instead, she walked out onto the pavement and around the corner.

"She's going to get soaked dressed like that," he thought, then remembered she hadn't been dressed like that. She'd been wearing a pink dress, not a green dress.

Confused, he climbed back out of his car and headed back toward the shop, turning where he'd seen her turn, walking into an alleyway just a few metres away from Aphrodite's Closet. But she was nowhere to be seen. Instead, there was a tall, stocky man climbing a tall ladder that led to Aggie's flat.

"Hey!" Kyle yelled. "What the hell do you think you're doing?"

The man growled and cursed under his breath, quickening his speed up the ladder.

Looking up, Kyle noticed that he was not alone. Another man had already reached the top and had broken the window into Aggie's living room.

"What the hell?" Kyle said to himself before he began climbing the ladder, without giving it a second thought.

"Hey," he yelled.

Being somewhat smaller than the big stocky man, Kyle reached him before he could reach the top and grabbed hold of his leg.

"Get off me, mate," he growled. "Or you'll be sorry." The man kicked as much as he could, but Kyle refused to let go, eventually pulling him so hard that he fell down a few rungs of the ladder, taking Kyle with him.

Not wanting the man to achieve his goal, Kyle grabbed both of his legs and pulled with all of his strength. Both of them ended up releasing their hold on the ladder and falling to the ground with a massive thud.

Winded like he'd never been winded before, Kyle could barely breathe. He tried to move but couldn't. He was either paralysed, or his arms and legs were pinned by something. A moment later, he lost consciousness.

CHAPTER 41

The sound of the bell ringing had alerted Aggie to the fact that Kyle must have given up waiting for her and left. She finished chatting and made her apologies to the couple talking to her and quickly made her way to the door.

Pushing it open, she rushed outside, looking left and right to see if she could determine which way he'd gone. Eventually, she spotted his car still parked on the kerb. Frowning, she bit the inside of her cheeks and wondered where he would have gone.

Turning back, she thought she caught sight of a woman in green running around the corner down the alleyway just past the shop. Then she heard some shouting and an almighty thud.

Her heart began to thud in her own chest, and she ran, not even noticing the pouring rain, toward the side of her building.

"Kyle!" she yelled at the sight of him on the ground, pinned by the big guy she recognised immediately. "Oh, God, Kyle, please be all right," she yelled, running to his side and trying to push Mr Jones from on top of him.

"Kyle?" she said, rain running down her cheeks, soaking her to the bone. "Kyle, please speak to me. Tell me you're all right?"

But Kyle said nothing. Mr Jones, on the other hand, grabbed her ankle, pulling her on to her bottom.

"Ow," she squealed, trying to kick at him to release his grip.

"Get off me, you pig," she shouted. But the man managed to use his other hand to pull her toward him, sliding her across the ground.

"Get off me," she screamed.

"Oi!" shouted a voice from above. "What are you playing at, Gavin? We're supposed to be in and out, not faffing about down there."

Aggie couldn't believe her eyes at the sight of another man, just as big and burly, inside her flat.

"Get out!" she screamed. "Get out of my house!"

Mr Jones clasped his hand over her mouth as she kicked and screamed, trying to get him off her. "Kyle, help!" she just about managed to yell before he pulled her upward, held her arms from behind, and used his other hand to cover her mouth.

It was no use, she was well and truly pinned. And Kyle was well and truly unconscious.

oOo

"Has anyone seen Aggie?" asked Trixie as she wandered around looking for her eldest daughter.

"I think I saw her go outside," said someone pointing to the door.

"What? In all this rain? In her new pink dress? Odd," Trixie said with a shrug before something even odder caught her attention.

It was Aggie in a green dress looking distressed by one of the windows. Trixie shook her head as if she was seeing things before she had the unusual thought that it wasn't Aggie at all.

"Aunt Petunia?" she whispered, and the woman walked toward the door, pointing.

Trixie nodded. Grabbing hold of her handbag, she rushed toward the door, ignoring everyone else at the party.

She followed Aunt Petunia outdoors and round the corner, down the alleyway that ran beside the shop. Her aunt put a finger over her mouth and pointed. Trixie nodded and tiptoed further down until she spotted them crouching on the ground. Kyle was lying on the floor, while Aggie was being held captive by Mr Jones, who hadn't noticed her.

Silently opening her handbag while she tiptoed closer and closer, Trixie pulled out what she needed and bit her bottom lip.

He felt the gun in his back before he even heard her behind and tutted to himself.

"Let her go and nobody gets hurt," Trixie said confidently.

Mr Jones immediately released Aggie who rushed over to Kyle's side.

"Is he all right, dear?" asked Trixie.

"I don't know, I really don't know, Mum."

"Call an ambulance, dear. And the police. Do it now. Don't worry about this great oaf. I've got it covered."

Aggie nodded as Trixie threw her handbag to her daughter. "Phone's in there, dear."

After she'd made the necessary phone calls to the police and to Coco inside the shop, Aggie squinted at her mother, who was clearly enjoying keeping Mr Jones "under arrest" with the so-called gun poking in his back. But it wasn't a gun. Aggie sniggered.

"Mum?" she questioned. "Oh, it's just a little something I bought yesterday. I swore Coco to secrecy," she said, trying not to laugh as Mr Jones continued to be held hostage with The Kinky Prince's latest vibrator.

"Aggie? Trixie? Kyle?" said Coco as people from the party began to gather in the alleyway.

"Aggie?" whispered a voice from the floor. "Aggie?"

"Kyle?" Aggie cried. "Can you move?" She took his hand in hers.

"I...I think so. I thought I was paralysed, but I must've just been pinned down by him," he muttered under his breath. "More importantly, are you okay?"

Aggie smiled.

"Never better," she grinned as they looked over to watch Trixie looking mighty proud of herself with her new Sonic Flutterer being used as a gun.

It didn't take long until everyone began applauding as the police arrived and arrested Mr Jones and his partner, who had become trapped inside Aggie's flat. Kyle was given the once over by the ambulance crew and, although they recommended he go to the hospital, he insisted he was fine for the time being. He told Aggie he didn't want to miss the rest of the party.

As the criminals were taken away, most of the partygoers returned to the shop to celebrate not only the life of Petunia Petal but also the end of a particularly nasty chapter.

CHAPTER 42

*L*ocal Vicar arrested on suspicion of arson and abuse
 Reverend Geoff Walters, the man responsible for the Frambleberry Church for the past decade has been arrested. It has been revealed that Geoffrey Walters (real name George Wally) is, in fact, a criminal wanted on several accounts of fraud in the Greater Manchester area.

Wally was caught by Mrs Trixabelle Trout, 71, after he created a grand scheme to bring down her daughter's business, Aphrodite's Closet, which included threatening behaviour, abuse, arson, and attempted theft. It has also recently come to light that Wally, while posing as a Reverend, molested several young adults over the past ten years.

"Well, there you go, Mum. You're famous now too," Aggie smiled as she finished reading the newspaper article and passed it on to her mother. "It's a great photo of you. Shame they didn't mention how you captured Wally's sidekicks though," she sniggered.

"Wouldn't that be a tale to tell," Ted roared with laughter. "I still can't believe it, myself. You do realise you're going to become a bit of a superstar in these parts, don't you?"

Trixie sat up straight and grinned, "I rather like the idea of being a bit of a superstar actually, darling," she joked. "Anyway, how's Kyle? He did go to the hospital after the party, didn't he, love?"

"Yes, and he's going to be fine. He's got a couple of fractured ribs though, which will take some time to heal. He's been told not to do any heavy physical work for a while."

"He's a bit of a hero, that boy is," Trixie smiled.

"He certainly is," Ted said as Aggie stood up and stretched her arms above her head.

"Well, I'd better go," she said. "Coco's waiting for me at the shop this morning."

"I thought you were closed today. It is Sunday, isn't it?" asked Ted.

"Yes, but we decided we'd hang out together today and have a girls' day out."

"I'll go and get your coat," Ted said, sensing that Trixie wanted to speak to her alone.

"That sounds lovely, dear. And so, well-deserved. Oh, Aggie?" Trixie asked.

"Yes, Mum?"

"About the other day, the party?"

"Hm-hm?"

"Did you...see anything out of the ordinary?"

"What do you mean?" asked Aggie.

"Well, I thought I saw someone familiar. Someone...oh it must be nothing. I think I must've just had a tad too much bubbly, that's all. Never mind, dear. Just ignore me."

Aggie, realising that perhaps her own vision hadn't just been her own, sat back down with a thump. "You saw her too, didn't you?" Aggie whispered.

Trixie's eyes widened, and she gulped. Sitting upright, she said, "...someone in a green dress?"

Aggie's heart began to thump harder in her chest, "Petunia?" she whispered.

Trixie sat back in her chair and let out a deep sigh, nodding.

"Great Aunt Petunia was there? I knew it. I've sensed her for a few months but never saw her until the party. She...Mum, she led me to Kyle."

"And she led me to you," Trixie whispered, her voice cracking as tears welled up in her eyes.

"I think that only means one thing, Mum," Aggie said quietly.

"That ghosts exist?" Trixie said, trying to make light of it.

"Well, yes, that too. But it means something far more important. It means she's forgiven you."

"I know, Aggie, I know," Trixie smiled as she squeezed her daughter's hands.

oOo

AGGIE PARKED her old Mini round the corner from the shop and climbed out. As she locked it and started walking, she smiled at the sight of Aphrodite's Closet up ahead. She could finally enjoy being the owner of such a beautiful building, not to mention a successful business too. The worries of being attacked and bullied were now behind her, and she looked forward to what the future held for her, Coco, Christie, and the business.

As she neared the door, she grinned when Coco pushed open the door from the inside.

"Oh, that was good timing," Aggie said, hugging her best friend.

"Not really," Coco laughed. "I saw you on camera." She pointed to the CCTV above the door. "Speaking of which, I watched what happened the other day. I still can't believe how stupid we were to think we were safe during the party and not one of us thought to keep an eye on the CCTV."

"I know," Aggie agreed. "But it doesn't matter now, does it? Everything's worked out for the best. We finally caught him and his goons, Coco. He's going to jail. We can finally breathe again."

"Absolutely," Coco smiled, linking arms with Aggie. "But there is one thing."

"What's that?"

"Something odd that's been bothering me since the party."

"Hm-hm?" asked Aggie.

"Kyle told me he kept seeing you in different dresses—a pink and a green dress. He was so confused. Then when I watched the CCTV footage, I never saw you in anything other than a pink dress, and I don't remember you changing either. Can you explain that?"

"He did have a nasty bump on his head, Coco," Aggie said with a smile.

"What aren't you telling me, girl?" Coco said, stopping and looking up at Aggie's grin.

"Nothing really, apart from the fact that Petunia was the one who saved us, Coco. It was Petunia."

"Huh?"

"She was there. She led me to Kyle, then when I got caught, she led Mum to me. My Great Aunt Petunia. She saved us."

Coco's face looked blank, "I...I...don't understand".

"The ghost of Petunia Petal has been with me all along, Coco. She's my...guardian angel," Aggie smiled.

"You mean you saw her ghost?" Coco asked, her mouth dropping open.

Aggie nodded, "Me, Mum, and Kyle. We all saw her."

"Wow, that's...that's...unbelievable."

"Close your mouth, Coco."

CHAPTER 43

It had been almost two weeks since Petunia's memorial party and business at the shop had skyrocketed. Not only had the local press featured the girls and the ghastly business with the Reverend, but the national media had picked up on it too. It seemed that Aphrodite's Closet was becoming famous. There were so many customers coming in and out of the shop every day that the girls were forced to take on extra staff.

"What should I do with these, dear?" Trixie asked Coco on her very first day.

Coco grinned, looking at the Sonic Flutterers in Trixie's hands. "I thought you knew, Trixie?" she joked. "Do you realise that we sold out of them last week?"

"Really?" Trixie asked.

"Yes, pretty much all of the ladies from your Ladies Luncheon Club came and bought one after you caught Mr Jones using one of them as a handgun."

Trixie's eyes bulged out of her head as she laughed out loud, "Well I never," she said.

"Just put them up there on that shelf," Coco instructed. "But keep the golden one out on display over there," she pointed.

"Absolutely," Trixie smiled, doing as she was told.

"Hello, darling," said Ted as he arrived for a visit following his game of golf that morning. "How's it going? Having fun?" he asked, looking at all the customers milling around on the first floor of the store.

"Hello, dear," Trixie said, giving her husband a discreet peck on the lips. "I'm having a wonderful time. Who'd have thought it, eh?" she laughed.

"I know I wouldn't have done," he chuckled. "If you'd have told me this time last year that you'd be working in a..." he stopped and looked around for a second before continuing in a hushed voice, "an adult shop, I'd have thought you'd gone bonkers, love."

"Me too, dear. Me too," she agreed. "Now I'd better stop chatting with you. I have work to do," she smiled and left him standing alone. With his hands behind his back, he casually looked around before something unusual caught his eye. Walking over to a display with a big "New" sign on it, Ted picked up the item which resembled an egg. Scrutinising it, he looked closer, wondering exactly what it was. As he twisted it, the two ends came apart, pulling out into a very long dildo, making him jump. As he did so, he dropped it on the floor. Trying to be casual, he picked it up and plonked it back on the display, but as he did that, he pressed a discreet button which made the item pulse and vibrate, causing it to slowly move across the shelf. His cheeks turning ruby red, Ted stepped back and put his hands in his pockets. Whistling, he moved away as fast and discreetly as he could.

Back downstairs, Trixie was now helping Aggie hang up a new delivery of workout wear, after having several clients inquire about yoga clothes.

"This is a lovely idea, dear," Trixie said as she pulled a couple of pairs of leggings out of the box. "Another line for the shop."

"Yes, actually it was Christie's idea. She started yoga a couple of weeks ago and has been reading up about it. Apparently, it's a booming business," she said, looking closely at the black and silver racer back vest. "And then Eric, one of our suppliers at the erotic show, recently sent us a brochure about a new line of yoga clothes they were developing, so it kind of seemed like fate. Like we were meant to sell this stuff."

"Really? That's lovely, dear. So the supplier has gone from erotica to yoga, eh?"

Aggie nodded, "He broke up with Edison, his partner and decided to launch his own range instead."

"Oh, how lovely for him. Well, not about the break-up, of course."

"Yes, he's a nice guy, Mum. He was the first person I talked to at the erotic show, and he made me feel at ease. We've kept in touch."

"But he's a homosexual, dear?"

Aggie nodded.

"Well, that's a shame," Trixie said, looking at her daughter. "Did you ever hear from that Cole fellow again?"

Aggie shook her head, "No."

"Oh, dear. Oh well, never mind. There's plenty more fish in the sea."

"I'm not worried about that, Mum. I'm quite happy on my own, you know."

"I know but…"

"No buts, Mum. I'm happily single and not looking for a man. I don't need one," she sighed as they finished hanging up the clothes. "That looks quite good, actually."

Trixie agreed, "Perhaps we should put an ad in the paper?"

"An ad? Are you mad, mother?" Aggie almost shrieked. "I said I'm happily single, and I certainly don't need to post an ad for a man!"

Trixie rolled her eyes, "I was talking about for the yoga-wear, dear."

"Oh, sorry," Aggie blushed.

"If you think I'd go as far as to place an advert for my eldest daughter to meet a man, then you really don't know me very well at all, do you?"

"Sorry, Mum," Aggie smiled, pulling her mother into a short embrace.

"However," Trixie continued. "Should you meet a man any time soon, there is something your father and I would like to discuss with you."

Rolling her eyes at her mother, Aggie stepped backwards. "And what is that? I hope you don't mean to give me the talk because I'm a little old for that, Mum," she winked.

"Oh, Agatha," her mother chuckled. "Nothing quite like that."

"What is it then?" she asked.

"We just wanted to talk to you about your wedding."

"But, Mum, I haven't even got a boyfriend. Why would you want to discuss that?"

"Well, you're almost thirty. We just wanted to know what your plans would be. We always planned to pay for your wedding, dear. We just wanted to know what your thoughts are on the matter."

"Oh, Mum, to be honest, I've never even thought about it. So there's nothing we can talk about. It's very sweet that you and Dad would've wanted to pay for it though. Thank you," Aggie said, giving her mother a quick peck on the cheek, feeling rather confused.

CHAPTER 44

Sitting at home with a glass of red wine in her hand, Aggie decided to take the plunge. Opening up her laptop, she took a swig as she waited for it to start. Once the wifi signal lit up, she opened her browser and logged in to Facebook just as her phone rang.

"Hey, Aggie," Christie said on the other end of the line.

"Hey, Sis, everything okay?" Aggie asked.

"Yeah, just put the kids to bed and thought I'd ring to see how Mum got on in the shop today?"

Chuckling, Aggie replied, "Pretty good, actually. She's very good with the clients, especially the older ones. She's got a knack of putting them at ease. She even sold a few Sonic Flutterers."

"Holy crap," Christie laughed. "I never would have seen that coming."

"I don't think Mr Jones did either," Aggie joked as both women started laughing.

"I'm still in shock about that."

"Me too," Aggie agreed. "So how are my little munchkins?"

"They asked about you tonight. They want to know when Aunt Aggie is coming over to help them bake fairy cakes again."

"Awww, tell them I'll be over next Sunday if that's okay with you?"

"That'd be brilliant. I was going to ask if you'd consider

babysitting some time over the next week or so anyway. Jonathan wants to take me out to that new Thai restaurant in town."

"Ooh swanky," Aggie said. "You know I'm delighted to look after the kids at any time."

"Thanks, how about Saturday night? Then you could stay over and bake on Sunday with them?"

"I'd love that."

"Fabulous. I'll tell Jonathan. So what are you up to?"

"Right now?" Aggie asked.

"Yup."

"I've finally decided to take the plunge and join Facebook."

"Shut the front door," Christie exclaimed. "But you've always been so anti."

"Yeah I know, but things have changed so much over the past year. I figured it's time I joined the rest of society and made an effort to be active online. Even Mum's on Instagram, you know?"

Aggie listened to Christie laugh for a moment.

"Yeah, I know. She posts all the time."

"Are you on there too?" Aggie asked.

"Me? Yeah. I'm active pretty much everywhere online. I started a blog a couple of months ago too."

"Why didn't you tell me?"

"Because you had a lot going on. I started it when you insisted I was safer at home. I was bored. I'll send you the link."

"Cool, thanks. So how do I do this Facebook thingy?" Aggie asked as she looked at the computer screen.

"Oh, it's super easy, just log on the to site and follow their instructions. You'll figure it out in no time. You're pretty computer-savvy. Once you're on, let me know, and we can work on a page for Aphrodite's Closet together."

"That would be great. I have had a few people ask for it," Aggie admitted.

"Yes, I've meant to talk to you about it too. We could do with the link for the website. Instagram and Twitter too. Oh and Pinterest."

Aggie cringed.

"I can hear you," Christie laughed.

"What?"

"Cringing."

"Yeah, I guess I was," Aggie said. "But I'll sort it, don't worry. I'll let you know when it's all up and running."

"If you link your email to your accounts, then all your friends should pop up and then you can add them easily enough," Christie suggested.

"Okay, I'll try and do that."

"Well, I'll leave you to it then. I'll be in to work tomorrow so I'll see you after I've dropped the girls off."

"Great. Have a fun evening."

"You too, Aggie. Love ya."

"You too," Aggie said as they put their phones down.

"So, Facebook, let's get this party started," Aggie whispered to herself as she followed the instructions and then linked her email to the account.

Soon, numerous people popped up, and she began willy-nilly clicking on then, adding them as "friends." Before she knew it, she found herself searching for the odd person she'd met over the years and hadn't seen for a long time, like old school friends and the children of her parents' friends.

"I wonder," she suddenly pondered to herself before tentatively typing in Cole's name. Taking a deep breath, she skimmed through a few guys with the same name until she spotted what looked very much like him. Before she clicked on his name, she sat upright, her finger hovering over the laptop. A feeling of guilt overwhelmed her like she was doing something she shouldn't. But her curiosity got the better of her, and she clicked the button.

While her other "friends" appeared to have some kind of privacy setting to stop everybody and anybody from seeing their posts, Cole's photos were there for the world to see. And he wasn't alone. As she started to scroll down, her mouth dropped open. All his recent pictures appeared to be of his own wedding.

CHAPTER 45

"Bastard," Coco seethed through gritted teeth. "How could he?"

Christie shook her head.

"Look, guys, I'm fine about it. I just wished he'd have told me the truth, that's all. It's been a few months anyway. He could have met her and married her within a few months, right?"

Both Coco and Christie looked at her and shook their heads.

"Well, it doesn't matter. It was just a fling anyway. It was fun while it lasted."

"Yeah, but he was engaged to be married…to another woman," Christie sighed.

"Who was engaged?" Trixie piped up as she walked into the shop just before nine the following morning.

"Oh, hello, dear. You're in early. I thought you usually dropped the girls off first thing?" she said, talking to her youngest daughter.

"Jonathan offered to do it this morning because he had a meeting in the same part of town," Christie replied as she accepted a kiss on the cheek from her mother.

"Morning, Coco," Trixie said, giving her a kiss too, followed by Aggie. "So, who was engaged? What have I missed?" she asked, hanging her coat up behind the counter before joining them.

"Cole," Aggie reluctantly said. "Apparently he was engaged to be married when he was over here sleeping with me."

"Bastard," her mother seethed.

"Mum!" Aggie said.

"Well, it's true. He'd seemed like such a nice young man too."

"Appearances can be deceiving," Coco added as she went into the kitchen. "Who fancies a cuppa?"

"Let me do it, dear," Trixie offered. "After all, I am the newest member of staff, and it was always the newest member of staff on tea duty when I worked in an office."

With her hands in the air, Coco stepped away from the kettle and nodded. "Thanks, Trixie. I'll be upstairs," she said.

At precisely nine o'clock, the bell above the door dinged, and clients started arriving, keeping the girls busy all the way through until just before midday when there was a temporary lull in business.

"Ooh look at that," Trixie pointed out the window. "Is that one of those stretch limousine thingies?"

"What? Here?" asked Christie, who rushed forward and peered out of the window. Sure enough, a black stretch limo was pulling up just outside the shop. "I think they're coming in here. Aggie quick, come and look."

Trixie, Christie, and Aggie all peered out of the window as the back door of the limo opened, and a man with dark hair wearing jeans, a black leather jacket, and cowboy boots stepped out.

"Oh my God," Aggie whispered. "It's Johnnie Blackburn."

"Johnnie Blackburn?" Trixie asked as they watched him walk toward the door.

"He's a rock star turned actor, Mum," Christie hyperventilated.

"Well, what's he doing here?" Trixie wondered out loud.

"I know what he's doing here," Aggie grinned as they all moved away from the window as quickly as possible and looked as if they were busy.

"What?" Christie asked dumbfounded.

"Coco," Aggie mouthed as the door opened and the star walked in.

All three women pretended not to have noticed him as he took a little time to check out his surroundings, admiring the architecture of the old building. He took a few steps toward the main counter, looking around for someone to speak to.

"Hello, dear," Trixie said before anyone else could speak. "Can I help you? Are you looking for anything special? Perhaps something a little kinky for your girlfriend?"

Aggie and Christie both looked at each other and went bright red. This was their mother?

Rushing forward, Aggie stepped in front of Trixie and looked at him apologetically.

"Sorry, can I help?" she asked.

"You're Agatha Trout," he said, clearly impressed.

Astonished that Johnnie Blackburn knew who she was, her mouth fell open, and she nodded her head.

"Yeah, I read about you in the paper," he nodded. "Cool place you've got here."

"Th...thanks," she gulped. "Were you looking for anything in particular?"

Johnnie shook his head before he began to nod, "Well, it's not what I'm looking for. It's whom."

Aggie nodded, "I assume you're looking for Coco," she smiled.

Looking a little taken aback himself, Johnnie half nodded. "How do you know I'm looking for Coco?" he asked.

"I was with her in Vegas," she smiled. "She told me she'd met you."

"Ahh yeah, that's right. Then she buggered off without another word."

"She got your number though," Aggie grinned.

"But she never rang," he said, his eyes looking a little sad.

"I know," Aggie agreed.

"And then I spotted her in the paper," Johnny grinned back at her. "So I thought I'd come and find out for myself why she never rang."

Thoroughly impressed that the superstar, Johnnie Blackburn, would make an effort to drive all the way up to Frambleberry just to see Coco, Aggie knew almost straight away that this guy was special. Rock star or not, he had a heart. And Aggie knew that he was perfect for Coco.

"Is she here?" he asked.

Aggie nodded and pointed toward the stairs, "You'll find her working on the second floor."

Grinning, Johnnie gave her the thumbs up before taking a deep breath. He walked up the stairs towards Coco's floor.

Coco was dusting the Sonic Flutterers when she felt someone standing behind her. All thoughts returned to when she was attacked, and so she immediately went on the defensive. Remembering the self-defence move Kyle had since taught her, Coco thrust her elbows outward, winding the poor man behind her, before she turned and grabbed him, pushing him to the floor and crouching over him, ready to attack.

"Coco?" he winced. "Coco Watson?"

"Holy shit," Coco wailed. "Johnnie Blackburn? What the hell are you doing here?" she said in dismay.

"Nice to see you too," he said, holding his stomach as if he was in agony.

"Oh shit, I'm so sorry. Are you okay? I kind of overreacted. Shit. Shit. Shit."

Bending down, she held out her hand to help him back up.

"Are you all right? I didn't hurt you, did I?" she asked.

"Not to worry," he whispered as he pulled himself up. "I'll live."

"What are you doing here?" she asked.

"I came to see you."

"Me? Why? And how?"

"It's a long story," he said, bending over to try and get his breath back.

"Let me get you some water," she said, going to walk away.

"No, don't go," Johnnie said. "You walked away once before, not again."

"That was Vegas, Johnnie, this is where I work," she sniggered, walking off and returning a few seconds later with a glass of water.

"So why are you here?" she asked, leaning against the counter, feeling like a total idiot.

"Because I haven't been able to get you out of my head," he admitted.

"You haven't?" she asked.

He shook his head.

"Why not?" she said without thinking.

Johnnie grinned, "Because you're bloody incredible, that's why not. You're the first girl ever to refuse to give me her number. I invited you out for a drink, and you didn't turn up. I gave you my number, and you didn't ring."

"So basically because I'm the one who got away?"

"I…guess. No, no that's not it at all. This isn't coming out right, is it?"

"Johnnie, I didn't want to be just another of your crazy one-night stands."

"Crazy one-night stands?"

"Yeah, I read the papers."

"You really shouldn't believe everything that you read."

"No?" she asked.

Shaking his head, Johnnie put the glass of water on the shelf beside the Sonic Flutterer, looking at it quizzically before continuing. "Coco, I'm not your usual run-of-the-mill rockstar. I don't sleep around, for one. I'm a one-woman man. And you've been on my mind ever since Vegas. I never thought I'd see you again, and then I spotted you in the paper!" he grinned. "Clearly I was meant to come and find you because I don't normally read the paper. I just happened to pick one up at the weekend, and there you were, surrounded by all this…stuff," he laughed. "Coco, this is destiny."

"Destiny?" she asked. "Really?"

"Yes!" exclaimed a voice from the top of the stairs. "Oops," said Trixie, trying to hide behind the bannister.

Johnnie and Coco both laughed as Trixie backtracked.

"Well? What do you say? Are you willing to take a chance on me?" he asked.

Coco looked toward the floor before she lifted her head, "You're really a one-woman kinda guy?" she asked.

"Totally. I've never cheated on anyone in my life, that I promise you. So, will you go out on a date with me?"

Turning to look at the stairs, she grinned at the sight of Aggie, Christie and Trixie all hiding and shook her head.

Johnnie's face dropped, "No?" he sighed.

"No, not you. I was shaking my head at them," she laughed, pointing toward the stairs. "But you, Johnnie Blackburn, if you're willing to come all the way up here just to find me, then, of course, I'll go on a date with you. I'm not that mean," she winked.

CHAPTER 46

She was dressed in a nineteen-twenties flapper dress, complete with pearls, and was doing the Charleston dance with Petunia, who was about the same age as her now. The two of them were giggling while the music abruptly changed. It was no longer the wonderful tunes from yesteryear but was an annoying buzzing sound. Suddenly coming to, Aggie sat up and rubbed her eyes. She looked at the clock on her bedside table and noticed that it was twenty past two in the morning. The buzzing continued.

Confused for a second, she realised it was the sound of her intercom. Climbing out of bed, she rushed to her front door and pressed the button.

"Hello?" she murmured. "Hello?"

"Aggie?" said a male voice.

"Yes," she replied. "Who's that?"

"It's me, Aggie. It's Kyle."

"Kyle? What on earth are you doing here? It's almost two-thirty in the morning. Are you drunk?" she asked before whispering, "You're not on drugs again, are you, Kyle?"

"No, no, of course not. I just needed to see you. Can I come up?"

"At two-thirty in the morning? Can't it wait?"

"No Aggie, it really can't."

Sighing, Aggie leaned back against the front door before she gave in and pressed the intercom, which opened the side door of the shop below.

Realising that she must look horrendous, she rushed to the bathroom and gargled a little mouthwash, before brushing her hair and wrapping herself in a dressing gown.

When there was a knock on the door, she took her time to open it.

Kyle stood there, carrying a small suitcase, soaked to the skin.

"Oh my God, Kyle, you're soaked. Are you all right? What on earth is wrong?" she asked, fetching him a towel.

"I'm fine, I'm fine. I just got back from Dubai. I got the bus from the airport and walked here from the station."

"Why did you get the bus? And why did you walk from the station?" she asked as she motioned for him to follow her into the living room where he could sit down.

"I...I just needed some time to think. I left my car at home this time."

"You should've got a taxi," she scolded.

"Yeah probably," he sighed, rubbing himself down with the towel.

"You're absolutely drenched, Kyle. Are there are any dry clothes in your suitcase? I think you should change."

"Yeah, probably," he said again.

"What's going on with you, Kyle? You've been acting weird the last few times I've seen you. Are you sure you're not back on the drugs again?"

Kyle stopped, "I will never, ever do that stuff again, ever, Aggie. You can trust me on that."

"Okay," she whispered, rubbing her eyes.

"I'm sorry to have gotten you out of bed."

"That's okay. I'm up now. I'll make us a hot drink. Why don't you get changed?" she suggested.

When she came back into the room with two cups of tea, Kyle, who was wearing a pair of dry jeans and a black T-shirt, was towel-drying his hair.

"Thanks, Aggie. Look, I'm sorry about this," he said as she handed him the tea.

"It's okay. Are you going to tell me what's going on now? Are you in some sort of trouble?" she asked, sitting across from him.

He shook his head, "No, it's nothing like that," he said.

"Then what is it? Why are you here and not at Coco's? She's normally the one you turn to when you need to talk, right?"

"Yeah, usually but she can't help me now. Besides, she's kind of tied up at the moment," he smiled. "She and Johnnie jetted off to the south of France for the weekend, remember?"

"How could I forget?" she smiled.

Kyle stood up and walked over to the window, watching the rain as it poured against the glass. He turned and put the cup of tea on the coffee table. Then he approached Aggie and crouched down in front of her.

Frowning, she sat back a little. Her heart began to thud harder in her chest.

"Kyle?" she whispered. "What's going on?"

"Aggie, I can't take this any more."

"Take what?" she asked.

"You," he sighed.

"You can't take me any more? Have I done something to upset you?" she asked, defensively.

"No, yes, no. I don't know."

"You don't know?"

"Aggie, I don't know how to say this."

"Perhaps you ought to just spit it out and get it over with, whatever it is," she suggested, taking a long swig of her tea so that the cup was empty. She stood up, practically knocking him to the carpet and walked back toward the kitchen.

"Refill?" she asked.

"No, no. Aggie, can you just stay still for a second. I need to tell you…"

"Tell me what, Kyle? You're making me nervous."

He got up from the floor and paced over toward her, "Aggie," he said, pushing her hair out of her eyes. "I can't stop this, this feeling inside."

"Christ, Kyle, you sound like you're going to burst into song or something…" she tried to joke.

"I'm serious, Aggie. Look, I need to get this off my chest."

"Then do it. What are you waiting for? A written invitation? Tell me, for God's sake. What the hell is wrong with you? Do you have some illness or something? Are you going to die? Are you gay? What? What is it?"

"Aggie, shut up woman. I'm trying to tell you that I'm in love with you," he shouted.

And the world stopped.

Well, just for a second anyway.

"Wh…what?" she whispered, steadying herself against the doorframe. "You're what?"

Kyle moved forward toward her and took her hands in his. "In love with you, Aggie."

Frowning, Aggie shook her head. "How can you possibly be in love with me? You've never suggested anything of the sort. We've been friends for years, and you've never said a word. Why? Why now? Why me? I don't understand, Kyle."

"Aggie, you've always been the one for me."

"Then why the hell didn't you tell me before?"

"Because I was a coward. Because I always thought you were too good for me."

Aggie's eyes widened, "Why would you even think that?" she said. "Kyle, I always thought you were too good for me."

"I was a drug addict, Aggie. I was a total mess."

Tears began to well up in her eyes, and Aggie shook her head, "You've never been a total mess, Kyle. You just got caught up in some bad shit. You went through hell. You lost your parents, both of them, at the same time. Yet you still managed to pull yourself out of it and look at you now. You're a successful businessman who frequently jets off halfway around the world to make deals. You're…you're incredible," she said.

Kyle's eyes began to well a little, too, and so he looked away. "You really think so?" he asked.

"I know so. But you can't possibly be in love with me, Kyle."

"Why not?" he asked.

"Because I'm just me, your sister's best friend. The snot-nosed, red-faced little girl from school who was always the coward, always the one too afraid to do anything."

"That snot-nosed, red-faced little girl has turned into a sexy woman not afraid to go out and get what she wants out of life. How can you not see yourself for what you truly are, Agatha Trout?"

Aggie screwed up her nose, "And what's that?" she asked.

"A true beauty, inside and out," he whispered, pulling her toward him. "And the woman Kyle Watson wants to be with."

"Really, Kyle?" she asked, "You really want to be with me?"

Nodding, he pulled her so close so that his nose was touching hers.

"Aggie, I've wanted to be with you for a long time, I was just too much of an idiot to admit it," he said as their lips touched for the very first time.

The kiss made Aggie's heart beat so hard, reminding her of the Sonic Flutterer, that she smiled, pulling away. "I've wanted to be with you too, Kyle. I just never dreamed that you would feel the same way."

"What?" he smiled. "You feel the same as me?"

Aggie nodded. "Even when we were kids, my favourite weekends were the ones I got to come and stay over with Coco because it meant hanging out with you too."

"Why didn't you ever say anything?"

Aggie shrugged, "I was a coward, remember?"

"I was so worried you were going to run off into the sunset with Cole," he sighed, pulling her into his chest.

"What?" she said. "Really?"

Kyle nodded. "Seeing you two together drove me insane with jealousy."

"He's married," she admitted. "I found out last week. He must've been engaged when we were…together."

"Bastard," Kyle said through gritted teeth. "But I'm glad," he grinned. "I was so relieved when he left you."

"Hey," she joked.

"I can't believe all these years we've fancied each other, and neither of us said anything."

"Then we were both cowards," Aggie smiled.

"But not any more."

"Nope, never again."

CHAPTER 47

"I can't believe it's been two whole years since we opened Aphrodite's Closet," said Aggie as she took the cake box from her mother and put it on the side in the kitchen of her flat.

"A lot has happened in the past twenty-four months, dear," Trixie said with a smile. "I'm so happy for you," she said, hugging her daughter tightly.

"Thanks for baking a cake for the occasion, Mum."

"It's a big day," she smiled, hugging her daughter. "Now, where's your dress?"

"In the bedroom," Aggie grinned. "Do you want to see it?"

"No, I'll wait until you're wearing it. I can't wait to see it on you, though. You're going to look beautiful. I'm so proud of you, sweetheart."

"Thanks, Mum. Where's Dad?"

"He's waiting for you downstairs with the girls. I'll go down and wait with them. You okay, getting dressed on your own?"

Aggie smiled and raised her eyebrows, "I've been doing it a few years now. I'll manage," she joked.

Her mother left the flat and went downstairs to wait with the rest of the gang.

Aggie took her time to put on the most exquisite sequinned dress she'd ever owned. She'd had it handmade by one of Christie's dressmaking friends, especially for the occasion. She slipped on her pale green T-bar shoes and finished it off with a pale cream feather in her hair. Looking in the mirror, she couldn't believe what she saw. It was like looking at a photo of Petunia. Smiling, she opened the door and made her way downstairs to the ground floor of the shop.

As she reached the staircase from the first floor, she stopped for a moment and looked around at the shop. Although little had changed in the design of the place, they now carried an awful lot more stock. It was full of kinky lingerie and gadgets galore in all kinds of colours and designs. Grinning, she turned to start walking down the last staircase. When she heard gasps from below, she stopped on the stairs and let her friends and family take in her beautiful dress.

"Wow," Trixie gasped. "You look stunning, dear. That dress is simply divine."

"What an absolute beauty, sweetheart," said her father. "You look breathtaking."

"The spitting image," Coco said as she turned to look at the photo of Petunia that they'd decided to keep on the wall by the entrance. "You look almost exactly the same."

"She does, doesn't she?" Christie whispered while her two daughters pointed and clapped at their auntie. One daughter was in Christie's arms while Jonathan held the other.

The bell above the door rang when it opened to reveal Kyle and Johnnie both arriving together.

"Looks like we're just in time for the party," Johnnie sang out loud before he wolf-whistled at the sight of Aggie in her new emerald green dress.

Kyle, on the other hand, remained silent. He just stood, speechless, at the sight of his girl looking so gorgeous.

"Aren't you going to say something?" Aggie laughed as she continued walking down the stairs until she stood beside him.

"Yeah," he muttered. "You look drop-dead gorgeous. Just like her," he whispered into her ear. "Exactly like when I saw her."

Aggie grinned, enjoying the moment as he bent down and kissed her gently on the lips before she pulled away and wiped the lipstick he now had on his face.

"I figured it would be a fitting homage to Great Aunt Petunia on the second anniversary of opening the shop, don't you agree?"

"I certainly do," he agreed. "But there's something else I need to do first."

"What's that?"

As she asked the question, he lifted her off her feet and carried her to the counter, where he sat her down before he kneeled in front of her. Looking backwards toward Johnnie, he nodded and grinned.

Johnnie began to sing her favourite song, while Kyle removed a small box from his pocket.

"Agatha Trout, I love you so much and want to spend the rest of my days climbing up and sliding down this bannister with you. Will you do me the honour of becoming my wife?"

Speechless, Aggie's eyes filled with tears, and she nodded. "Yes, yes, of course, I will," she said.

"I'm so glad you said that," he laughed as he picked her up and held her tight before putting the most beautiful emerald on her finger.

"Oh wow, it's stunning," Aggie cried, while the rest of the gang applauded.

"It's an antique. I've been searching for the right one for a few months now and ended up asking for your mum's help," he admitted.

They both looked up to see Trixie in Ted's arms as they smiled in utter delight at the young couple.

"Thanks again, Trixie," Kyle said.

"It was an absolute pleasure, dear."

"So you knew all this time and managed to keep it a secret?" Aggie asked. "Unbelievable."

As Johnnie finished singing the song, everyone clapped loudly.

"Hurray!" yelled the two children. "Sing another one, Uncle Johnnie, sing another one," they demanded, as he started to belt out another popular love song before he took both young girls by their hands and began to dance with them on the black and white shop floor.

"They're loving that," Aggie said, sighing with happiness as she gazed down at her beautiful engagement ring.

"You didn't suspect a thing?" Kyle asked.

"Not a thing," she smiled. "Where did you find it?"

"America, actually," he grinned. "I found a jeweller in Charleston who deals exclusively with vintage and antique pieces. I knew it had to be an emerald, but I couldn't decide which one. That's when I asked your mum for her advice. She knew straight away, which one was right."

"You both did a wonderful job," she grinned. "I absolutely love it."

"Okay, everyone, it's time," Ted announced as they all gathered beneath the photo of Petunia. In his hand was an envelope. He went to hand it to Aggie, but she shook her head.

"You do it, Dad. You read it, please."

Ted nodded and released the seal, opening it up, he pulled out a letter and started to read.

DEAR AGGIE,

In my last video, which you will have seen some two years ago, I mentioned that there was an addition to my final will and testament. I neglected to tell you what that was because it was important to me that a couple of years pass before you were given the final part. So, here we are two years later, and I'd like to finally give you what remains of my estate. The sum of fifty thousand pounds is to be used for a wedding. Yes, Agatha, I'd like very much that you marry. Choose someone you deeply love, my dear, and enjoy every moment. For you never know how long you will have with him. My hope for you is that you will get a lifetime of love, joy, and happiness with whomever you choose as your husband. Sadly, I never got a whole lifetime with any of my husbands because they kept dropping dead on me! But the short time I did have, I made sure it counted. This is what I want for you.

As for your sister, Christie, I leave a further fifty thousand pounds, which I imagine she will pass on to her children, but she may use the money for whatever she fancies, to be honest.

And finally, to my niece, Trixie, and her husband, Ted, I leave the sum of seventy thousand pounds, which they must use for travel, perhaps a cruise or two. I don't care where they go, I just want them to see the world and open their eyes to new possibilities. We never saw eye to eye, but I have a feeling things might have changed over these past few years.

And that's it, my dearest great-niece, Aggie. For you all, I wish only the best. And that's it. It's time for me to go now. You see, I'm on my dying death bed as I dictate this. Know that you were all always on my mind...
;)

"And at the end, there's a semicolon and a bracket," Ted said, looking little confused.

"She's winking, Dad," Aggie chuckled.

"Oh I see," he said, turning the paper on its side to make out a wink.

"Well I never," Trixie whispered. "Seventy thousand pounds? Why would she have left all that money to us, Ted?"

"Because she wants us to travel, I suppose," he grinned. "And isn't it something you've always wanted to do? To go on an exclusive cruise?"

Tears began to fall out of Trixie's eyes, and she sobbed into her husband's chest.

"There, there," he whispered.

"Is she all right, Dad?" asked Christie as she pulled her daughter, Matilda, up into her arms and over her heavily pregnant belly.

Ted nodded. "Just a bit overwhelmed, love," he said.

"....A cruise," Trixie cried. "And a wedding too. It's just too much. It's too much."

"Yes, it is," Aggie reassured her mother. "But it's exactly what she wanted to do, Mum. I love that she waited two years to do this. It's like she knew things were changing for us all."

Trixie lifted her head up from Ted's chest and nodded. "She must've known," she sobbed. "What a dear, dear woman."

Aggie smiled at her mother and looked down at her own hand intertwined with Kyle's, the man of her dreams. Pulling him toward her, she led him away from her family and friends, around the corner from the main entrance until she pulled him down to sit on a chair near the changing rooms. She sat on his lap and smiled.

"So what are we doing over here?" he asked, grinning.

"I just wanted to be alone with you for a minute," she whispered.

"Oh, really?" he asked.

"Of course. Plus, I wanted to show you something."

"Oh yeah, what's that?"

"Over there," she pointed toward the grand staircase.

Looking up, Kyle gasped at the sight of a woman wearing the same green dress as Aggie. She was sitting in the middle of the stairs watching everyone having a wonderful time. She turned to look at Aggie and Kyle and smiled. Lifting her hand, she waved before standing up. She began to walk away, her transparent figure eventually disappearing into nothing.

"Goodbye, Great Aunt Petunia," Aggie whispered as she rested her head against Kyle's.

"She's gone, hasn't she?" he asked.

Aggie nodded, "She did what she set out to do, so I doubt we'll be seeing her again. At least not for many, many years to come."

"What she set out to do?" asked Kyle.

"Bring us all together at last," Aggie smiled.

She turned to face her future husband and leaned in to kiss him, knowing deep down that they would be together for a long and happy life. All thanks to Great Aunt Petunia.

THE END

GET A FUN FREE READ...

FREE DOWNLOAD

Willow Tree Farm

Nestled among a thicket of weeping willows deep in the heart of Dartmoor, lies a house like no other. A house defying the laws of logic–and gravity for that matter. Some might even say it had a mind of its own. They wouldn't be wrong.

Affectionately known as Willow, this house has been an integral part of the Winterbourne family for over 400 years, and it is very, very protective of the Winterbournes, so woe betide anyone who dares to wrong this family of witches...

Compatible with all reading devices.
Exclusively available, and never before published.

Get your FREE COPY of Willow Tree Farm when you sign up to the author's VIP mailing list. **Get started here:**

www.suzyturner.com/free-book

OTHER BOOKS BY SUZY TURNER:

Forever Fredless
Stormy Summer
And Then There Was You
The Chick Lit Box Set

Suzy also writes YA fiction under the pen name,
SG Turner
The Raven Saga:
Raven
December Moon
The Lost Soul

The Praxos Academy:
Daisy Madigan's Paradise
The Ghost of Josiah Grimshaw
The Temporal Stone
Looking for Lucy Jo
We Stand Against Evil

The Winterbourne Witches:
Willow Tree Farm

ABOUT THE AUTHOR

Suzy Turner wrote her first chick lit novel in her early twenties, but it wasn't until much later that she decided to focus on writing full time. It was during a visit to Canada in 2009 when the ravens within the dark eerie forests of British Columbia called to her. The story of Lilly Taylor was born soon after and the first novel in The Raven Witch Saga was created. Suzy has since published several more urban fantasy books (under her pen name SG Turner) and contemporary women's novels.

Having lived in Portugal since childhood, Suzy, who is originally from Yorkshire in England, loves to travel. She finds inspiration wherever she goes. Old decrepit buildings, graveyards, cathedrals and castles are just a few of the things that can be found within the worlds of her urban fantasy books, and her contemporary women's fiction novels are filled with fun friendships, ordinary people in extraordinary circumstances and quirky characters you'd want as friends.

Suzy lives in the Algarve with her husband, three cats and a dog, where she does yoga every morning and bookish stuff for pretty much the rest of the day!

For more books and updates, visit www.suzyturner.com